BOOKS

Simply Learning, Simply Best

Simply Learning, Simply Best

倍斯特出版事業有限公司
Best Publishing Ltd.

BEST BOOKS

MP3

Follow
30 場票房電影
實現你的
旅遊英語夢

李佩玲/ Bella ◎著

由票房電影 **蜘蛛人2 (L.A.)、魔戒 (New Zealand)**
和 **哈利波特 (London)**…等,引領你進入魅力城市、
飽覽旅遊勝地、享用垂涎的佳餚…

健行者和背包客【強推】的
【太平洋屋脊步道】
冒險經歷+++

嚴選城市介紹

大自然愛好者【熱愛】的
【可愛島】
極富綠田秋持色+++

攝影同好【口耳相傳】的
【阿拉巴馬州】
秀麗風景和踏遊勝地+++

文藝復興的搖籃+++

藝術家和建築師
【靈感泉源之地】的【佛羅倫斯】

單車族【讚不絕口】的
【阿姆斯特丹】
騎腳踏車最方便的城市+++

文學A咖【爭相走訪】
的【都柏林】
呼者倒流段的寧靜跟喜喔+++

　　我想旅遊最為迷人的地方就是，你可以遇見許多的不同。世界這麼大，可以想像有多少的不同在等著我們和他們巧遇。我們一邊看著旅遊節目或電影，一邊編織著我們自己的嚮往。"那可能就是我蜜月旅行想去的地方吧！"，"哇！那好像是另一個世界。"，"如果可以去那裡有多好。"隨著越來越多的嚮往堆積起來，我們也漸漸地習慣他們就那麼地堆積在我們內心的一個角落，直到他們又再次被提起，我們才會抖抖灰塵，再次看到他們。

　　世界那麼大，人生實在太短。如果可以在短短的人生中，精彩的度過如同電影般的精彩那該有多好！這本書衷心希望可以藉由經歷和簡介，世界 30 個小角落和電影景點的介紹幫你抖抖灰塵，重新激發你探險世界的勇氣和熱誠。書中也有包含情境對話，旅遊小貼士來幫助你置身其中。還在等什麼？該出發囉！

Bella Lee／李佩玲

Editorial

　　Follow 30 場票房電影實現你的旅遊英語夢由【城市介紹】讀者對該城市的地方特色和風俗民情有更多認識。而【情境對話】富趣味性且全然跳脫瞎聊式對話內容，對話的口語內容道地，多為作者與當地人互動的對話內容，無疑是活教材，更能現學現用呢！在【特別景點報導】的部分包含 30 個電影取材景點，為許多遊客朝聖之地，許多遊客更在這些景點流連忘返呢！【饕客園地】的部分包含許多美食菜餚，旅遊之餘也別忘了吃些美食，感受一下當地的飲食風例如南方美食玉米粉丸子和 39 號碼頭的酸麵包蛤蜊巧達濃湯都是首選喔！【旅遊愛玩咖】則包含許多旅遊勝地，除了拿自拍神器拍閃光照以及打卡之外，映入眼簾的美景跟氣氛更是讓人回味無窮喔！。【詞彙和慣用語】包含文章中出現過的重要字彙。最後的是【旅遊小貼士】包含許多旅遊小提醒。

　　　　　　　　　　　　　　　倍斯特編輯群

Contents 目次

Contents

Unit 01

Honolulu 夏威夷
Kawela Bay Huger Games:
Catching Fire
奇微拉海灣，飢餓遊戲 2 星火燎原

城市介紹 ▶

Whether you are an active person, beach bum, or nature enthusiast, Hawaii has plenty of natural resources to offer you a memorable time. It is perhaps the turquoise sea, swaying palm trees and the soft white sand, or possibly the gentle trade wind, the golden sunset and the twinkling stars that make Hawaii one of the most popular vacation spots. Walking down on the streets in Honolulu, you see lots of tourists from all over the world, and local people who are mostly made of North Americans or Haole in Hawaiian, Asians, and Polynesians due to its mid pacific location. Even if Hawaii is the 50th state of the United States, Hawaii is quite distinguishable from the rest of the states.

The word "Aloha" is well known worldwide to be the greeting and farewell word of Hawaii. However, what most people do not know is that Aloha is a word in Hawaiian which means peace, love, affection and mercy. Through time, Aloha has become a way of life, through which people learn to respect each other and the environment. Aloha spirit can be seen everywhere in Hawaii. From yielding seats, letting you cut in while stuck in traffic, sharing waves... that also explains why Hawaii is also called the "Aloha State".

夏威夷 - 檀香山

　　無論你是一個喜好活動，熱愛海灘者或是大自然愛好者，夏威夷都有足夠的自然資源提供您一個難忘的時光。或許是那湛藍的海水，搖擺的棕櫚樹，柔軟的白沙；又或者是那輕柔的季風，金黃色的日落和閃爍的星空使得夏威夷成為最受歡迎的度假勝地之一。走在夏威夷的街上，你會看見許多來自世界各地的遊客，以及因為夏威夷位在太平洋中的地理位置，由大部分北美洲的白人，或是夏威夷語中的 Haole（歐洲裔白人），亞洲人，和波利尼西亞人所組成的當地居民。即使夏威夷為美國的第五十州，夏威夷和美國其他州還是大有所不同。

夏威夷
威尼斯
紐約
曼谷
哥斯大黎加
舊金山
倫敦
都柏林
巴塞隆納
洛杉磯

　　阿囉哈這個字廣泛被世人認知為打招呼和道別的意思。然而大部分的人不知道的是其實阿囉哈在夏威夷文，意思是和平，愛，情感和憐憫。隨著時間，阿囉哈已經成為一個生活方式，夏威夷的居民隨此精神尊重彼此和環境。阿囉哈精神也在夏威夷隨處可見，從讓座，塞車時讓彼此切車，分享浪等等。這也解釋了為什麼夏威夷的別名為：阿囉哈州。

Dialogue 情境對話 ▶

Emily is visiting Hawaii by herself. She is talking to a local girl Leah at the hotel front desk.
艾蜜利一個人到夏威夷自助旅行！她正在和飯店櫃台的一個當地的女孩莉雅聊天。

Leah: Aloha, how may I help you?

莉雅：阿囉哈，請問我可以幫你嗎？

Emily: Hi! I just got here this morning. I'm wondering what I can do here?

艾蜜利：嗨！我今天早上剛到這裡！我想請問我在這邊可以做什麼呢？

Leah: Okay, so we're at Waikiki area. One popular activity is surfing. Do you like surfing?

莉雅：好的，我們這邊是威基基地區。這裡受歡迎的活動是衝浪！你喜歡衝浪嗎？

Emily: I have never tried it before! Is it for beginner?

艾蜜利：我從來沒有試過！初學者可以嗎？

Leah: Yes, the waves are pretty small today. There are surf lessons as well, so you should be in good hands!

莉雅：可以啊！今天的浪蠻小的！這邊也有衝浪課程，所以你應該不用擔心！

Emily: Wow, okay. I will give it a try! What else do you recommend to do on the island? I want to go for something exciting!

艾蜜利：哇！好！我會試試看！在這個島上你還有推薦玩什麼嗎？我想要嘗試刺激一點的活動！

Leah: Hmm… Let's see. There are plenty to do on the island. What do you think about shark cage tours?

莉雅：嗯…我想想。在這個島上可以做的事很多！你覺得鯊魚籠這個行程如何？

Emily: What is that!? Shark cage tours? How does that work?

艾蜜利：那是什麼！？鯊魚籠？！要怎麼進行活動？

Leah: It is an activity at north shore Oahu where you are put in a cage under water near where the sharks are. That way, you will be able to see sharks in a short distance safely. That's pretty exciting in my opinion…

莉雅：這是一個在歐胡島北海岸的活動。你會被放在籠子裡，然後再放到水裡。這樣一來你才可以安全地近距離欣賞鯊魚。對我而言，這是一個還蠻刺激的活動…

夏威夷
威尼斯
紐約
曼谷
哥斯大黎加
舊金山
倫敦
都柏林
巴塞隆納
洛杉磯

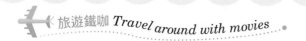
Emily: Terrific! How do I sign up for it again?　艾蜜利：太棒了！你剛剛説我要怎麼報名？

Special Sites Introduction 1: 特別景點報導 ▶

Honolulu Kawela Bay Huger Games: Catching Fire

 MP3 01

Kawela Bay, also known as Secret Beach by many people, is an exclusive beach located at the north shore of Oahu. Its protected location allows visitors to swim and paddle boards in the calm water. It is part of the luxurious Hawaiian resort, Turtle Bay's property. At times, you could see people kayaking or horseback riding at the beach. The Hollywood Blockbuster, Hunger Games: Catching Fire, was shot here for the starting scene of the game. Katniss Everdeen (Jennifer Lawrence) and the other Tributes started the game from this beach. The cast spent their free time learning to paddle boards in here too! The actors also stayed at the Turtle Bay resort at the time. Compared to other popular beaches in Hawaii, not too many people know about this place yet, so if you enjoy beaches that offer that extra bits of tranquility and peace of mind, Kawela Beach will be your best bet! One magical bonus is that turtles are often spotted here at Kawela Bay. Make sure you observe them from a distance. Do not disturb the turtles as disturbing turtles in Hawaii is considered illegal!

夏威夷奇微拉海灣，飢餓遊戲 2 星火燎原

　　奇微拉海灣，或是許多人稱之為秘密海灘，是一個位於歐湖島北海岸獨家的海灘。它天然受保護的位置使遊客可以在平靜的水面游泳，及玩水上滑板。這個海灣是夏威夷豪華的度假飯店 Turtle Bay 的資財之一。好萊塢熱門大片，飢餓遊戲：星火燎原，在這裡拍攝比賽的首發現場。凱妮絲・艾佛丁（珍妮佛・勞倫斯）和其他競爭者開始從這些平靜的水域比賽。劇組利用空閒時間也在這裡學習水上滑板呢！而演員們也在拍攝期間下榻於 Turtle Bay。相比其他在夏威夷受歡迎的海灘，不會有太多人知道這個地方，所以如果你喜歡特別寧靜，平和的海灘，奇微拉海灘將是您最好的選擇！一個神奇的加分點是，海龜經常會出現在這裡。確保你遠遠的觀察他們，不打擾海龜，因為打擾海龜在夏威夷是被認為是非法的喔！

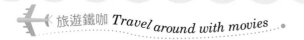

Onolicious Food　　MP3 02

Speaking of local Hawaiian food, you would not want to miss Poke. Poke, which is cubed raw tuna fish seasoned with sea salt, soy sauce, onions, limu seaweed and other variations. However, there are more and more variations of Poke. You may also find raw octopus in some places. One all time favorite would be spicy tuna Poke. (Below is the recipe if you feel like making your own).

You can find Poke in local Hawaiian families a restaurant and even almost every grocery store in Hawaii. It is considered a comfort food for Hawaiians. Besides Poke, you may also ask for a Poke Bowl if you are feeling hungry. Poke Bowl is Poke of your choice with a bowl of rice.

當地美食 Poke

　　說到夏威夷當地的美食，你一定不會想錯過 Poke。Poke 也就是切丁的生鮪魚用海鹽，醬油，洋蔥，海藻，以及其他的調味所完成的一道菜。然而，現在有越來越多不同口味的 Poke，你在某些地方也可以找到用生章魚做成的 Poke。一個一直很受歡迎的口味是辣鮪魚 Poke（以下有食譜如果你想要試著自己做看看）

　　你可以在夏威夷人的家裡，餐館，或是幾乎每一間超市找到 Poke。Poke 也被夏威夷人認為是慰藉食物的一種。除了只有 Poke，你也可以點 Poke 飯！Poke 飯也就是在你喜歡的 Poke 口味下鋪了一碗飯！

夏威夷

威尼斯

紐約

曼谷

哥斯大黎加

舊金山

倫敦

都柏林

巴塞隆納

洛杉磯

Spicy Tuna Poke 辣鮪魚 Poke

Ingredients 原料

3 yellowfin tuna steak	3 片鮪魚排
1tbsp Soy sause	1 大匙醬油
1/2 tbsp sesame oil,	½大匙的麻油
2 green onions chopped	2 把切好的青蔥
1/4 onion, sliced	¼個洋蔥，切片
2 tbsp mayonnaise	2 大匙美乃茲
2 tbsp Chili sauce	2 大匙的辣椒醬

Instructions 作法

1. Slice the tuna into cubes.

   把鮪魚切丁

2. Combine tuna in a bowl with 1 tbsp soy sauce, 1/2 tbsp sesame oil, and 1 chopped green onoion.

   把鮪魚丁，一大匙的醬油，½大匙的麻油，和一把切好的青蔥放到碗裡

3. Put it in the refrigerator for 30 minutes.

   把那碗放到冰箱裡醃三十分鐘

4. Combine 2 tbsp mayonnaise, 2tbsp chili sauce, remaining green onions (save some for the end)

   綜合兩大匙的美乃茲，兩大匙辣椒醬，和剩下的青蔥（留一點到最後）

5. When tuna is chilled, add the spicy mayo and mix them to-gether.

當冰箱的鮪魚已經涼了，拿出來並將剛綜合的美乃茲辣醬跟鮪魚混合

6. Top with more green onions! Enjoy!

再把最後剩下的青蔥放到美乃茲辣鮪魚上！好好享受！

夏威夷

威尼斯

紐約

曼谷

哥斯大黎加

舊金山

倫敦

都柏林

巴塞隆納

洛杉磯

Vocabulary and Idioms ▶

❶ **distinguishable**
　adj 可辨別的

❷ **affection** n 感情

❸ **be in good hands**
　Idiom 得到妥善照顧的

❹ **go for** Phrase 選擇

❺ **exclusive** adj 獨家的

❻ **luxurious** adj 奢華的

❼ **tranquility** n 平靜，安寧

❽ **variations** n 不同，差別

1. The fake purse is barely distinguishable from the original one.

　那個假的包包幾乎跟真的無法分辨。

2. He is showing a lot of affection towards his cat.

　他對他的貓展現了許多感情。

3. Your children are in good hands. They have a very good teacher.

　你的小孩都會得到妥善地照顧的。他們有一個好老師。

4. I'm going to go for the red dress for tonight's banquet.

　我決定今天晚上的宴會我要選擇穿那件紅洋裝。

5. This private beach is totally exclusive for the guests from this hotel.

　這個私人的海灘是只有這家飯店的客人可以獨家使用的。

6. The winners will be able to stay at the luxurious villa for two nights.

　贏家可以在這奢華的別墅住上兩晚。

7. The sound from the waves adds on the tranquility of the night.

海浪的聲音為夜晚增添了平靜。

8. There are some variations in prices, so you have to compare the prices before you buy anything.

這裡都有價差，所以你在買東西之前一定要比價。

旅遊小貼士 ▶

　　俗話說出外靠朋友！這句話在夏威夷會非常適用因為夏威夷當地有當地人的折扣（kama'aina）中文音為：卡馬愛那。而且一般折扣都會在八折到七折以上有些甚至免費！而要得到這個當地人的折扣，結帳時必須要秀出當地人的證件。所以說囉！如果在旅途中有認識當地人的話，結伴出遊的時候千萬不要忘記這個小撇步！當然，結交朋友時也是要格外的小心！若是沒有當地的朋友的話，有國際學生證也是有些折扣！沒有的話或許問問有沒有 kama'aina 卡馬愛那，有時候運氣好也是會有折扣的！得到折扣後也別忘記像當地人一樣說一聲 Mahalo（謝謝）喔！

Unit 02

Venice 威尼斯 - Hotel Danieli - The Tourist 達涅利酒店 - 色遇

城市介紹▶

The moment you step in this ancient city at the northeast Italy, it is a lot like traveling back in time. Renaissance architectures can be found all over the place and on top of that there are no vehicles allowed on Venice, so you have no other choice but to walk or take the gondolas around the city. Perhaps it is the atmosphere in Venice or the unusual scenes around you, you would not mind slowing down and appreciating what the city has to offer in front of you. Sitting down by the canal sipping a cup of coffee can just be the perfect thing to do. The whole city is consisted of 117 small islands and they are connected by the canals and the bridges. Venice is a city built in water. Therefore, Venice is often called "the City of Water", "City of Canals" or "the Floating City".

Following the intricate, narrow roads on Venice, street maps seem not to do its trick as it normally does. However, getting lost seems to be part of the experience you will get in Venice. Try asking the local Venetians directions, reckoning from their response, you will know you are surely not the first ones asking them!

✈ ◀ 威尼斯 - 水上之都 ▶

　　在你踏上義大利東北方這個古老的城市，你就會覺得好像時光倒流。文藝復興時期的建築隨處可見，加上在威尼斯車輛是禁止進入的，所以你也沒有其他的選擇，只好走路或是搭貢多拉（義大利平底船）在城市中行動。可能是威尼斯的氛圍，或是你身邊那不尋常的景象使你不介意慢下來並欣賞這個城市提供在你眼前的美景。坐在運河旁啜飲一杯咖啡似乎再適合不過了！這整個城市是由 117 個小島由運河和橋所連接起來，威尼斯是一個在水中建起的城市。因此，威尼斯也時常被稱之為 "水之都"， "運河城" 或是 "水上城市"。

　　在威尼斯交錯複雜並窄隘的街道，街道地圖似乎發揮不了平常的功用。然而，迷路也是在威尼斯旅行的經驗之一。試著向當地威尼斯人問路，從他們的反應來推測，你就會知道你應該不會是第一個問他們路的

夏威夷
威尼斯
紐約
曼谷
哥斯大黎加
舊金山
倫敦
都柏林
巴塞隆納
洛杉磯

人！

Dialogue 情境對話 ▶

Kim and Royce are walking around Venice when they come across the love locks on the bridges.
琴和羅伊斯正在威尼斯散步，他們走著走著遇到一座充滿了愛鎖的橋。

Royce: What are all these locks for? What are people trying to do with the padlocks here?

羅伊斯：這些鎖是幹嘛的？人們在這裡用這些鎖幹嘛？

Kim: Don't tell me you don't know about this!

琴：不要跟我說你不知道這個！

Royce: What do you mean? What's the story behind these locks? Or whatever they are?

羅伊斯：什麼意思？這些鎖背後的故事是什麼？還是不管它們叫什麼？

Kim: Love locks! They are called love locks!

琴：愛鎖！他們叫愛鎖！

Royce: Love locks? I've never heard of them in my life.

羅伊斯：愛鎖？我這輩子沒聽過這個！

Kim: These are from lovers who wrote their names on the padlocks, swore on their love, and then they locked the padlocks on the bridges and threw the keys in the river. That way their love will be locked forever.

Royce: Do you actually believe in this ritual, too?

Kim: Well... it is a popular thing to do and there's a trend of love locks around the world! You can find them in Paris, New York City, and Canada...etc.

Royce: I don't know about this trend! Venice is a very old city, I don't think it can take all the weight of people's love at this point.

Kim: You know what? You're spot on this one. Local people are trying to do a campaign on "unlocking your love" since the love locks are really

琴：這些是由情侶們在鎖上寫上他們的名字，對他們的愛發出誓言，然後他們把這些鎖鎖在橋上，再把鑰匙丟到河裡！這樣他們的愛就永遠被鎖住了！

羅伊斯：你真的相信這個儀式嗎？

琴：嗯…這個很受歡迎耶！而且還在全世界帶起愛鎖的風潮！你在巴黎，紐約市，加拿大…等等都可以看到！

羅伊斯：我不太確定這個潮流！威尼斯已經是一個很老的城市了！我不知道它現在能不能承受大家愛的重量。

琴：你知道怎麼著？這個論點完全被你說中了！當地人都在宣傳要 "解放你的愛" 因為愛鎖真的對威尼斯來說

夏威夷
威尼斯
紐約
曼谷
哥斯大黎加
舊金山
倫敦
都柏林
巴塞隆納
洛杉磯

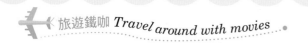
weighing Venice down! 太重了！

Royce: Yes! Free your love, people!!　羅伊斯：沒錯！解放愛吧人
　　　　　　　　　　　　　　　　　　　們！

Special Sites Introduction 2: 特別景點報導 ▶

Venice Hotel Danieli - The Tourist　💿 MP3 03

　　Remember the scene in the movie "the Tourist" When Elise (Angelina Jolie) and Frank (Johnny Depp) are in a luxurious Gothic style Hotel suite? It is the very Hotel Danieli from Venice! There is also a brief shot of the famous Danieli staircase in the film as well. The building was originally built at the end of the 14th century, only till 1824 a housekeeper nicknamed "Danieli" rented the building and turned it into a hotel. He finally purchased the hotel, realizing the great location of the hotel and spent a lot of money, time, and love to turn the hotel into something extraordinary! With its rich history and great location overlooking the Venice Lagoon, and only a few minutes away from St. Mark's square, Hotel Danieli is one of the five most luxurious hotels in Venice. Either you are craving for a special encounter like the movie the Tourist, or you just want to pamper yourself with a luxurious stay, Hotel Danieli would be an excellent choice.

威尼斯達捏利酒店 - 色遇

　　還記得在電影 "色遇" 中，伊莉絲（安潔麗娜裘莉）和法蘭克（強尼戴普）在一間華麗哥德式的飯店套房嗎？那正是在威尼斯的達涅利酒店！電影中也有短暫一幕從達涅利酒店出名的大廳的樓梯拍攝。這棟建築最早是在十四世紀末所興建，一直到 1824 年由一名小名為達涅利的管家所承租下來並把它改建為一個飯店。他發現這飯店具有極佳的地點而最終買下這個飯店並花費大量的金錢，時間和愛將飯店改的不同凡響！由於飯店豐富的歷史，絕佳的地理位置（可以俯瞰威尼斯潟湖，以及幾分鐘即到聖馬可廣場）達涅利飯店成為威尼斯五大最豪華飯店之一！不論你渴望得到像色遇中男女主角的際遇，或是想要寵愛自己一個豪華的一晚，達涅利飯店都是一個很不錯的選擇！

 旅遊愛玩咖 ▶

What comes to your mind when I say "opera"? Did you imagine an orchestra, great opera singers on stage and a huge concert hall that houses many people? Yes, that is the traditional type of Opera. However, here in Venice, there is an exclusive opera experience that you will hardly find anywhere else. All of your imagination of the opera was true besides the fact that it happens in one of the most intriguing Venetian palaces: Palazzo Barbarigo Minotto, which only welcomes no more than 70 guests each time. The opera is performed in three parts and each part is done in a different hall. With the beautiful setting, top rated singers and a 360° performance in the same room, the experience is unbeatable. Expect some interactions from the singers at times and be ready to improvise! There will be fine wines and snacks during the intermissions to better ensure you having a great evening! Have you ever watched an opera from within? Well, next time you visit Venice, don't forget to look them up! It will absolutely be worth your while!

獨家歌劇院

　　當我說"歌劇"的時候，你會想到什麼？你是否想像有一個交響樂團，超棒的歌劇歌手，和一個可以容納很多人的歌劇廳嗎？是的，那就是傳統的歌劇型態。然而，在威尼斯有一個獨家的歌劇體驗，是你在其他地方都很難找到的。你剛剛所有的想像都是對的，除了不是在很大的歌劇廳，而是在一個非常耐人尋味的威尼斯宮殿-Palazzo Barbarigo Minotto 舉辦！每次都只限定 70 個觀眾！歌劇本身分成三個部分，而每個部分都是在不同廳內表演。華麗的場景，頂尖的歌手，和三百六十度的表演，這個體驗是無人能敵的！和歌手間的互動是有可能的，所以要隨時準備好即興演出！中場休息也會有好酒和點心來更加確保觀眾度過美好的一夜！你有身歷其境地看過歌劇嗎？下次你到威尼斯，別忘了查一查這個獨家歌劇！絕對值回票價！

夏威夷
威尼斯
紐約
曼谷
哥斯大黎加
舊金山
倫敦
都柏林
巴塞隆納
洛杉磯

Vocabulary and Idioms ▶

❶ **ancient** `adj` 古老的　　❷ **intricate** `adj` 錯綜複雜的

❸ **ritual** `n` 儀式　　❹ **spot on** `Phrase` 精準的

❺ **extraordinary** `adj` 出眾的

❻ **encounter** `v` 遇到

❼ **intriguing** `adj` 令人感興趣的

❽ **intermission** `n` 中場休息

1. The moment we stepped in the ancient house, we were very impressed by the old designs.

   當我們走進這個古老的房子的時候，我們就對它古老的設計感到印象深刻。

2. The intricate pattern of the spider web is amazing.

   蜘蛛網錯綜複雜的圖案真是太驚人了。

3. There are a lot of rituals that need to be done when a girl is getting married in Asia.

   當一個女孩要在亞洲結婚時，會需要做許多儀式。

4. Your prediction was totally spot on!

   你的預測超級精準的！

5. Without a doubt, he got promoted for his extraordinary performance this year.

   毫無疑問的，他因為他今年傑出的表現而被升職了。

6. She encountered great difficulties learning Spanish.

她在學西班牙文的時候遇到了極大的困難。

7. The novel was getting intriguing, so I did not go to bed until 4 am!

小說越來越有趣,所以我昨天凌晨四點才睡。

8. They serve refreshments and drinks during the intermission of the show.

他們在中場休息時間會供應點心和飲料。

旅遊小貼士 ▶

　　去威尼斯旅行還有一個很重要而且不能錯過的行程-面具節!在全世界總共有三個最有名的嘉年華會:法國尼斯(Nice)和巴西里約熱內盧(Rio de janeir)與義大利威尼斯(Venice)!嘉年華會的起源其實要追溯到當人們要進入齋期前大肆宴會,作樂開始;嘉年華的真正意思其實是"再見了,肉!"。每年舉辦嘉年華會的時間都不太一樣,不過大約都在一、二月之間,精確的時間必須要上官網查詢才準確,面具節期間到處都可以看見穿戴面具、華服的人們,在嘉年華會最後一天在大運河上也會有璀璨的煙火!喜歡不一樣文化體驗的你,不要錯過了噢!

夏威夷
威尼斯
紐約
曼谷
哥斯大黎加
舊金山
倫敦
都柏林
巴塞隆納
洛杉磯

Unit 03

New York 紐約
Serendipity 美國情緣

城市介紹 ▶

A lot is happening when you are in New York City. If you are looking for places to slow down and relax, you have probably come to the wrong place. However, possibilities, excitement, and opportunities would be the correct words for you to describe New York. Just like any other big city, the moment you step in New York City, you will find yourself walking among tons of people. On the other hand, the facilities of the city are great and very convenient. You will be able to find anything you need within walking distance or a few subway stops away. From museums, restaurants, Broadway shows, shopping malls, to parks, you can also find the world-famous Statue of Liberty here.

New York has the nickname Big Apple. This can be traced back to the 1600s when a guy compared New York City to a big apple that everyone would like to take a big bite. The statement is still true even till this day. The city continues to prosper and thrive, every year, millions of tourists pour in from all over the world!

紐約市 - 大蘋果

當你身在紐約的時候，身邊很多的事都會發生的非常快！如果你是在找地方放慢腳步和放鬆，那你可能來錯地方了！然而，可能性，刺激，和機會都是描述紐約市比較正確的字眼。就像其他的大城市，當你踏入紐約市的時候，你會發現你置身於很多人之中。另一方面來說，城市中的設備都非常好又便利！你所有需要的東西都會在走路範圍中或是地鐵幾站之內。從博物館、餐廳、百老匯、購物中心到公園。你也可以在這看到世界聞名的自由女神像。

紐約有一個小名為大蘋果，因為追溯到十七世紀的時候，有一個人把紐約比喻為是人人都想分一杯羹的城市！這個聲明到現在都還是適用。紐約市持續繁榮興旺，每年都還是有上百萬的旅客從世界各地湧進！

夏威夷
威尼斯
紐約
曼谷
哥斯大黎加
舊金山
倫敦
都柏林
巴塞隆納
洛杉磯

Dialogue 情境對話 ▶

Amy and Jason are waiting in line at Times Square on New Year's Eve.
艾咪和傑森正在紐約時代廣場排隊等跨年夜。

Amy: Oh my goodness, it's only 2 p.m. and there are so many people already!

艾咪：天啊！現在才下午兩點就已經這麼多人了！

Jason: I thought we are one of the early birds! Looks like we've got some competition.

傑森：我以為我們是早鳥之一！看來我們有很多競爭者。

Amy: Luckily, we got in before they blocked the whole area!

艾咪：幸好我們在他們關閉整個區域前進來！

Jason: You really know how to look on the bright side!

傑森：你還真會往好的方面想。

Amy: I don't know Jason. I don't think I can stay outside for another 10 hours or so.

艾咪：傑森我不曉得。我不知道我能不能在戶外再待十多個鐘頭。

Jason: Oh tell me about it! We

傑森：就是說嘛！我們當初

shouldn't have put this on our bucket list in the first place.

不應該放到我們人生一定要做的清單上。

Amy: It is too late now. I'm sure we had our reasons, and we'll find out tonight to see if it's worth it!

艾咪：太遲了。我相信我們當初一定有什麼好理由，而且我們今天晚上就知道值不值得了。

Jason: You're right. So what's gonna happen anyway?

傑森：對。所以等下到底會發生什麼事？

Amy: So the New Year's Eve Ball will light up at 6 p.m. and all the performances will start at 8 p.m. So that's another 4 hours we're looking at. Much better.

艾咪：所以新年球會在六點的時候亮起，然後表演會在八點開始。所以我們現在只要再等四個小時。好多了。

Jason: 4 hours till the Ball lights up? Great.

傑森：再四個小時等球亮？好極了。

Amy: Yeah, no wonder people go all out dancing here. We'll need it then before we are all frozen.

艾咪：對啊，難怪大家最後都大跳特跳舞。我們在凍僵前也很需要！

Jason: Hahaha... so that explains

傑森：哈哈哈…原來如此。

夏威夷
威尼斯
紐約
曼谷
哥斯大黎加
舊金山
倫敦
都柏林
巴塞隆納
洛杉磯

everything.

Amy: The part I'm really excited about is 60 seconds before midnight, the Ball will start to descend, and when the big moment comes, lots of confetti will be released from the roof top!!

艾咪：我最期待的是在午夜前六十秒，球會開始下降，然後當時間到的時候，滿天的彩色紙花會從屋頂被釋放出來！

Jason: Yeah, that sounds really cool! Hey! Do you know where the bathroom is?

傑森：對啊，聽起來好棒！欸！你知道廁所在哪嗎？

Amy: Oh... I forgot to tell you...

艾咪：喔…我忘了跟你說…

 Special Sites Introduction 3: 特別景點報導 ▶

New York City - Serendipity **MP3 05**

On the Upper East Side of New York City, in between Second and Third Avenue is a delicate restaurant called "Serendipity III". As its website demonstrates, "Serendipity is the art of making happy discoveries, or finding the unexpectedly pleasant by chance or sagacity." Indeed, in the movie "Serendipity" released in 2001, Jonathan (John Cusack), and Sara (Kate Beckinsale) meet randomly in a department store before Christmas by accident and decide to share a dessert at Serendipity III, where Sara took Jonathan because she liked the sound of "Serendipity" and also the meaning: a fortunate accident. Perhaps their encounter reminded her of the restaurant, and it certainly made their connection that much more magical. They hit it off right away, but Sara wasn't sure about their affection, and decided to leave it to fate.

At the restaurant, the two shared the dessert: Frozen Hot Chocolate, which tastes creamy and insanely dreamy! The restaurant has brought people from all corners of the world to taste not only their famous Frozen Hot Chocolate, but also their other heavenly desserts.

紐約 - 美國情緣

在紐約市上東城區，有一間精巧可愛的餐廳叫 "緣 III" 位在第二和第三大道之間。就如同它的網站上所說：緣分就是隨機製造快樂發現，或找到意料之外喜悦的藝術。沒錯，在 2001 年上映的電影 "美國情緣" 中，強納森（約翰·庫薩克）和莎拉（凱特·貝琴薩）聖誕節前隨機地在一間百貨公司相遇並決定要一起去 緣 III 分享一個甜點。莎拉帶強納森到那裡因為她喜歡 "緣" 聽起來的聲音還有它的意思：幸運的意外。或許是他們的相遇令她想到這間餐廳，而這也絕對為他們之間的聯結增添了神奇氛圍。他們立刻就一見如故，但是莎拉不確定他們之間的感情，並決定交給命運來決定。

在這間餐廳，他們兩個分享的甜點是：情緣巧克力冰沙。巧克力冰

夏威夷
威尼斯
紐約
曼谷
哥斯大黎加
舊金山
倫敦
都柏林
巴塞隆納
洛杉磯

沙吃起來既濃郁也有令人發瘋的夢幻！這間餐廳吸引了世界各個角落的
人前來品嚐他們熱門的情緣巧克力冰沙和其它天堂般的甜點！

MP3 06

Coming to New York, besides exploring the city, don't miss the chance to go to one of the Broadway shows at the Broadway Theater in Manhattan. Here in New York, there are plenty of splendid Broadway shows to choose from. From the most popular show Lion King, Les Miserables, Mamma Mia, Blue Man to some of the newest shows depending on the time you go. One thing that is almost guaranteed is that you will most likely have a memorable and unforgettable evening! There are certain things you would thing that is better kept in your imagination. However, the actors in Broadway can really bring your imagination alive and even better!

Most people know about the discounted tickets for the Broadway shows. Broadway will sell the leftover tickets at half price on the day before the show starts. However, there is an easier way out! A good website to find discounted tickets is www. broadwaybox.com. You will be able to read the descriptions of the shows, select the time that is most convenient for you, and choose your own seat on the website!

百老匯

　　來到紐約除了在城市中探索，也千萬別錯過到曼哈頓百老匯劇院看一場表演的機會！在紐約，你有許多非常輝煌精彩的秀可以選擇。從很受歡迎的獅子王，悲慘世界，媽媽咪呀，藍人到許多依照你到紐約的時間而定的新秀。有一件事是幾乎可以確定的，你非常有可能會渡過一個十分印象深刻且難忘的夜晚！有些事情你會認為想像會比真實的好，但是在百老匯的演員，他們真的可以將你的想像帶到真實世界，甚至又詮釋的更好！

　　許多人都知道百老匯折價的票。百老匯會在當天表演開始之前釋出低至五折的票券。然而，現在有一個更簡單的辦法！一個很不錯的網站是 www.broadwaybox.com 你可以在上面讀每個表演的劇情簡介，選你最方便的時間，和選擇自己喜歡的座位喔！

Vocabulary and Idioms ▶

❶ facility n 設備

❷ compare... to Phrase 比喻

❸ bucket list

　　n 人生目標清單

❹ descend v 下降

❺ delicate adj 精美細緻的

❻ serendipity n 緣分

❼ hit it off Idiom 相處融洽

❽ splendid

　　adj 輝煌的，壯麗的

1. The facilities in this kitchen are lousy.

　　這間廚房的設備糟透了。

2. He compared his girlfriend to the sun that brings him warmth constantly.

　　他把他的女朋友比喻為一直帶給他溫暖的陽光。

3. He has so many things on his bucket list, but he has already finished half of them!

　　他的人生目標清單上有好多項目，但是他已經完成一半了！

4. You need to be very careful when descending off the steep rock.

　　你在從陡峭的石頭垂降時務必要小心。

5. Look at this delicate dish she made me.

　　你看她做給我的精美餐點。

6. Serendipity happens when you are least expecting it.

　　緣份在你最不預期時發生。

7. They hit it off right away from the beginning.

他們從一開始就相處得很融洽。

8. The new house they built is splendid. There is even a fountain in front of the house.

他們新建的房子十分的壯觀。房子的前面甚至有噴泉。

旅遊小貼士 ▶

　　到紐約也別忘了到小義大利走走，小義大利，照著名字的意思來說就是紐約一小區塊充滿了義式餐廳的地方！在這裡對喜歡享受義式美食的人來說，是一小塊天堂！但是在來訪之前，請務必做好功課才可以享受到真正到地的美食，還有要注意的是，這裡的服務生時常會推薦他們菜單上沒有的獨家美食，這時候開心之餘，千萬別忘了向服務生尋問價錢以便衡量是否是在自己的預算範圍之內！時常發生的誤會是服務生會端出比菜單上高出許多的一道菜！避免到時候的尷尬，建議務必要先詢問價錢噢！

夏威夷

威尼斯

紐約

曼谷

哥斯大黎加

舊金山

倫敦

都柏林

巴塞隆納

洛杉磯

Unit 04

Bangkok 曼谷 - Hangover 2 醉後大丈夫 2

城市介紹 ▶

Taking a stroll on the streets of Bangkok, depending on your mood, you might feel intrigued by everything and everyone around you like a kid in the candy shop. However, you might also feel overwhelmed at times because of the crowd and the sweltering heat. That said, Bangkok is a very popular tourist attraction for either sight seeing or the authentic experiences of the Southeast Asia. Therefore, almost everyone speaks and understands English in this busy city. Day in and day out, you hear the hustle and bustle of Bangkok, and see tourists explore and splurge. It's a city that awakes early and goes on all night long. It would be a challenge to be bored in this city for there are all sorts of things you can get into. Whether you are feeling adventurous for food or local experiences, or you just crave for a relaxing vacation. Bangkok has it all. It has several convenient metro systems if you don't feel like getting involved in the hectic rush hour. If your wild heart desires, you can jump on one of the Tuk Tuks by the street. Tuk Tuk is a three-wheeled cabin vehicle that provides an unusual experience for you on the street of Bangkok. Make sure you buckle up for all the fun Bangkok offers!

◀ 曼谷 ▶

漫步在曼谷的街上，看你的心情，你可能會像一個小孩到糖果店一樣對周遭所有的人事物的覺得很新奇，但也有時候，你可能會被周遭的人群和悶熱的熱氣壓迫得喘不過氣。也就是說呢，曼谷是一個十分受歡迎的觀光景點，不論是為了風景或是道地的東南亞體驗。 所以當地幾乎大家都會說也聽得懂英文。日復一日的，你聽見曼谷城市的喧囂，看見遊客探索和享樂。這是一個很早起，但到深夜也很熱鬧的城市。在這個城市裡有許多不一樣的事你可以嘗試，所以要很無聊也是一個挑戰。不管你有冒險精神想嘗試不一樣的食物和當地體驗，或是你嚮往一個放鬆的假期，曼谷什麼都有！如果你不想參與曼谷瘋狂的尖峰時刻交通，它也有許多方便的地鐵系統可以搭乘。但如果你狂野的心想嘗試看看，你也可以跳上路邊的嘟嘟車。嘟嘟車是一個三輪有車廂的車，它可以帶給你在曼谷街上不一樣的體驗。記得要繫好安全帶，好好享受曼谷帶給你的樂趣！

夏威夷

威尼斯

紐約

曼

谷

哥斯大黎加

舊金山

倫敦

都柏林

巴塞隆納

洛杉磯

Dialogue 情境對話 ▶

Alan and Ivy are on the long-tailed speedboat at the Amphawa Floating Market.
艾倫和艾薇正在安帕瓦水上市場裡的一艘長尾船上。

Ivy: Hey! Alan! Are you filming this? This is so cool!

艾薇：嘿！艾倫！你有沒有在拍這些？超酷的！

Alan: You bet I am! Look at the camera! Where are we?

艾倫：那當然囉！欸看鏡頭！我們在哪裡啊？

Ivy: HI! Alan and I are at the Amphawa Floating Market in Thailand! Look around us; people here sell all kinds of produce, food and just anything here! We are about to go on a treasure hunt!

艾薇：嗨！艾倫和我現在在泰國的安帕瓦水上市場裡！你看我們周遭的人，他們在賣各式各樣的農產品，食物，還有很多東西！我們即將要展開尋寶之旅！

Alan: Yeah, wow Ivy look, people actually live by this canal here and they sell things on their balcony!

艾倫：對！哇艾薇你看！這些人住在這運河上耶，他們直接在他們的陽台賣東西！

Ivy: That's convenient. You don't have to commute to work!

艾薇：好方便噢！都不用通勤去上班！

Alan: Yes, but that's annoying, too. It must get noisy here at times.

艾倫：對啊，但是也很煩。這裡有時候應該很吵！

Ivy: Yeah. Hey, I'm starving, should we stop somewhere to try some food?

艾薇：對啊。欸！我好餓噢！我們要不要停在哪裡吃個東西？

Alan: Sure, but I don't know how clean the food is going to be. I hope they don't wash their ingredients in this water.

艾倫：好啊，但是我不知道這裡的食物有多乾淨！我希望他們不是用這水來洗食材！

Ivy: Oh come on Alan. When in Rome?

艾薇：噢拜託，入境？

Alan: Do as the Romans do! I know. It's just I have a very delicate stomach.

艾倫：隨俗！我知道！只是我有一個很脆弱的胃！

Ivy: Oh please!! Hey look at that! Mango with the sticky rice! Should we split one?

艾薇：拜託！欸你看那個！芒果糯米耶！我們要不要平分一個？

Alan: Sure, what's that again?

艾倫：好啊，不過你說那是什麼？

Ivy: It's mango, sticky rice and condensed milk. Absolutely genius! Who would have thought they all go so well together!

艾薇：是芒果，糯米，和煉乳！真是太天才了！誰能想到把這幾樣東西加在一起會這麼好吃！

Alan: Did they just throw the peel in the water…

艾倫：他們剛剛是把皮丟到水裡嗎…

 Special Sites Introduction 4: 特別景點報導 ▶

Bangkok 曼谷 - Hangover 2　 MP3 07

Remember the scene when the Wolf pack went up to a bar that overlooks Bangkok to switch Chow's (Ken Jeong) money to get their missing buddy, Teddy (Mason Lee)back? That's the Sky Bar Rooftop in Bangkok. Getting of at Saphan Taksin BRT station, you can easily walk to the Sky Bar and enjoy a cocktail with the spectacular panoramic view around you.

Their cocktails are famous for their creativity. If you are a fan of Hangover II, try their "Hangovertini". It is made of green tea liquor, apple juice, Martini Rosso, and rosemary honey. If you want to have the bar all to yourself, plan to arrive before sunset. Otherwise, expect to share the bar with a thirsty crowd. There is also an oyster bar right by the cocktail bar. It may not be the most relaxing bar, but definitely one of the most unique ones you'll ever experience. Next time you're in Bangkok, don't forget to stop by Sky Bar Rooftop to enjoy a fancy cocktail!

曼谷 - 醉後大丈夫 2

還記得在醉後大丈夫第二集裡，瞎狼幫到 Sky Bar 裡用老周的錢去換泰迪回來嗎？那就是曼谷的 Sky Bar Rooftop。從曼谷 Saphan Taksin BRT 站下車只要走路就可以抵達 Sky Bar 並享用一杯調酒和很壯觀的曼谷全景。

他們的調酒是以創意聞名。如果你是最後大丈夫的影迷，不仿點一杯醉後馬丁尼。它是以綠茶烈酒，蘋果汁，馬丁尼羅索，和迷迭香蜂蜜所調成！想要一個人在 Sky Bar 裡輕鬆享用調酒，計劃日落前到 Sky Bar，不然的話就得預期和一群飢渴的群眾一起享受 Sky Bar。這裡也有一個生蠔吧！這裡或許不會是最令人放鬆的酒吧，但絕對會成為你最獨特的經驗之一！下次你到曼谷，千萬不要忘記到 Sky Bar 裡想用一杯精美的調酒噢！

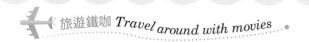

Chatuchak Weekend Market   MP3 08

If you are going to be in Bangkok on the weekends, make sure not to miss the Chatuchak or Jatujak Weekend Market! It only opens on Saturdays and Sundays from 9 in the morning to 5 in the afternoon. The scale of the market is enormous. It houses around 15,000 vendors. Be prepared if you are planning a day treasure hunting here. From clothing, food, second hand goods to bars and hardware stores. You can find pretty much everything within this gigantic weekend market. Needless to say, it also attracts tons of tourists. Unless you are a local or have been to this market many times before, expect to get lost and enjoy being lost in the alleys. You never know what you will find turning into the next narrow alley. This is essentially a large-scaled treasure hunt in real life. When you find something you like, don't hesitate to buy it at once because chances are that you will not find your way back to the shop you lingered at. To avoid the crowd, plan to be there around 11 am and leave around 3 pm so that you do not put yourself in the center of the crowd madness. Good luck! Happy treasure hunting!

恰圖恰週末市集

　　如果你週末會在曼谷，記得別錯過恰圖恰或是扎都甲週末市集！這裡早上九點開市，五點收市。這個市級的規模也十分的巨大！它可以容納 15000 個攤販！如果你計劃來這裡尋寶記得要有心理準備！從衣服，食物，二手商品，到酒吧和五金行。你在這龐大的週末市集裡幾乎什麼都可以找得到！不用說，它也吸引了許多的觀光客。除非你是當地人或事先前來過這裡許多次，不然的話，預期你會迷路，而也要享受在巷弄中迷路的過程！你永遠不知道在轉進下一個窄巷會找到什麼！這其實真的就是在現實生活中大型的尋寶。當你找到你喜歡的東西，千萬別遲疑要不要，立刻買下來，因為你會再回到先前徘徊的店的機率是微乎其微！要避免人潮，計劃大約到市集的時間是十一點，然後在大約三點鐘離開以避免把自己置身於瘋狂的人潮中！祝你們好運！尋寶快樂！

Vocabulary and Idioms ▶

❶ **stroll** n 散步

❷ **overwhelmed** adj 受不了的，喘不過氣的

❸ **splurge** v 揮霍金錢

❹ **crave** v 渴望獲得

❺ **produce** n 農產品

❻ **panoramic** adj 全景的

❼ **essentially** adv 實質上，本來

❽ **linger** v 徘徊

1. They are taking a stroll in the park now.

   他們現在在公園裡散步。

2. He is a little overwhelmed by his work.

   他現在被工作壓得有一點喘不過氣。

3. It is alright to splurge a little when you are on vacation.

   在度假的時候可以稍微揮霍一點沒關係。

4. It is so bad that I always crave fried chicken at nighttime.

   我晚上都會很想要吃炸雞，真是不好。

5. There is a lot of fresh produce at the Farmer's Market.

   農夫市集裡有很多新鮮的農產品。

6. You can get a panoramic view from the lookout.

   你從那個景觀台可以看到全景。

7. They are essentially good people. They just made a mistake that's all.

   他們其實是好人。只是他們犯了個錯。

8. He lingers at the coffee shop for a while, hoping to see the girl again.

他一直在咖啡店徘徊，希望可以再見到那個女孩一面。

旅遊小貼士 ▶

　　來到曼谷坐計程車時，和一般計程車不一樣的是，你必需要先問計程車司機有沒有要到你要到的目的地！有的時候目的地太遠，司機還會拒絕你！這是因為或許你要到的地點很遙遠他或許也沒有辦法載遊客回來，這麼一來他的油錢回程也只好自付。一開始不了解還會覺得莫名其妙，竟然還有司機拒絕的道理！一個好的辦法是你可以選擇搭到中間較受歡迎的地點再轉乘另一個計程車前往想去的地點！不然的話，你可能會遭受到一連串計程車司機的拒絕！另外，坐上計程車後第一件事是要問司機是否是 "by meter" 照里程數算，如果不是的話可能會流為司機亂喊價，所以不要客氣要立刻下車喔！

夏威夷

威尼斯

紐約

曼谷

哥斯大黎加

舊金山

倫敦

都柏林

巴塞隆納

洛杉磯

Unit 05

La Fortuna 哥斯大黎加 - Arenal Volcano National Park After Earth

（阿雷納爾）火山國家公園地球過後

城市介紹 ▶

Costa Rica has always been known for its abundant natural resources. Several parts of the country remains untouched and it's no wonder several movies were filmed in this beautiful site. Besides its lushness, seemingly limitless coastlines and palm trees, the local people (or Ticos) are all very friendly and appreciative of life in general. Pura Vida is a phrase characterizes the Costa Rican life. It means pure life literally. However, the real meaning is closer to "this is real living". The phrase can be used in a variety of ways. For instance, it can be used as a greeting or a farewell, a reply for life's going well, or a gesture to give thanks.

Entering La Fortuna, a small village in San Carlos by the foot of the Arenal Volcano, all sorts of resorts and restaurants come into sight. The temperature compared to San Jose is relatively lower and cooler, but that just makes the natural hot springs in La Fortuna that much more enjoyable. Tourists are drawn here for several of its tourist attractions, such as resorts with natural hot springs, hiking in Arenal Volcano National Park, waterfall trail trekking, horseback riding, kayaking, zip-lining, whitewater rafting, bungee jumping, and etc. Pay a visit to La Fortuna as your adventurous heart demands!

✈ 哥斯大黎加 ▶

　　哥斯大黎加一直以來都是以它豐富的自然資源而被大眾所知。在這個國家還有很多個部分都還未被開發，而這也難怪許多部電影都是在這個美麗的地方拍攝的！除了它綠意盎然的翠綠，似乎無止境的海岸線，和棕櫚樹之外，當地人（或是 Ticos）也都非常的友善和對生活充滿感激！Pura Vida 是一個哥斯大黎加特有的當地片語，它字面上的意思是單純的生活。然而，他真正的意思比較接近“這就是真正的生活”。這個片語有很多用法。例如，它可以被用來打招呼或是道別，或是回覆別人自己過得很好，亦或是一個表達謝意的表示。

在進入聖卡洛斯裡的小村子，Arenal 火山國家公園腳底下的 La Fortuna 之後， 映入眼簾的是各式各樣的飯店和餐廳。這裡的溫度和聖荷西相比低了一些，也涼了一點，但這也使得這邊的溫泉更令人覺得享受。觀光客們被 La Fortuna 許多的觀光景點所吸引：例如附有天然溫泉的飯店，在 Arenal 火山國家公園健行，瀑布步道健行，騎馬，皮筏艇，鋼索滑行，泛舟，高空彈跳，等等。下次就依你冒險的心要求而到 La Fortua 玩吧！

Dialogue 情境對話 ▶

Sarah and Mia just finished hiking in the Arenal Volcano National Park, and they are now at a local diner in La Fortuna.

莎拉和蜜雅剛結束了在 Arenal 火山國家公園裡的健行，而現在他們在一個 La Fortuna 當地的小餐館裡。

Sarah: I'm starving! Thankfully, this restaurant is still open. I can't believe most restaurants are closed, considering it's only 8 p.m.!

莎拉：我餓死了！好險這間餐廳還開著。我不敢相信大部分的餐廳都關了，現在才八點耶！

Mia: Well, I guess it's not the peak season right now. We did not run into too many tourists earlier as well.

蜜雅：嗯，我想是因為現在不是旺季吧。我們剛剛健行的時候也沒有遇到很多觀光客！

Sarah: True that! Anyways, let's order, shall we? If we can understand any of these.

莎拉：也是啦！好啦，我們來點餐吧，好不好？如果我們可以看得懂菜單的話！

Mia: Oh I know Casado! It's basically rice, black beans, plantains, salad, a tortilla, and an optional entrée that may include chicken, beef, pork, fish and so on. Simple and quite healthy! And Casado means married man. It's pretty much what a married man here eats at home.

蜜雅：噢我知道什麼是卡薩多！是用米飯，黑豆，大蕉，沙拉，玉米餅，和一個可選的主菜，其中可能包括雞肉，牛肉，豬肉，魚等。很簡單也很健康！卡薩多的意思是已婚男士。因為那就是哥斯大黎加已婚男士在家吃的！

Sarah: Wow that sounds pretty awesome, but I'm afraid I might need to eat more than a married man eats here now. I might need to eat a married couple's meal right now.

莎拉：哇聽起來好棒，可是我現在想吃的比這裡已婚男士吃的還要多。我可能需要吃一對已婚夫婦的餐。

Mia: Haha… I know! You really went all out for hiking earlier. You were so fast!

蜜雅：哈哈⋯我知道！你今天健行的時候真的全力以赴！走超快的！

Sarah: I had to. I just wanted to see it

莎拉：一定要的啊！我想要

all! Hmm… I might order this one here, Olla de Carne. The picture looks pretty amazing.

全部都看看！嗯…我可能會點 Olla de Carne。照片上這看起來超好吃！

Mia: I'm just going for something I know I think. I'm gonna get the Casado with Chicken, and we can always order more if we need to afterwards!

蜜雅：我想我只想點我知道的。我要點卡薩多和雞肉，我們想多點的話等下也可以多點！

Sarah: Right on!

莎拉：好！

 Special Sites Introduction 5: 特別景點報導 ▶

La Fortuna - Arenal Volcano National Park After Earth

 MP3 09

In the moive "After Earth", which was released in 2013. When Cypher (Will Smith) and son Kitai (Jaden Smith) were accidentally sent back to the dangerous Earth, parts of Cypher and son Kitai's fights against the evil creatures in the jungle were filmed in Arenal National Park, Costa Rica. Arenal Volcano National Park is a national park that is located in the central part of Costa Rica. The national park encompasses Arenal Volcano which was considered to be dormant until an eruption in 1968. Within the national park, there are trails that you can hike, up to several different lookouts to get a better view of either the Arenal

Volcano, or the Lake Arenal Dam. However, you will have to check the weather in advance to prevent going there in vain since at times La Fortuna can be pretty foggy. Hiking up the trail, you will need hiking shoes, mosquito repellent and a bottle of water. Once you are at the lookout, you will be amazed to see how perfectly symmetrical Arenal Volcano actually is.

哥斯大黎加 - 火山國家公園地球過後

在 2013 年上映的電影地球過後，當西佛雷吉（威爾史密斯）和他的兒子奇泰（傑登史密斯）意外地回到危險的地球，片中西佛雷吉和奇泰和邪惡的生物對決的叢林場景就是在哥斯大黎加的 Arenal 火山國家公園所拍攝。Arenal 火山國家公園是位於哥斯大黎加中部的國家公園。整個國家公園含括 Arenal 火山，這個火山曾被認為是休眠狀態，直到 1968 年爆發。

在這個國家公園中，有很多步道可以帶領你到不同的觀景台以較好的角度看 Arenal 火山，或是 Arenal 大壩。然而，在你去之前，請特別注意氣象報導，以免得白去了！因為 La Fortuna 有時候會起大霧！爬上這些步道，你會需要登山鞋，防蚊液和一瓶水！當你到了觀景台之後，你會很驚訝 Arenal 火山有多麼的對稱！

夏威夷
威尼斯
紐約
曼谷
哥斯大黎加
舊金山
倫敦
都柏林
巴塞隆納
洛杉磯

旅遊愛玩咖 ▶

Natural Scene　MP3 10

There is a local natural hot spring river in La Fortuna. It is totally free, wild and full of charm. People usually recommend that you should have walk down to the river in the dark, and just follow the sound of people and random flashes from the lights people bring with them down to the hot spring. As the splashing sound gets louder, you will know you are getting close to the hot spring. Walking into the hot spring will be such a treat in a chilly night at La Fortuna. With the river babbling and murmuring, sour whole body will quickly loosen up from the hike you did or stress from life in general. You can smell the aroma from the forest and hear the chirps from the insects. It is just like one of those relaxing music CDs. You can stay there until your fingers get all wrinkly. Nobody will rush you. It will certainly be wonderful to experience what the Ticos do in Costa Rica.

夏威夷

威尼斯

紐約

曼谷

哥斯大黎加

舊金山

倫敦

都柏林

巴塞隆納

洛杉磯

自然場景

在 La Fortuna 裡有一條當地天然的溫泉河水。它完全免費，野外的，並充滿了魅力！人們通常會建議你晚上去這條河。只要隨著人聲和從人們帶到溫泉的手電筒隨機的閃光，就可以抵達。當河水的飛濺的聲音變大，你就知道你已經接近溫泉了。在 La Fortuna 寒冷的夜晚裡走進溫泉真是莫大的幸福。隨著涓涓河水，你全身很快的就會立刻從早先爬山的痠痛或是生活帶來的壓力中放鬆下來。你可以聞到來自森林裡的芳香，和聽到蟲鳴如同那些令人放鬆的 CD 音樂一般。你可以待到手指都發皺也沒有人會催趕你，那也將會一個很棒的經驗體驗當地人（或是 Ticos）喜歡在哥斯大黎加做的事！

Vocabulary and Idioms ▶

❶ abundant `adj` 充足的 　　**❷ lushness** `n` 翠綠茂盛

❸ appreciative `adj` 感激的 　**❹ trek** `v` 長途艱苦跋涉

❺ diner `n` 小餐館 　　**❻ eruption** `n` 爆發

❼ mosquito repellent
　防蚊液 　　　　　　　**❽ splash** `v` 潑，濺

1. Looks like they will have abundant water for the next week.
   看來他們下禮拜會有充足的水。

2. The lushness of this forest is beyond description.
   這片森林的翠綠茂盛是無法形容的。

3. He was very appreciative for what his parents did for him.
   他十分感激他的父母為他做的一切。

4. They trekked for 11 hours straight and made it to the top.
   他們長途辛苦的跋涉了十一個小時攻頂。 ‘

5. There are several nice diners around this neighborhood.
   這附近有許多很好的小餐館。

6. She is about to have an emotional eruption.
   她即將要情緒爆發了。

7. Don't forget to bring the mosquito repellent to the campsite.
   記得別忘了要帶防蚊液到營地。

8. The water is splashing from the waterfall.
   水由瀑布飛濺下來。

旅遊小貼士 ▶

　　在哥斯大黎加有一個怪事就是他們的住址其實根本就不存在！他們並沒有街名！很令人吃驚吧！那他們要怎麼報路，而郵差又要怎麼寄信呢？當地人其實是用相對方位來報路。譬如說，他們會跟你說麥當勞就是在加油站東邊 200 公尺，或是在水果攤往東邊走 300 公尺等等！所以說囉，當你在問方向的時候，千萬別太驚訝你必須要多問好幾個地方的方向才會到達你想去的地方！因為其實他們給的方向是非常精確的喔！出門前只要多記幾個大的路標即可！

夏威夷

威尼斯

紐約

曼谷

哥斯大黎加

舊金山

倫敦

都柏林

巴塞隆納

洛杉磯

Unit 06

San Francisco 舊金山 Golden Gate Park - The Pursuit of Happyness 金門大橋公園當幸福來敲門

城市介紹

If you are looking for a city that bridged the gap between East and West with innovating technology, you will find San Francisco.The seemingly limitless museums matched with a wide variety of cuisine will leave one filed with lots to explore.

San Francisco bay has become and remains for most of the American settlement and business city of the «Far West». This port helped to bring in influences to the Americas from Asia and other parts of the pacific. As years rolled on, the bay became home to the world known monument known as the Golden Gate Bridge.

Surrounding the bay is a city full of this heritage that many people come from near and far to indulge themselves in art and food today. Indeed, there are plenty of hidden gems in food, art, history, and adventurous activities. Surrounded by the water, San Francisco is like a city coming out from a painting. That is no wonder San Francisco houses and inspires several well-known artists of all kinds. Take a few art classes when you are in San Francisco next time! You just might meet the artist inside you!

舊金山 ▶

如果你想找一個擁有創新科技並連接東西方的城市，舊金山就是你想找的！似乎無盡的博物館和豐富多樣的料理會留給你很多去探索。

舊金山海灣曾成為並還是大多美國人"遠西"的居留和商業城市。這個港口曾幫助美洲帶入由亞洲和太平洋其他部分所帶來的影響。幾年過後，這個海灣成為世界聞名的金門大橋的家。在這個海灣的周遭是一個充滿歷史遺產的城市。現今，人們從世界各地來到這個城市來沈浸在藝術和美食中。確實，這裡有許多隱藏的美食，藝術，歷史，和冒險活動珍寶。被海水環繞，舊金山就像是從畫中走出一般，這也難怪舊金山住了和成就了許多世界聞名的各類藝術家。下次你來舊金山，去上幾堂藝術課程。或許你會遇到你自己內心深藏不露的藝術家！

夏威夷 威尼斯 紐約 曼谷 哥斯大黎加 舊金山 倫敦 都柏林 巴塞隆納 洛杉磯

Dialogue 情境對話 ▶

Ryan and Dylan just jumped on the cable car to go to the Fishermen's Wharf.

萊恩和迪倫剛跳上噹噹車前往漁人碼頭。

Ryan: Wow, this is so neat!! Definitely one of the best ways to explore this city!

萊恩：哇！這個好棒喔！絕對是探索這個城市最好的辦法之一！

Dylan: Yeah, I agree! Come to this side, you can see the view of the bay!

迪倫：對啊，我同意！你來這邊，這邊可以看到海灣的風景喔！

Ryan: I think I'm better off staying on this side. This ride is pretty rough!

萊恩：我覺得我是在這頭抓緊就好了！這段旅程好顛簸！

Dylan: Yeah, I believe the driver just said: "Hang on or get killed!"

迪倫：對啊，我相信剛剛司機說了："抓緊或是喪命！"

Ryan: Seriously? He was joking, right? I mean there are children and old people, too.

萊恩：真的假的？他只是在開玩笑，對嗎？我的意思是說，車上還有小孩和老人。

Dylan: Well… I do think he has a good point. The streets here are so steep!

迪倫：嗯…我覺得他說得有道理。這裡的街道都好陡峭喔！

Ryan: It's like a roller coaster ride. Must be fun to drive the cable car here.

萊恩：就像雲霄飛車一樣。在這裡開噹噹車一定很好玩。

Dylan: It's fun to watch the driver ring the bell nonstop, too!

迪倫：看司機不停地響鈴噹也很有趣！

Ryan: Yeah, he's getting on my nerves, though. We are going to arrive soon, correct?

萊恩：恩，但是他已經開始讓我覺得有點煩了。我們快到了，對嗎？

Dylan: Negative. I think it's still going to take a while. You'd better hang tight and enjoy the breeze!

迪倫：不對！我想應該還要一下喔！你最好抓緊跟享受這微風！

Ryan: It beats walking all this way to the Fishermen's Wharf I suppose.

萊恩：總比走去漁人碼頭好，我想。

Dylan: Yeah, we had enough walk from the Golden Gate Park yesterday…

迪倫：對啊，我們昨天在金門大橋公園走夠了！

夏威夷
威尼斯
紐約
曼谷
哥斯大黎加
舊金山
倫敦
都柏林
巴塞隆納
洛杉磯

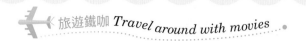

Ryan: Hang on!! Big drop ahead!!

萊恩：抓緊了！前面有很大的下坡！

Special Sites Introduction 6: 特別景點報導 ▶

San Francisco - Golden Gate Park - The Pursuit of Happiness

MP3 11

Remember the heart-warming movie, the Pursuit of Happyness, released in 2006? In the movie the desperate Dad, Chris Gardener (Will Smith) was looking at his Son, Christopher (Jaden Smith) play in the children's playground while spotting a homeless man carrying his stolen X-Ray machine. Chris ran and got the X-Ray machine back from the homeless man soon afterwards. This scene was shot in the Golden Gate Park in San Francisco.

Golden Gate Park is located on the northwest side of San Francisco. It is 5 kilometer in length and 800 meters in width. It includes 359 streets and is by far the biggest man-made Metropolitan Park. You can find gardens, lakes, huge playgrounds, trails, golf courses, tennis court, soccer fields and more here. What's more? On the weekends, from JFK Drive to 19th Ave. will only be open for pedestrians. All vehicles are not allowed at this part of the park. People may dance, roller skate, or bike in the middle of the street without worrying about getting in the cars' way. Golden Gate Park just might be the perfect urban escape for you!

舊金山 - 金門大橋公園當幸福來敲門

還記得 2006 年上映溫馨感人的片子，當幸福來敲門嗎？在電影中當那絕望的爸爸，克里斯（由威爾史密斯飾演）正在公園看著他的兒子克里斯托福（傑登史密斯）在公園裡的遊樂場玩的時候，他突然看見一個流浪漢提著克里斯被偷走的 X 光機。克里斯立即奔跑並把他的 X 光機拿回來。這個場景就是在舊金山的金門大橋公園所拍攝。

金門大橋公園是位於舊金山的西北岸。這個公園長 1.5 公里，寬 800 公尺。公園包含了 359 個街道，並是至今最大的人造都會公園。在其中你可以看到花園，湖，巨大的遊樂區，步道，高爾夫球場，網球場，足球場，還有更多。除此之外還有什麼呢？在週末，從約翰甘迺迪大道到第 19 大道只開放給行人。所有的車輛都禁止進入公園的這個區域。人們可以在其中跳舞，輪式溜冰，或是在路中間騎腳踏車，並無需擔心擋到車的路。金門大橋公園可能就是你那最好的城市解悶最佳去處！

夏威夷
威尼斯
紐約
曼谷
哥斯大黎加
舊金山
倫敦
都柏林
巴塞隆納
洛杉磯

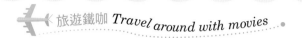

饕客園地 ▶

Pier 39-Clam Chowder and Sourdough Bread Bowl

 MP3 12

If you are a foodie, then you really cannot miss this signature dish at Pier 39 in San Francisco. Seafood has always been the favorite dish by the locals and the tourists at Pier 39. The origin of clam chowder can be dated back to the 16th or the 17th century when San Francisco was still just a fishing village. Villagers would cook up a big pot of broth with vegetables, and waited for the fishermen to come back with whatever seafood they caught on the day and they threw it in the soup. As for the sourdough in San Francisco, when the French baker Isidore Boudin immigrated here in 1849. He made the sourdough and it became so popular. However, some said that it was perhaps the chilly bay breeze that first inspired the marriage of Clam Chowder and Sourdough Bowl. Whoever it was, this dish has certainly spread its name around the world. People come to Pier 39 from far and wide to see the wild sea lions that have been living there since 1990 and enjoy a bowl of clam chowder with sourdough bread bowl. Choose a chilly, and misty afternoon, and come by pier 39 to try a bowl of clam chowder with the sourdough bread bowl. Guarantee it will be worth your while!

夏威夷

威尼斯

紐約

曼谷

哥斯大黎加

舊金山

倫敦

都柏林

巴塞隆納

洛杉磯

39 號碼頭-酸麵包蛤蜊巧達濃湯

　　如果你是一個食客的話，那你就絕對不能錯過這個舊金山 39 號碼頭的招牌菜。在 39 號碼頭，海鮮一直都是這裡當地人和遊客的最愛。蛤蜊巧達濃湯的來源可以被追溯回十六或十七世紀時，當舊金山還是一個小小的漁村。村民們會煮好一鍋由蔬菜所熬煮而成的大鍋高湯，並等著漁民們當天捕捉回來的海鮮在一起煮成一鍋湯。至於舊金山的酸麵包,當法國的麵包師 Isidore Boudin 在 1849 年移民到舊金山，他做了酸麵包並使得酸麵包在舊金山一舉成名。然而，有些人説或許是那寒冷的海風才造就了巧達濃湯和酸麵包的結合。不論一開始究竟是誰發明了這道菜，酸麵包蛤蜊巧達濃湯已經是家喻戶曉了！人們從世界各地來到 39 號碼頭來看從 1990 年就住在這裡的海獅，並享用一碗酸麵包蛤蜊巧達濃湯。選個寒冷並起霧的下午來 39 號碼頭，試一碗酸麵包蛤蜊巧達濃湯。保證值回票價！

Vocabulary and Idioms ▶

❶ **innovating** adj 創新的   ❷ **cuisine** n 料理

❸ **heritage** n 遺產   ❹ **indulge** v 沈迷於

❺ **neat** adj 很棒的   ❻ **get one someone's nerves**
Idiom 使某人開始煩躁

❼ **pedestrian** n 行人   ❽ **signature dish** n 招牌菜

1. Their innovating products have become a big success in the market.

   他們創新的產品已經在市場上締造佳績。

2. We are going to try the French cuisine at a local diner tonight.

   我們今天晚上要到當地的一家小餐館吃法式料理。

3. A clean environment is the best heritage we can leave for our descendants.

   一個乾淨的環境是我們可以留給我們子孫最好的遺產。

4. He indulged in the video games all day, and forgot to go to the class tonight.

   他一整天都沈迷於電玩，而且晚上還忘了去上課。

5. That idea is so neat!

   這個點子真是太棒了！

6. He is really getting on my nerves this time.

   他真的開始讓我生氣了。

7. Watch out for the pedestrians when you are riding the bike on the street.

你在街上騎腳踏車的時候要小心行人喔。

8. Paella is his signature dish. You cannot leave without trying it.

西班牙海鮮燉飯是他的招牌菜。你不能沒試過就離開！

旅遊小貼士 ▶

　　來到舊金山，一個小小的提醒是，記得要以洋蔥式穿衣法穿衣服，雖然處於加州，舊金山的天氣還是早晚溫差很大！甚至在白天的時候，也像小時候北風和太陽的故事一樣，在太陽曬得到的地方時，你會熱到脫掉你的外套，在大樓遮蔽，只有陰影的地方的時候，舊金山的風一吹，你也會忍不住立刻穿起外套，在城市中遊走也就在你脫脫穿穿外衣中渡過，所以囉，在舊金山別忘了準備穿脫方便的外衣喔！

夏威夷
威尼斯
紐約
曼谷
哥斯大黎加
舊金山
倫敦
都柏林
巴塞隆納
洛杉磯

Unit 07

London City 倫敦市 – 哈利波特熱潮 The craze for Harry Potter

城市介紹 ▶

Claiming fame to the Capital of Britain, you will find London. The huge city of over 7.5 million people is a huge draw from tourists and residents from all over the globe. Residing among these people you will find the Royal Family. Even though we may not have the same accommodations as the Royals do, it seems as if the honor and royal service can be felt throughout the entire city.

Some of the traditions, such as changing the guards at Buckingham palace or the Changing of Keys at the tower of London whose origins can be dated back to the. Going back even further than the traditions, are some of the myths and legends off the streets; such as "pea-soupers", which is a "white out" fog that occurs every 50 or so years.

London is famous in the world for both its history and diversity. You could be relaxing in a centuries old pub or find yourself dining in a trendy new restaurant. Hosting the 2012 Olympics brought about even more modernizations without affecting the history of this exciting city.

倫敦市

在英國享有首都名聲的倫敦，超過七百五十萬人的這個城市是一個吸引觀光客和世界各地的居民來一探究竟的城市，在這些居民當中，你會找到皇室家族。雖然我們沒有像皇室般的住處，但那皇室的榮譽和服務似乎在整個城市都可以感受到。

倫敦有些傳統例如更換白金漢宮的守衛，或是變更倫敦塔的鑰匙都可以追溯回 1600 年代，追溯回這些比傳統更早發生的是一些神話和街上的傳說。例如黃色的濃霧，也就是一片不透明的濃霧每隔 50 年左右就會發生一次！

倫敦是在世界上是以它的歷史和多樣性而成名。你可以在一個百年老酒吧放鬆喝酒， 或是在一個新潮的新餐廳裡享用餐點。在 2012 年倫敦主辦奧林匹克賽事，那也為倫敦帶來更多的現在化的事物而沒有影響到這個刺激城市的歷史。

Dialogue 情境對話 ▶

Melissa and Travis have a transit flight at London and they decide to go for a ride on the London Eye.

梅利莎和崔佛思在倫敦轉機，所以他們決定要去倫敦眼。

Melissa: I had no idea how spacious each capsule in London Eye is!

梅利莎：我從來不知道倫敦眼每一個座艙都那麼寬敞！

Travis: Yeah, I read from the brochure that it can take up to 28 people in each capsule.

崔佛思：對啊，我從這個小冊子裡讀到倫敦眼每個座艙可以乘載高達 28 人！

Melissa: Wow, there are 32 capsules in total and it's around 20 euros per person...can you imagine how much money they are making every day?

梅利莎：哇，倫敦眼總共有 32 個座艙耶！一個人至少要 20 歐元…你可以想像他們每天賺多少錢嗎？

Travis: Well... life is not fair sometimes. You gotta admit it's a pretty genius idea though. I can't think of a better way to spend our short time in London better. We only have 1.5 hour till the next flight.

崔佛思：嗯。人生有的時候是不公平的，但你必須承認這是個蠻好的主意！我無法想出一個更好的辦法來利用我們在倫敦的短暫時間。到下一班機起飛前我們只有一個半小時。

Melissa: You're right. I think this is the biggest Ferris wheel I've ever been on. I can only imagine how romantic it will be at nighttime.

梅利莎：你說的對，這是我坐過最大的摩天輪！我只能想像晚上在這一定很浪漫！

Travis: They are only open till 8:30 pm though!

崔佛思：他們只開到晚上八點半耶！

Melissa: Yeah, a perfect way to start a date before dinner!

梅利莎：對啊，在晚餐前，這是個很好的辦法來開始一個完美的約會！

Travis: Wait a minute... What are you implying?

崔佛思：等一下…你是在暗示什麼？

Melissa: We can stay till 8 pm and go for a dinner before we have to go!

梅利莎：我們可以在這待到八點，然後在要離開前去吃個晚餐吧！

Travis: Sounds great! I'd like that!

崔佛思：聽起來不錯。我喜歡這個主意！

夏威夷
威尼斯
紐約
曼谷
哥斯大黎加
舊金山
倫敦
都柏林
巴塞隆納
洛杉磯

Special Sites Introduction 7: 特別景點報導 ▶

London - The Craze for Harry Potter   MP3 13

Before entering the enchanting and exciting scenes of the world-renowned Harry Potter films, loyal fans of Harry Potter will not miss the fascinating scene where Harry (Daniel Radcliffe), Ron (Rupert Grint) and Hermione (Emma Watson) have to push the trolleys through the brick wall between platform 9 and 10 to access platform 9 ¾. At 9 ¾ platform, they will be able to catch the train to go back to Hogwarts before the school year starts.

The train station in all Harry Potter movies is the very Kings Cross Station in London. It has become a pretty touristy spot ever since Harry Potter movies won hearts of every household in the world. When you arrive at Kings Cross Station, it will be pretty easy to find the 9 ¾ platform and a trolley that is half way out of the wall since there is always a long line waiting for picture taking at the site. You are allowed to take your own photo if you wish not to spend any money there. You will get to pick a scarf for your photo shoot, and if you are not satisfied after that, feel free to pop in a souvenir store next door that has a Harry potter theme. Enjoy, and stay imaginative!

倫敦 - 哈利波特熱潮

　　在進入世界聞名的哈利波特電影那些神奇又刺激的畫面前，哈利波特的忠實粉絲們一定不會錯過那有趣的場景。當哈利（丹尼爾雷得克里夫），榮恩（魯博特葛林）和妙麗（愛瑪華森）必須推著推車穿過第九和第十月台中間的磚牆來到九又四分之三月台。在九又四分之三月台，他們才可以在新學年開始前搭乘火車回去霍格華茲。

　　那個在所有哈利波特電影中出現的火車站就是在倫敦的國王十字火車站。自從哈利波特贏得了世界各地人們的心之後，它就變成一個蠻觀光客的地方。當你到了國王十字火車站時，就會很容易就找到了九又四分之三月台，以及一個一半在牆裡的推車，因為那裡會有很長的人龍等著要拍照。如果你不想花錢的話，你也可以自己拍照。你可以選擇自己的哈利波特圍巾來照相。如果拍完照後你還是不盡興的話，你也可以到隔壁的哈利波特主題紀念品店裡逛逛。好好玩，並且繼續保持充滿想像力！

夏威夷
威尼斯
紐約
曼谷
哥斯大黎加
舊金山
倫敦
都柏林
巴塞隆納
洛杉磯

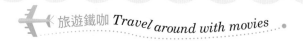

  MP3 14

Coming to London, you should not leave without trying the food that is originated from London: Fish and Chips. Different from what the name suggests, chips here do not mean potato chips but deep-fried French fries. The fish is usually Atlantic cod or haddock covered with batter and then deep-fried. If you do some research, you will find tons of restaurants that sell this hot item in London. New or old, each has its own fans. What makes everyone go nuts about their fish and chips are the succulent, fresh fish that flakes off so easily, and the crispy chips that are not too greasy and are still good even when they get cold. Sounds a bit heavy for you? Try it with the side dish coleslaw, which consists of finely shredded cabbage and is often dressed with salad vinaigrette and mayonnaise.

Fish and Chips was originally a stock meal for the working class when fresh fish was often delivered when troll fishing was at its peak in London. Who would have thought that years later, this dish has become something that characterizes London.

夏威夷

威尼斯

紐約

曼谷

哥斯大黎加

舊金山

倫敦

都柏林

巴塞隆納

洛杉磯

炸魚薯條

　　來到倫敦，你沒試過源自倫敦的炸魚薯條的話，你就不應該離開。跟它名字不同的是 Chips（薯片），在此並不代表馬鈴薯片，而是指薯條。魚通常是亞特蘭大的鱈魚，或是黑線鱈，覆蓋麵糊之後再油炸。如果你研究一下的話，你就會發現超多的餐廳賣這道熱門的菜。新的餐廳也好，舊的也罷，他們都有自己忠實的群眾。令許多人為這道菜瘋狂的是那多汁，新鮮的魚肉，一片魚肉輕易地就會掉下來。和他們酥脆卻不會太油膩的薯條，就算冷掉了也還是很美味。聽起來還是有點油膩嗎？試著跟一個旁邊的小菜，涼拌捲心菜一起吃吧！涼拌捲心菜包括了切得很細的高麗菜和油醋沙拉醬以及美乃茲所組成。炸魚薯條一開始其實是倫敦在拖釣釣魚巔峰時期時是勞工階層囤積的餐點。誰想得到數年之後，這道菜竟然成為象徵倫敦之一的特色！

Vocabulary and Idioms ▶

❶ **resident** n 居民　　❷ **accommodation** n 住宿

❸ **myth** n 迷思　　❹ **spacious** adj 寬敞的

❺ **brochure** n 小冊子　　❻ **Ferris wheel** n 摩天輪

❼ **imply** v 暗示　　❽ **succulent** adj 多汁的

1. You get more discounts if you are a resident here.

   如果你是當地居民的話你會有比較多的折扣。

2. Did you figure out your accommodation in London?

   你在倫敦的住宿已經安排好了嗎？

3. It's a myth why girls love the color pink.

   女生喜歡粉紅色真是一個迷思。

4. His new apartment is very spacious and clean.

   他的新公寓很寬敞又乾淨。

5. We should get a brochure about the show. We barely know what it is about!

   我們應該要拿個關於這個表演的小冊子。我們幾乎完全不知道這個表演的內容。

6. We used to eat our lunch in the Ferris wheel on a field trip.

   我們以前郊遊的時候都會在摩天輪上吃午餐。

7. He implied that I would get a promotion very soon this morning.

   他今天早上暗示我很快就會被升遷了。

8. The steak here is very succulent and flavorful.

這牛排很多汁又很有風味。

旅遊小貼士 ▶

　　在倫敦市玩的時候，你會發現這裡不僅是有來自世界各地的遊客，還有許多當地的居民行走在城市中。如果你仔細地觀察的話，就會發現這裡的人們大多都會好好的打扮自己之後再出門，不只是女士們打扮的得體合宜，男士們也都是十分有自己的時尚風格。所以囉，當你來到倫敦，行走在街道上的時候也要注意自己的穿著。旅行的時候雖然以穿著輕鬆便利之外，還代表了自己的國家行走在街道上。來到倫敦，出門前打扮一下，以免穿著夾腳拖鞋出門後懊悔不已！

夏威夷
威尼斯
紐約
曼谷
哥斯大黎加
舊金山
倫敦
都柏林
巴塞隆納
洛杉磯

Unit 08

Dublin 都柏林 –
P.S. I Love You P.S.我愛你

城市介紹 ▶

Dublin is the capital of Ireland, and it is also the biggest city within Ireland. Dublin takes you back in time just by having you walk down any of its street. Surrounded by old buildings, a walk down the street can be quite peaceful and delightful. A book and a pot of Assam tea cannot be better enjoyed anywhere else. From churches to statues, beautiful gates to fountains, the beauty of Dublin can be seen just about anywhere.

Dublin is one of the places that is most well-known for its bar culture. Irish people celebrates food, drinks, and music alto-gether on the south bank of river Liffey. The Temple Bar area comes alive at night time with lots of tourists and a variety of beers and liquors at your choice. There are dances, music, art galleries, food, and drink. It is definitely a must-go if you want to experience the historical and modern Dublin. The actual Temple Bar can be traced back in 1840, with the quaint decoration and joyful atmosphere. It is still the most popular bar till today.

◀ 都柏林 ▶

　　都柏林是愛爾蘭的首都，也是愛爾蘭境內最大的城市。只是在任何一條都柏林的街上走著都仿佛時光倒流一般。這裡被古老的建築物圍繞，走在街上都覺得格外的平靜和喜悅。一本書和一壺阿薩姆紅茶跟這裡比起不能在別處更令人享受了！從教堂到雕像，華美的大門到噴水池，都柏林的美隨處可見。

　　都柏林是以酒吧文化最為聞名的地方之一。愛爾蘭人在麗妃河的南岸一次享用美食，美酒，和音樂。聖殿酒吧區在夜晚會變得十分活躍，有許多的觀光客會來到這邊，也有許多啤酒和利口酒供你選擇！舞蹈，音樂，畫廊，美食，美酒都會在這區等著你！如果你想要體驗歷史和現代的都柏林文化，這區是一定要去的！而真正的聖殿酒吧可以被追溯回 1840 年開店，可愛的裝飾和令人開心的氣氛都是令它至今都還是最受歡迎的酒吧的原因！

夏威夷
威尼斯
紐約
曼谷
哥斯大黎加
舊金山
倫敦
都柏林
巴塞隆納
洛杉磯

Dialogue 情境對話 ▶

Marie and Jesse just sat down at one of the bars for breakfast.
茉莉和傑西正在一間酒吧坐下來點早餐。

Marie: Wow, I would have never guessed they serve breakfast in a bar!

茉莉：哇，我永遠都不可能會猜到他們的酒吧有賣早餐！

Jesse: Yeah, I know. I didn't know about this, either. A friend of mine told me about this!

傑西：對啊，我知道。我之前也不知道。是我一個朋友跟我說的！

Marie: What should we order? I'm starving!

茉莉：我們該點什麼呢？我好餓喔！

Jesse: I'm gonna start with an Irish coffee!

傑西：我要先點一杯愛爾蘭咖啡！

Marie: What exactly is in an Irish coffee?

茉莉：愛爾蘭咖啡裡面到底有什麼？

Jesse: It's pretty much, black coffee, Irish whisky, sugar with cream!

傑西：其實就是黑咖啡，愛爾蘭威士忌，糖和奶油！

Marie: Yum! Sounds perfect on a chilly day like today! I'll take one, too!

茉莉：好吃耶！在像今天天氣冷的時候喝一杯最棒了！我也要點一杯！

Jesse: Yeah, let's try the Irish breakfast since we're here!

傑西：好，既然我們在這就點這個愛爾蘭早餐吧！

Marie: Alright! Let's do it! A full Irish breakfast experience! I like it!

茉莉：好啊！我們就這樣點吧！一整套的愛爾蘭早餐體驗！我喜歡！

(After the waiter served their breakfast)

在服務生上菜之後

Marie: What on earth is this black thing?

茉莉：這個黑黑的東西到底是什麼？

Jesse: Oh, that's black pudding! Don't tell me you don't know about this.

傑西：喔，那是黑布丁！不要跟我說你不知道那是什麼！

Marie: Am I supposed to know about this? Do I want to know?

茉莉：我應該要知道嗎？我想知道嗎？

Jesse: It's not a big deal! It's just pig

傑西：這沒有什麼大不了的

夏威夷
威尼斯
紐約
曼谷
哥斯大黎加
舊金山
倫敦
都柏林
巴塞隆納
洛杉磯

blood with oatmeal. It's just like a blood sausage.

啦！就是豬血和燕麥。就像是血香腸。

Marie: A blood sausage?! That does not make it better at all!

茉莉：血香腸？！那聽起來沒有比較好噢！

Jesse: Oh come on, you won't know whether you like it or not until you try it!

傑西：噢拜託，你不試就不會知道你究竟喜歡還不喜歡！

Marie: I'm pretty sure it's not my thing.

茉莉：我蠻確定我不會喜歡。

Jesse: You will always wonder about this black pudding. You're so close! Come on!

傑西：你永遠會一直想著這黑布丁。你已經這麼接近了！試試看嗎！

Marie: Okay! I will try a small bit of it.

茉莉：好啦！我試一小口。

Jesse: Well? What do you think?

傑西：怎麼樣？你覺得如何？

Marie: Now we know I don't like it. Thanks Jesse!

茉莉：現在我們都知道我不喜歡這個了！謝謝你傑西！

Special Sites Introduction 8: 特別景點報導 ▶

Dublin - P.S. I Love You　　MP3 15

Remember in the movie "P.S. I Love You", released in 2007, Gerry (Gerard Butler) and Holly (Hilary Swank) demonstrated the true love that does not cease by death? In this romantic film, Gerry was dying from an incurable disease. However, determined to help Holly get over grieving over his death, Gerry wrote ten letters, each was sent with a specific instruction to help Holly move on with her life. One of the letters instructed Holly's best friend to take Holly to "Whelan's pub" where Gerry and Holly met for the second time and where Gerry was performing on stage in that very pub.

Whelan's pub is located on 25 Wexford St. in Dublin. The pub is big enough to house two gigs each night thanks to the 2 stages in the pub. The place celebrates Irish music as well as world music. A lot of international musicians claim this was the birthplace for their music. So next time when you are in Dublin, why not follow what Gerry said to Holly's friend: "Whelan's, my favorite pub. There's beautiful music to be heard, beautiful people to be around."

夏威夷
威尼斯
紐約
曼谷
哥斯大黎加
舊金山
倫敦
都柏林
巴塞隆納
洛杉磯

都柏林 - P.S. 我愛你

還記得在 2007 年上映的電影 "PS 我愛你" 中，傑瑞（傑哈德巴特勒飾）和荷莉（希拉蕊史旺飾）呈現了真愛不會因為死亡而結束？在這個浪漫感人的片中，傑瑞得到了不治之症。然而，決心要幫助荷莉走出他死亡的陰霾，傑瑞死前寫了十封信，每一封都有特別的指示來幫助荷莉繼續她的人生。其中一封信指示荷莉最好的朋友帶荷莉去 Whelan's 酒吧，荷莉和傑瑞第二次見面的地方，而那也正是當時傑瑞在台上演出的地方。

Whelan's 酒吧是為在都柏林 25 號 Wexford 街上。這個酒吧因為有兩個舞台，所以可以容納兩個樂團在同一個晚上演出。這裡也是以愛爾蘭音樂和世界音樂為主流。很多國際樂手宣稱這個地方是他們音樂的孕育地。所以下次當你人在都柏林，何不遵從傑瑞給的指示："Whelan's，我最喜歡的酒吧。那裡有美妙的音樂可以聽，美麗的人們陪伴在你身旁。"

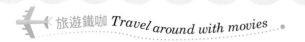
 旅遊愛玩咖 ▶

Legend of the Leprechauns · MP3 16

The legend of the Leprechauns was said to come from the Irish Mythology and is folklore. A Leprechaun is a fairy that has the look of an old man and is always nicely dressed in green. They are about three feet tall with a beard and a hat. It is said that they are the mischievous, and devious fairies that store coins and gold at the end of the rainbow. They have magical powers to guard their pots of gold. Therefore, if you have ever caught one, which is highly unlikely due to the fact that they would do about anything to escape, in exchange for release, the Leprechaun will grant you three wishes with their magical powers. However, every Irish person would tell you that you should never trust a Leprechaun when making your three wishes since the Leprechauns are great mind players and by making the wrong wishes, you might end up with more troubles than joyful things.

Leprechauns are shoemakers. They are busy all day making shoes. It is said that they love to dance all day, and that is precisely the reason why they need shoes constantly. They are also known to be great musicians. They can play several traditional Irish instruments.

夏威夷

威尼斯

紐約

曼谷

哥斯大黎加

舊金山

倫敦

都柏林

巴塞隆納

洛杉磯

矮精靈的傳說

　　矮精靈的傳說聽說是來自愛爾蘭的神話和民間傳說。矮精靈是一個看起來像老人並穿著綠衣服的精靈。他們大多是三呎高，都有留鬍子和戴帽子！他們聽說是非常頑皮，狡詐的精靈，他們在彩虹的盡頭裡儲存了硬幣和金礦。這也是為什麼他們都有神奇的魔法來守衛他們的金礦。如果你真的抓到了一個矮精靈（十分不可能因為他們會用盡所有的辦法逃跑），為了恢復自由，他門會用他們神奇的魔法給你三個願望。然而，每個愛爾蘭人都會跟你說許願時千萬別相信矮精靈說的話，因為矮精靈們是很厲害的心智玩家，而如果你因此許了不好的願望，你可能到後來會得到更多的麻煩而非開心的事。

　　矮精靈們也是鞋匠。他們總是在做鞋子。傳說他們喜歡成天跳舞，而這也是為什麼他們會需要那麼多的鞋子。他們也是很厲害的音樂家，他們會演奏幾乎所有傳統的愛爾蘭樂器！

Vocabulary and Idioms ▶

❶ **statue** n 雕像

❷ **something is not my thing!**
Idiom 我對這沒興趣！

❸ **incurable** adj 無法治癒的　　❹ **gig** n 演奏，表演

❺ **mythology** n 神話　　❻ **folklore** n 民間傳說

❼ **mischievous** adj 調皮的　　❽ **devious** adj 不光明的

1. The statues are so real that the dogs thought they are strangers.
   這些雕像實在是太逼真了以至於狗群都以為它們是陌生人。

2. Hiking is not my thing. I'd rather go swimming.
   我對健行沒興趣。我寧願游泳。

3. He got an incurable disease, but he is still very positive.
   他得到了一個不治之症，但他還是十分的正向。

4. He has two gigs at two different places tonight.
   他今天晚上在兩個不同的地方有表演。

5. I think mythology is just the explanation people come up with when they see something they don't know.
   我認為神話只是人們對於他們不知道的事物的解釋。

6. Folklores reveals a lot about the town.
   民間傳說可以透露很多關於這個鎮的資訊。

7. He always has this mischievous smile on his face when he is up to something.
   他在計劃什麼事的時候臉上總是掛著一個調皮的笑容。

8. He became rich through devious ways.

他以不光明的方式變得富裕。

旅遊小貼士 ▶

　　在愛爾蘭吃飯時， 去餐廳吃飯記得要給小費噢！小費大約在 10% 左右！但是記得到酒吧或是小酒館時就不必給小費了！由此得知愛爾蘭人其實不常在外吃飯！除非是比較富有一些才會在外吃飯一週一至二次！而他們大多也以他們的家常菜為最受歡迎的餐廳。當你被當地人邀請至他們家吃飯，切記一定要等所有人就定位再開動，還有就是盤子中夾的食物一定要吃完噢，否則可能會被視為浪費食物和不喜歡他們的菜色！

夏威夷
威尼斯
紐約
曼谷
哥斯大黎加
舊金山
倫敦
都柏林
巴塞隆納
洛杉磯

Unit 09

Barcelona 巴塞隆納
Vicky, Christina, Barcelona
情遇巴塞隆納

城市介紹 ▶

    The smell of paella, nuts, dried cod fish fills in the air of La Ramba, the street that is always crowded with lots of tourists. The tree-lined, 1.2-kilometer street offers a lot to try and lots to buy. People try to bargain with their broken Spanish while taking pictures of all sorts of souvenirs that they have never seen before. All the while, several ancient cathedrals are overlooking the street around it. Every corner can be a perfect setting for your selfies or photos. Sitting down at a tapas bar with an open mind, you just might run into backpackers around the world to share their exclusive stories around the world with their exceptional story-telling skills! While in Barcelona, surrounded by history, architectures, arts, and music, expect that anything can happen. Sitting down at a store by the street eating, someone might come and take your food away. Just when you are about to tell the person you are not done yet, the person walks out of the store. You look at the owner of the vendor, he would just shrug and tell you: "Welcome to Barcelona!"

巴塞隆納

　　在蘭布拉大道，空氣中充滿了海鮮燉飯，核果，和鱈魚乾的香味。蘭布拉大道總是充滿了許多的觀光客，這兩旁有樹，長為 1.2 公里的街道上提供了許多可以試和可以買的東西。人們試著以簡陋的西文向攤販殺價並同時拍下許多他們從未看過的紀念品。始終，許多古老的大教堂都在大道的周遭俯瞰這一切。每一個轉角都可以是你自拍或是拍照最完美的背景。而如果以開放的心胸坐進任何一家西班牙風味小館，都有可能會遇見在環遊世界的背包客以他們卓越的説故事技巧和你分享他們的獨家故事！身在巴塞隆納，被歷史，建築，藝術，和音樂環繞，預期什麼都有可能發生。坐在一個路邊的店家吃東西，有人可能會走近並收走你的食物。正當你想跟那個人説你還沒吃完，那個人就走出店外了！你看著店家，他也可能只會聳聳肩並跟你説：「歡迎來到巴塞隆納！」

夏威夷
威尼斯
紐約
曼谷
哥斯大黎加
舊金山
倫敦
都柏林
巴塞隆納
洛杉磯

Dialogue 情境對話 ▶

Samuel and Amy are walking in La Sagrada Familia
山姆和愛咪正在走進聖家堂。

Amy: Oh my, Gaudi must have lost it at the end!

艾咪：我的天啊！高第最後一定是瘋了！

Samuel: What do you mean?

山姆：你是什麼意思？

Amy: I think this building is beyond anyone's imagination. This is more than a cathedral, more than architecture, and more than anything you could possibly think of!

艾咪：我覺得這個建築物已經是超乎任何人的想像力了！這不只是一個大教堂，不只是一個建築物，也不只是任何你可能想得出來的東西！

Samuel: I know what you mean. I feel extremely humble in front of a magnificent building like such.

山姆：我知道你的意思。我在這麼樣宏偉的建築前覺得超級謙卑！

Amy: And it's not done yet! He started building this since 1884, and after he died in 1926, the rest of the crew continued to work on this until today! It

艾咪：而且它還沒建造完！它從 1884 年開始建造，在高第於 1926 年死後，剩下的人繼續建造到今天！他們

is estimated that La Sagrada Familia will be finished in 2020!

估計在 2020 年會完工！

Samuel: Oh wow, impressive! Look at how detailed every part of the building is!

山姆：哇，真厲害！你看這個建築物的每個部分都做得好仔細喔！

Amy: Tell me about it! You can totally tell how obsessed Gaudi was to this!

艾咪：對啊！你完全可以看出當初高第有多麼地著迷！

Samuel: I'm going to pick up an audio tour, do you want one?

山姆：我要去拿個語音導覽，你要嗎？

Amy: Sure! Thanks a lot!

艾咪：好啊！謝啦！

Samuel: Before I go, should we get a picture in front of La Sagrada Familia?

山姆：在我去之前，我們要不要在聖家堂前照張相？

Amy: I don't know if that is possible. This building is huge.

艾咪：我不曉得那有沒有可能。這個建築物超大的。

Samuel: Let's hope we pick a good photographer then!

山姆：那就希望我們挑個很好的攝影師囉！

夏威夷
威尼斯
紐約
曼谷
哥斯大黎加
舊金山
倫敦
都柏林
巴塞隆納
洛杉磯

Special Sites Introduction 9: 特別景點報導 ▶

Barcelona 巴塞隆納 - Vicky, Christina, Barcelona

 MP3 17

The alluring film directed by Woody Allen that was released in 2008. Some said Woody Allen was still new and fresh at the age of 72 when the movie was first brought to the big screen. In the movie, the adventurous Christina (Scarlet Johansson) and her friend Vicky (Rebecca Hall) who is a bit more refrained met the free-spirited artist Juan Antonio (Javier Bardem) in the romantic Barcelona.

In the movie when Vicky bumps into Juan at the fountain in Guell Park, he explained the reason why he did not call her. That particular scene was shot in one of Gaudi's most popular sites: Guell Park.

The Guell family was one of wealthiest families at the time and when they met their dear friend Gaudi, they gave Gaudi all the freedom to create a park that fulfills his imagination. One of the most significant part of the park and the most popular part is right by a flight of stairs with something between a dragon and a lizard. It is fairly hard to take a picture with the creature since the line in front of you is unimaginable.

巴塞隆納 - 情遇巴塞隆納

　　這由伍迪艾倫所執導的迷人的電影是在 2008 年上映的！有些人說伍迪艾倫在他七十二歲時將這部片搬上大螢幕時還是一樣的新潮和令人覺得煥然一新！在電影中，熱愛冒險的克里斯蒂娜（史嘉蕾喬韓森飾）和略為保守的朋友微琦（麗貝卡豪爾飾）在浪漫的巴塞隆納遇見了自由精神的藝術家簧安東尼（哈維爾巴登飾）。

　　在電影中微琦在奎爾公園的噴水池旁遇見了簧，他解釋了為什麼他在沒有打給她。而那個場景正是在高地最為文明的建築物之一：奎爾公園。

　　奎爾家族在當時是最富有的家庭之一。當他們遇見了他們親愛的朋友高第時，他們給予了高地所有的自由去創造符合他想像力的公園。在公園中最重要也是最受歡迎的地方就是在樓梯旁，有一隻介於龍和蜥蜴之間的生物。但很難能和這個生物拍上一張照，因為在你前面排隊的隊伍是你無法想像的！

Gaudi 　　　MP3 18

You will not be able to leave Barcelona without visiting any of Gaudi's works within the city. There are several tourist attractions within Barcelona that is featuring Gaudi's works. For instance, the world-famous La Sagrada Familia, the fairy-tale-like Casa Batllo, the grand Guell Park, and etc.

If you take a closer look at all Gaudi's buildings, his works have two distinct features: nature and animals. As a young boy, Gaudi enjoyed hiking. While he was on a hike, Gaudi would take notes of everything he saw. He put a lot of these into his works later on. You can see insects on the door-knockers, leaves on the doorways, and vines twisting around the stairs. Also, when you are looking at Gaudi's buildings, you would forget these enchanting buildings are actually made of stone, wood and concrete since they are just so imaginative and seem like they pop out from a storybook. They are precisely the results of a fairy moving in and using magic to decorate everything. It is the ability to let his imagination go wild and manage to turn his fantasies into reality that make Gaudi so irreplaceable. Barcelona would never be as charming without Gaudi.

高第

　　你絕對不可以在沒看過高第的建築前離開巴塞隆納。在巴塞隆納有許多景點是以高第的作品為主軸。例如，世界聞名的聖家堂，如同童話故事般的巴特尤之家，還有那廣大的奎爾公園等等。

　　如果你仔細看高第的建築物，他的作品有兩個明顯的特色：大自然和動物。當高第還是一個小男孩，他非常喜歡健行。而當他在健行的時候，他會對他所看到的一切做記錄。他將許多當時的筆記放到之後的建築當中。你可以看到昆蟲在敲門的門環上，門口有些葉子的裝飾，還有樓梯上有纏繞的藤蔓。另外，當你在看著高第的作品時，你會忘記這些充滿魔力的建築物其實是以石頭，木材，和石灰所建造而成因為它們實在是像從童話故事中跳出般地有想像力！精確地說，它們其實像是精靈搬進這個建築物並用魔法佈置好一切之後的結果！就是高第這有辦法將想象變換為現實的能力讓他這個的無法取代。巴塞隆納沒有了高第就不會像現在這般的迷人。

Vocabulary and Idioms ▶

❶ **bargain** ⓥ 討價還價　　❷ **exceptional** adj 卓越的

❸ **lose it** Idiom 失去理智　　❹ **humble** adj 謙卑的

❺ **obsessed** adj 著迷的　　❻ **alluring** adj 迷人的

❼ **unimaginable** adj 無法想象的　　❽ **fantasy** ⓝ 幻想

1. She enjoys bargaining so much that I almost think she enjoys it more than shopping itself.

   她喜歡討價還價到我以為比起購物本身，她更喜歡討價還價。

2. Her performance on stage was exceptional.

   她在台上的表演真的超棒的。

3. He almost lost it when his girlfriend kept on being very rude to him.

   當他的女朋友一直對他很沒禮貌，他差點就失去理智。

4. He remains humble even if he is very successful at what he does.

   即使他現在在他的領域十分成功，他還是十分的謙卑。

5. She is obsessed with the boy groups in Korea.

   她對於韓國的男子團體很著迷。

6. There are a lot of alluring advertisements in the magazine.

   在這本雜誌裡有很多迷人的廣告。

7. If he keeps smoking so much, the consequences are unimaginable.

他如果再繼續抽這麼多煙,後果是無法想像的。

8. He always lives in fantasy instead of working hard for what he wants.

他總是活在幻想中,而不是為他想要的努力工作去爭取。

旅遊小貼士 ▶

　　來到巴塞隆納旅行一直是許多人心中的夢想,然而,到了歐洲旅行,千萬別自以為聰明,為了不想隨身攜帶大量現金而去和銀行兌換旅行支票!在歐洲,幾乎沒有商店會收旅行支票,而銀行也是少之又少會收旅行支票,所以千萬不要攜帶旅行支票來到這邊旅遊喔!可以以歐元現金和攜帶信用卡為主!不然你也只能望旅支興嘆!和想買的東西說Adios!!

夏威夷
威尼斯
紐約
曼谷
哥斯大黎加
舊金山
倫敦
都柏林
巴塞隆納
洛杉磯

Unit 10

Los Angeles 洛杉磯
Spider Man 2 蜘蛛人 2

城市介紹 ▶

Located at the southern California region, Los Angeles enjoys sunshine and agreeable climate. It is a big city mixed with beach scenes. You might run into fashionably dressed office workers, celebrities, and roller skaters with casual outfits passing through the tourists on the street. Los Angeles is the second biggest city in the United States. It is also the most populous city right after New York. Wonder why? In addition to the pleasant weather in this region, L.A. is also where dreams do come true. Filmmakers, actors, and actresses crowd into the city looking for a chance to become famous and get some big bucks. However, behind the relaxing beach scenes, the intense business competitions, non-stop hustles within the city can be quite overwhelming. The city runs towards the glamorous end. It is the place where a Pilates studio would thrive, and the healthy juice bar will be worth investing. Needless to say, shopping malls, and celebrity culture is wildly celebrated within the city. Bag some of L. A.'s glamour home with you next time when you are there!

◀ 洛杉磯 ▶

　　位於加州南部的洛杉磯享有陽光和怡然的天氣。它是一個大城市加上海灘場景的地方。在街上你可能會遇到穿著時尚的上班族，名人，和穿著休閒的直排輪者穿梭在觀光客之間。洛杉磯是全美第二大城市，而它也是居於紐約之後人口最多的城市。想知道為什麼嗎？除了它美好的天氣之外，洛杉磯也是一個夢想會成真的地方。許多製片家，演員，會湧入這個城市只求一個成名和賺大錢的機會。然而，在輕鬆的海灘場景之後，許多緊張的商業競爭，無止境的忙碌也是十分令人喘不過氣的。整個城市都有著十分繁華的氛圍。這是一個皮拉提斯教室會成功，健康果汁吧值得令人投資的地方。不用多說，購物中心，名人文化也是在城市中十分的流行。下次你來洛杉磯，打包一些洛杉磯的奢華回家吧！

Dialogue 情境對話 ▶

Molly and Tom are entering the "House of Horrors" at the Universal Studio.
茉莉和湯姆正在走進環球影城的環球恐怖城堡。

Molly: I'm getting so scared! I don't know if I can handle this! Don't let go of my hands Tom!!

茉莉：我越來越害怕了！我不知道我可不可以撐過這個！千萬不要放掉我的手湯姆！

Tom: It's not real Molly! Come on! It's gonna be fun!

湯姆：這都不是真的啦，茉莉！拜託！一定會很好玩的！

Molly: I can hear people screaming! They can't touch us, right?

茉莉：我可以聽到別人的尖叫聲！他們不能碰我們對不對？

Tom: Who knows? There are so many other ways to scare people anyways!

湯姆：誰知道？反正還有很多其它嚇人的方式！

Molly: Oh my god, I feel like we are in the movies, these props are so real!

茉莉：我的天啊，我覺得我們好像在電影裡，這些道具都好逼真噢！

Tom: Maybe they're real.

湯姆：說不定他們是真的！

Molly: Not funny Tom. This is actually so cool! Man you gotta admire

茉莉：湯姆，不好笑。不過這真的好酷噢！天啊你必須

their skills to make all these props! | 敬佩他們製作這些道具的技巧！

Tom: Hey Molly! Are those dead babies? Are we supposed to walk through them?! | **湯姆：** 欸茉莉！那些是死掉的嬰兒嗎？我們是必須要走過他們嗎？！

Molly: Wow, amazing!! Gosh, how did they come up with so many sick ideas anyways? | **茉莉：** 哇，太厲害了！！天啊，他們到底怎麼想出這麼多變態的點子？

Tom: Molly wait up! Where are you going? | **湯姆：** 等等茉莉！你要去哪裡？

Molly: Tom! Check this out! The blood is so gluey and sticky! | **茉莉：** 湯姆！你看！這血好黏稠噢！

Tom: Molly! That's gross. Come on, let's get out of here. | **湯姆：** 茉莉！那很噁心。拜託，我們趕快離開這裡。

Molly: Do you think this is made of corn syrup? | **茉莉：** 你覺得這是玉米糖漿做成的嗎？

Tom: Molly! | **湯姆：** 茉莉！

Molly: Your face turned white, and your palm's so sweaty! Wait, are you fainting Tom??? 茉莉：你的臉色好蒼白，而且你的手心流好多汗！等等，湯姆你要昏倒了嗎？？

Special Sites Introduction 10: 特別景點報導 ▶

Los Angeles - Spider Man 2　　MP3 19

An amusing scene in the movie "Spider Man 2" is when Peter Parker (Toby Maguire) was running late for Mary Jane's (Kirsten Dunst) play "The Importance of Being Earnest", the usher of the theater, played by Bruce Campbell, kindly reminded Peter to tie his shoe laces, and his tie, only to find that he stopped Peter from getting in the theater to watch Mary Jane's performances for the quality of the performance. Meanwhile, Mary Jane was performing on stage and got distracted when she saw the empty seat of Peter's in the theater.

The splendid theater is the very Ivar Theatre which is located at 1605 North Ivar Avenue in Hollywood. The theater first opened in 1951, and several movies and plays were performed in the site. The grand theater can seat up to 350 people and during its peak, celebrities including the legendary rock star Elvis Presley performed movies in the theater. However, the theater had been through quite a rough ride for its survival. It later became a rock club, nudity strip club, picture-shooting rental, and it has currently been renting the theater to people for filming purposes. One regular user is the Los Angeles Film School.

洛杉磯 - 蜘蛛人 2

在電影蜘蛛人 2 中其中一個好玩的一幕是當彼得帕克（陶比麥奎爾飾）去瑪麗珍（柯絲婷鄧斯特飾）的演出 "真誠的重要" 遲到時，劇場的接待員，由布魯斯坎貝爾飾演，好心提醒彼得繫他的鞋帶，以及整理他的領帶，結果在彼得照做之後，他卻因為維護表演品質而不讓彼得進入戲院看瑪麗珍的表演。在同時間，在台上表演的瑪麗珍因為看到彼得沒來的空位而分心。

這個華麗的戲院正是位於好萊塢區 1605 號 North Ivar 大道的 Ivar 戲院。這個戲院最早是在 1951 年開幕，這裡也有許多的戲劇和電影的演出。這個廣大的戲院可以容納 350 人，而在它的高峰時期，許多的名人，包括傳奇的搖滾巨星貓王的電影演出也是在這裡。然而，為了生存，這個劇院經歷了很多辛苦的歷程。它後來演變為一個搖滾夜店，脫衣舞店，拍照出租，而現在他們將戲院出租為拍片場地。一個固定的常客是洛杉磯電影學校。

夏威夷
威尼斯
紐約
曼谷
哥斯大黎加
舊金山
倫敦
都柏林
巴塞隆納
洛杉磯

In-N-Out MP3 20

A very popular fast food chain that first opened in 1984, In-N-Out, has now reached nearly 300 stores on the west coast of America. Therefore, when you are in Los Angeles, you wouldn't want to miss this big timer! What are the differences between In-N-Out and the world-famous McDonalds is that they are more flexible for the customers' choices. Unlike most fast food chains, In-N-Out only has a few choices list on their menu in store. However, if you are a loyal fan of In-N-Out, you will know about the secret menu of theirs. An easy way to understand the secret menu is that the first number represents meat patties, and the second number represents the number of the slices of cheese you want. For instance, ordering a 3 by 2 would mean that you want to have 3 meat patties with 2 slices of cheese. Another hot item is called Animal style that is a mustard cooked beef patty with pickle, extra spread, and grilled onions. There is also vegetarian burger that is basically a burger without the patty. So there, I hope you won't feel too out of the loop the next time you are at In-N-Out!

一個在 1984 十分受歡迎的速食連鎖店，In-N-Out，最一開始是在 1984 年開店，到現在已經在美國西岸有將近 300 家分店。所以囉，當你身在洛杉磯，你一定不想錯過這個大咖！In-N-Out 和麥當勞最大的不同點就是 In-N-Out 對顧客的選擇漢喜好比較有彈性。不像大部分的速食店，In-N-Out 在他們的店裡沒有列出很多選擇。但是如果你是比較忠實的客戶的話，你就會知道他們有秘密菜單！一個很簡單的方式來瞭解秘密菜單就是第一個數字代表的是多少塊漢堡肉，第二個數字代表的是幾片起司片。例如，3×2 就是三個漢堡肉漢加兩片起司的意思！另外一個熱門的菜是 "animal style"。也就是在芥末醬中烹煮的漢堡肉，加上酸黃瓜，更多抹醬，和烤洋蔥。他們也有素食漢堡，其實就是漢堡但是沒有漢堡肉！希望下次你去 In-N-Out 的時候不會覺得自己很像門外漢噢！

夏威夷
威尼斯
紐約
曼谷
哥斯大黎加
舊金山
倫敦
都柏林
巴塞隆納
洛杉磯

Vocabulary and Idioms ▶

❶ **agreeable** adj 怡人的　　❷ **populous** adj 人口眾多的

❸ **crowd into** v 湧入　　❹ **glamorous** adj 繁華的

❺ **gluey** adj 黏稠的　　❻ **gross** adj 噁心的

❼ **faint** v 昏倒　　❽ **peak** n 高峰

1. The agreeable weather and the extraordinary scenery make Hawaii one of the top tourist attractions in the world.

   怡人的天氣和卓越的風景都使得夏威夷成為世界最棒的觀光景點之一。

2. Taipei is the most populous city in Taiwan.

   台北是台灣人口最多的城市。

3. Many people crowd into his house to watch Super Bowl.

   很多人湧入他家去看超級盃。

4. She looked so glamorous tonight at the party.

   她在今天晚上的派對上看起來美極了。

5. The common mistake in making mashed potatoes is that people forget to drain the potato and end up with gluey mashed potatoes.

   一個做馬鈴薯泥時很常犯的錯是大家忘記要把馬鈴薯瀝乾，以至於最後作出黏膩的馬鈴薯泥。

6. What the movie was showing was really gross. I almost threw up during the movie.

電影上演的真的很噁心。我在電影播放時差點吐了。

7. He fainted the moment he saw blood.

他一看到血就昏倒了。

8. August is the peak season for tourism.

八月是觀光的旺季。

旅遊小貼士 ▶

　　來到洛杉磯，除了安排住宿及想要去的各大景點，千萬別忘了安排租車或是包車的服務！洛杉磯路大地大，通常你想去的景點和景點之間都是走路無法快速到達的！所以囉，無論是選擇自己租車或是尋找包車的服務都是比較好的選擇噢！因應這個需求，洛杉磯也不乏包租車的服務，若是選擇包車服務，有較多人一起分擔費用的話，其實也是不會很貴的，而司機也通常可以給一些當地的資訊噢！

夏威夷

威尼斯

紐約

曼谷

哥斯大黎加

舊金山

倫敦

都柏林

巴塞隆納

洛杉磯

Unit 11

Vancouver 溫哥華
Twilight 暮光之城

城市介紹 ▶

Whether you are a city person at heart or nature explorer at times, Vancouver seems to cover it all. It is the place where you can ski at the mountaintop in the morning and come back to swim and roll on the beach sands in the afternoon. If you'd rather just chill and relax in the craft beer pubs, it's not a problem at all! This new trend of Vancouver seems to draw even more people to come to Vancouver and try out different kinds of refreshing beers. Did I forget to mention their fine cuisine and top-notch restaurants? From one of the best Chinese foods in North America to fresh seafood, Vancouver can bring them all. It is certainly the greenest city in Canada and the amazing climate has made

Vancouver one of the best cities for living. You wonder why so many people immigrate to Canada every year? Go figure! Great weather, scenic trails, plenty of activities to do, modern restaurants and thriving businesses. Reasons for not coming to Vancouver? None!

✈ 溫哥華 ▶

　　不論你內心是喜歡都市，還是你時常喜歡探索大自然，溫哥華都有！這是一個你可以早上在山頂滑雪，下午回到海邊游泳和在沙上翻滾。如果你比較想要放鬆在手工啤酒吧裡，也沒問題喔！這個溫哥華新興的風潮也吸引了更多的觀光客來品嘗許多不同的清涼的啤酒！我忘了提到他們的美食和一流的餐廳了嗎？從北美最棒的中國餐廳到新鮮的海鮮，溫哥華什麼菜都端的出來。這裡也絕對是加拿大最綠的城市而這超棒的天氣也使得溫哥華是最適合人居住的城市之一。你懷疑為什麼每年那麼多人移民來溫哥華？想想看！好天氣，風景般的步道，許多活動可以玩，摩登的餐廳和興隆的商機。有任何理由不來溫哥華呢？沒有！

溫哥華
佛羅倫斯
柏林
洛桑
阿姆斯特丹
阿拉巴馬州
聖安東尼奧
波哥大
太平洋屋脊步道
紐西蘭

Dialogue 情境對話▶

Mindy and her Taiwanese friend Ping are walking around the Chinatown in Vancouver.
明蒂和他的台灣朋友萍正走在溫哥華的唐人街裡。

Mindy: It is so fun to step in this side of the city. The decoration and the atmosphere change the moment we step in here.

明蒂：走到城市的這區總是很好玩。當我們一踏進來這區感覺裝飾和氛圍就立刻改變了！

Ping: Yeah, definitely. It is a very different culture after allm even for me. This part of the town is pretty old. A lot of the store reminds me of the old Chinese movies!

萍：對啊，真的！這畢竟是十分不同的文化，就算對我來說也是。這區其實蠻老的。很多店都讓我想到以前的中國電影。

Mindy: Oh really? And I have been to many Chinatowns, but I gotta say this one is pretty big. We have been walking for 2 hours already, and we're not done yet!

明蒂：真的？而且我有去過很多唐人街，但我必須說，這一個真的很大。我們已經走了兩個小時了，還沒走完！

Ping: This is the second biggest Chinatown in north America.

萍：這是北美第二大的唐人街啊！

Mindy: Where's the biggest? New York?

明蒂：那哪裡是最大的呢？紐約？

Ping: No, actually it's San Francisco! It's pretty fun over that one, too!

萍：不是，其實是舊金山。那個也蠻好玩的！

Mindy: I'm a bit hungry, should we find some food to try?

明蒂：我有點餓了，我們要不要找東西試吃看看？

Ping: Absolutely. All this walking makes me so hungry as well.

萍：好！！一直走路我也好餓了喔！

Mindy: What should we try? There are so many quaint-looking tea-shops!

明蒂：我們該試試什麼呢？這裡有好多雅緻的茶店！

Ping: Maybe we can try some Dim Sum with tea?

萍：或許我們可以試試港式點心和茶？

Mindy: I love Dim Sum! They are such delicious delicacies!

明蒂：我愛港式點心！他們真是美味的佳餚！

Ping: Let's do it then!

萍：那就這麼決定了！

溫哥華

佛羅倫斯

柏林

洛桑

阿姆斯特丹

阿拉巴馬州

聖安東尼奧

波哥大

太平洋屋脊步道

紐西蘭

Special Sites Introduction 11: 特別景點報導 ▶

 MP3 21

Bella Swan (Kristen Stewart) and most of the Cullen family went to Forks High school, which was first described by Bella that most of the students in the school know each other and their grandparents had been toddlers together, and that she thought she would be a freak coming from the big city. In the movie New Moon and Eclipse, several scenes were actually shot at the "Forks High School" at Vancouver, where the crew thought they would be able to get more producing values in Vancouver.

"Forks High School" in Twilight New Moon and Eclipse was actually shot at David Thompson Secondary School at 1755 East 55th Avenue, at Gordon Park, south Vancouver. David Thompson Secondary School had opened back in 1958. If you want to get a glimpse of where Bella and Edward (Robert Pattinson) went to school in the movie, drop by David Thompson Secondary School and you might find yourself walking the same school corridor as the cast!

溫哥華 - 暮光之城

　　貝拉・史旺（克莉絲汀史都華）和大部分庫倫家族的人都去福克斯高中上學。福克斯高中一開始就被貝拉描述大部分的學生都認識彼此，而他們的祖父母大概從小就認識了。她一定會成為一個來自大城市的怪胎。在電影"新月"和"月蝕"中，很多在福克斯高中拍攝的場景其實是在溫哥華所拍攝的。劇組人員認為在溫哥華拍攝他們可以得到比較多的製作價值。

　　在暮光之城第二、三集中的"福克斯高中"其實是在南溫哥華，Gordon Park 區，第 55 東大道，1755 號的大衛湯普森高中所拍攝。大衛湯普森高中是在 1958 年開校。如果你想看看貝拉史旺和愛德華（羅柏派丁森）在電影中去的學校，拜訪一下大衛湯普森高中！你可能會發現自己走在跟他們一樣的走廊喔！

溫哥華

佛羅倫斯

柏林

洛桑

阿姆斯特丹

阿拉巴馬州

聖安東尼奧

波哥大

太平洋屋脊步道

紐西蘭

 旅遊愛玩咖 ▶

Stanley Park MP3 22

Stanley Park was named "Top Park in the entire world" by Trip Advisor in 2004. This gigantic space spreads out along the waters of Vancouver Harbor and English Bay. It is one of the places you must visit when you are in Vancouver. This park offers a lot for you to explore. Rather than a regular man-made park, Stanley Park is more or less the results of how people preserved and used this space over the time. The park still maintains how it looked like back in the late 18th century. The wild life, dense rainforest, the majestic trees, beautiful beaches and traces of the places that were left by history can all be found within this park. There are several trails that are waiting for you to explore and there are also children's playgrounds, and an aquarium for the little ones in your family! It is the oasis in the middle of the well-developed urban areas of Vancouver. So come and get in touch with nature when you are in Vancouver.

史丹利公園

　　史丹利公園在 2004 年被 Trip Advisor 選為"全世界最好的公園"。這個龐大的空間沿著溫哥華港口的水域和英吉利灣展開。這裡絕對是你在溫哥華一定要來一探究竟的地方！這個公園提供你很多去探索。有別於一般的人造公園，史丹利公園比較像是隨著時間人們如何保存和使用這個空間的結果。這個公園大部分都還是跟十八世紀末時看起來很像。野生動物，茂密的雨林，巨大的樹，美麗的海灘，和歷史留下的痕跡都可以在這個公園裡被你發現！這裡有許多步道等著你來探索，也有小孩的遊戲場和水族館給你們家的小孩遊玩。這是在發展良好的溫哥華市區的綠洲。所以當你來溫哥華來這和大自然接觸吧！

溫哥華

佛羅倫斯

柏林

洛桑

阿姆斯特丹

阿拉巴馬州

聖安東尼奧

波哥大

太平洋屋脊步道

紐西蘭

Vocabulary and Idioms ▶

❶ **chill** v 放鬆	❷ **craft beer** n 手工釀造啤酒
❸ **top-notch** adj 第一流的	❹ **Dim Sum** n 港式飲茶點心
❺ **toddler** n 幼童	❻ **freak** n 怪胎
❼ **corridor** n 走廊	❽ **majestic** adj 雄偉的

1. Today is my day off. I just want to chill and read a book at home.

   今天我放假。我只想放鬆和看本書。

2. The make the best craft beer in town.

   他們有整個鎮上最棒的手工釀造啤酒。

3. They have top-notch engineers and great skills. No wonder their products are so popular.

   他們有第一流的工程師和良好的技能。難怪他們的產品那麼受歡迎。

4. We should drink tea and eat Dim Sum for lunch.

   我們午餐應該去喝茶和吃港式點心。

5. When she was just a toddler, she always ran around in her diaper.

   她還很小的時候，她總是包著尿布到處跑來跑去。

6. Everyone thought he was such a freak as he doesn't even own a phone.

大家都覺得他真是一個怪胎因為他沒有手機。

7. The bathroom is at the end of the corridor.

廁所就在走廊的盡頭。

8. The majestic building makes us feel so humble.

這個雄偉的建築使我們覺得格外的謙卑。

旅遊小貼士 ▶

　　在溫哥華記得出門都要擦防曬油！據統計，這裡可是世界上皮膚癌罹患率最高的的地方呢！所以在溫哥華即使溫度沒有很高，日照也還是很強。溫哥華的冬天溫度大約在攝氏五度，夏天約為攝氏 24 度左右！雖然天氣十分的宜人，勤擦防曬油還是一定要做的功課喔！要不然玩了一天之後，你的皮膚可能會已經受到相當程度的傷害囉！

Unit 12

Florence 佛羅倫斯 - Hannibal 人魔

城市介紹 ▶

This is probably how time travel would feel like when you walk in Florence. Ancient Florentine statues and buildings proved Florence to be the cradle of the renaissance. Famous artist like Michelangelo, Leonardo da Vinci, and etc. left traces all around the city. Cathedrals and monuments all stand tall for the splendid Florentine history. Simultaneously, tourists are taking pictures with selfie sticks and looking up information for each museum, debating if it is worthwhile to visit. If we can overlap time, could we be walking pass Leonardo da Vinci, and what would he be doing? Florence would not strike you as a big city, but through the narrow streets, it evokes you to see more and understand more about the stories of the city. What is it about this city that enlightened so many poets, artists, philosophers and architects? And what is it that makes the people celebrate food and wine so much here? You will have to see it by yourself. Bring a big appetite and curious mind. I am certain that Florence will not let you down.

✈ ◀ 佛羅倫斯 ▶

　　走在佛羅倫斯的路上，你會覺得這大概就是時光旅行會給人的感覺吧。古老的佛羅倫斯雕像和建築證明了佛羅倫斯正是文藝復興的搖籃。出名的藝術家譬如米開朗基羅，達文西等都在城市四處留下了痕跡。大教堂和紀念碑也都為了佛羅倫斯光輝的歷史而高站。同時，觀光客們正在使用自拍器拍照，以及查詢關於各個博物館的資料，盤算着是否值得進場。如果我們可以重疊時間的話，我們是不是是有可能會和達文西擦肩而過，而他又會正在做些什麼呢？佛羅倫斯不會讓你覺得它是一個大城市，但它窄隘的小巷卻會引發你想要看更多以及瞭解更多關於這個城市的故事。是這個城市的什麼啟發了這麼多的詩人，藝術家，哲學家和建築師呢？又是什麼使得這裡的人們如此歌頌他們的美食和好酒呢？你必須要自己來到這裡判斷。帶著一個大胃口和一顆好奇的心。我相信佛羅倫斯不會讓你失望的。

溫哥華

佛羅倫斯

柏林

洛桑

阿姆斯特丹

阿拉巴馬州

聖安東尼奧

波哥大

太平洋屋脊步道

紐西蘭

Dialogue 情境對話 ▶

Nina and Ryan are trying to figure out what flavor of Gelato to get.

妮娜和萊恩正在想要買哪一種口味的義式冰淇淋。

Nina: Look at the selection of the flavors! What are we going to do?

妮娜：看看這些口味的選擇！我們該怎麼辦？

Ryan: Yeah, they got some funky flavors, too. Rose caramel?

萊恩：嗯，他們還有一些奇怪的口味。玫瑰焦糖？

Nina: Can be good, you never know!

妮娜：可能很好吃也說不定！

Ryan: I think I'm going to go with Passion fruit and dark chocolate.

萊恩：我想我要點百香果和黑巧克力。

Nina: I'm getting peach and the coconut one.

妮娜：我要水蜜桃和椰子。

Ryan: I literally cannot wait to try.

萊恩：我真的等不及了。

(After they get their gelato)

（等他們拿到他們的義式冰淇淋後）

Nina: Oh my god, Ryan, this is the bomb! You've got to try the coconut one! It's so creamy and rich.

妮娜：我的天啊，萊恩，這個超屌！你一定要試試看這椰子口味的！超綿密又濃郁！

Ryan: Mine's also really good. The dark chocolate one is really good.

萊恩：我的也很好吃耶！這黑巧克力很好吃！

Nina: Yeah, the peach one is also very good. You can tell they put in really good ingredients.

妮娜：對啊，水蜜桃也好好吃。你真的可以吃得出來他們用很好的食材。

Ryan: There's a sign saying they don't put in any preservatives. That's good!

萊恩：有一個標示寫他們沒有放任何防腐劑。很好！

Nina: No kidding. I definitely think two scoops of this divine gelato will do you good in some way.

妮娜：真不是開玩笑的。我真的覺得每天吃兩球這個一定會對你身體某方面很好。

Ryan: Definitely want to live longer for this anyways.

萊恩：的確是會想要為了吃這個而多活兩年。

Nina: Do you want to split another one? I'm done with mine!

妮娜：你想要再分一支嗎？我吃完了！

溫哥華

佛羅倫斯

柏林

洛桑

阿姆斯特丹

阿拉巴馬州

聖安東尼奧

波哥大

太平洋屋脊步道

紐西蘭

Ryan: What, how did that happen?　　莱恩：什麼，這怎麼發生
　　　　　　　　　　　　　　　　　　　　的？

 Florence - Hannibal　　🎧 MP3 23

Hannibal, a sequel to the classic Academy Award-winning thriller "The Silence of the Lambs", was released in 2001. Set ten years after the last film, the FBI agent Clarice Starling (Julianne Moore) and Hannibal (Anthony Hopkins) met again, only this time in Italy. In the movie a very significant clue was that when someone sent Clarice a letter, while there were no words written in the letter but only a strange fragrance. Clarice investigated on the fragrance and traced it back to Florence, Italy. The spooky thriller is actually based on a true story in Florence between 1968 and 1985.

There are several scenes in the movie that were shot in Florence. One of them is the Pharmacy of Santa Maria Novella, where Hannibal bought almond soap and other perfumed products for Agent Starling. It is, even today, still a very popular spot for souvenir shopping. Another scene is the Porcellino Fountain where Hannibal killed a gypsy guy and washe his bloody hands at the fountain. Porcellino means little pig in Italian and legend has it that if you put a coin in the piggy's mouth for it to fall off smoothly, then you will get good luck. Then you touch the pig's nose, it means you will be able to come back to Florence.

佛羅倫斯 - 人魔

　　人魔，是在 2001 年繼金像獎得主沈默的羔羊之後的續集。場景設在距上片十年之後，FBI 警員克莉絲史黛林（茱利安摩爾）和漢尼拔（安東尼霍普金斯）又再次見面，只是這次是在義大利。在片中一個關建設當有人寄信給克莉絲，但信中沒有任何的內容，只有一抹奇怪的香味。克莉絲調查之後發現香味來自義大利佛羅倫斯。這個驚悚的恐怖片其實是根據一個介於 1968 到 1985 年的真實故事改編。

　　片中有許多場景都是在佛羅倫斯所拍攝，例如，藥妝店 Santa Maria Novella。那裡就是漢尼拔買杏仁香味的肥皂給史黛林探員，還有其他的香水產品。那裡一直到現在也都是十分熱門的紀念品採買地點之一。另外一個場景是在 Porcellino 噴水池當漢尼拔殺了一個吉普賽男人之後在噴水池下洗淨他血腥的手。Porcellino 在義大利文中指的是小豬。傳說如果你把一個硬幣放入小豬的嘴中，它順利滑落之後你便可以得到好運。然後如果你摸摸小豬的鼻子，代表你未來將會回來佛羅倫斯！

 MP3 24

A fascinating place to visit is the bustling Central Market or "Mercato Centrale". It is located near the San Lorenzo market, so after shopping for crafts, leather, and perhaps some souvenirs, follow the smell to come to Central Market to take your pick among myriad vendors that sell fresh product and meat. This is definitely one of the best, unexpected food places in the world. You can find everything from sheets of tripe, pig's feet, sausages, whole chickens, rabbits, to cheeses and olives to dedicate your exotic food list. One of the popular items in the market is the tripe sandwich. Foodies might want to sample everything and arouse different parts of your palate in Central Market. At the north tip of the market you can find seafood from Italy and the rest of the world. Central market is open Monday to Saturday from 7 a.m. to 2 p.m. with additional hours on Saturday from 4 p.m. to 7 p.m. Planning on cooking Italian tonight? Why not stop by Central Market first and get inspired!

中央市集

　　一個十分有趣的地方是忙碌的中央市集或是義文的 "Mercato Centrale"。他是位於佛羅倫斯皮革市場的旁邊。所以當你買完手工藝品，皮件，和或許一些紀念品之後，跟著香味來中央市集來從許多種賣蔬菜水果和肉的不同的攤販選擇。這或許是世界上最好也是最出乎人意料的美食市集之一。從一片一片的牛肚，豬腳，香腸，全雞，兔肉，到起司和橄欖你都可以在這找到能夠加到你異國食物的菜單上。其中一個受歡迎的一道菜是牛肚三明治。饕客要試試每道菜和喚醒你不同部位的味覺。在市集的北邊賣的是從義大利及來自世界各地的海鮮。中央市集每週一到週六從早上七點開到下午兩點，星期六還會加開下午四點到七點。晚上想煮義大利菜嗎？來趟中央市集來搜集靈感吧！

Vocabulary and Idioms ▶

❶ cradle n 搖籃

❷ splendid adj 輝煌的

❸ simultaneously adv 同時地

❹ enlighten v 啟發

❺ funky adj 古怪的

❻ sequel n 續集

❼ fragrance n 香味

❽ myriad adj 各式各樣的

1. New Orleans is said to be the cradle of Jazz in the U.S.

   紐奧良聽說是美國爵士的搖籃。

2. The chandelier makes the living room even more splendid.

   這個水晶燈使得客廳更加的輝煌。

3. They were talking simultaneously, so it was really hard to understand them.

   他們同時間說話，所以非常難懂他們想說什麼。

4. Enlightened by her kids, she wrote a picture book of bears.

   受到她的小孩的啟發，她寫了一本關於熊的圖畫故事書。

5. Her taste in dresses is funky, so it's best not to buy her dresses.

   她對洋裝的品味很古怪，所以最好還是不要買洋裝給她。

6. The sequels of the movies are usually not as good as the first one.

   電影的續集通常都沒有第一集好看。

7. I can smell the fragrance from the flowers in the garden.

   我可以聞到來自花園的花香味。

8. One of the selling points of the night markets is the myriad vendors.

夜市其中一個賣點是有各式各樣的攤販。

🎓 旅遊小貼士 ▶

　　來到佛羅倫斯不能忘記去的地方是前面介紹過的烏非茲美術館，但是因為他的知名度還有他收藏豐富的文藝復興時期的作品，每每在烏非茲美術館的人潮總是數都數不清。一個小小的撇步是去烏非茲美術館之前可以打電話或是上網預約噢！如果有住在民宿或是飯店的話都可以詢問他們有沒有幫忙預約的服務噢！這樣一來你就可以省掉在排隊時的時間了！

溫哥華
佛羅倫斯
柏林
洛桑
阿姆斯特丹
阿拉巴馬州
聖安東尼奧
波哥大
太平洋屋脊步道
紐西蘭

Unit 13

Berlin 柏林 -
Unknown 狙擊陌生人

城市介紹 ▶

Berlin is the capital of Germany and one of the most important cities during World War II. Since the reunification of the two sides of Berlin, it has thrived and changed itself into a fast-paced, thrilling city that claims to be one of the most exciting cities in the world. Threading around the historical monuments are some of the most modern restaurants and cutting edge clubs in the world. Berlin had certainly picked up its pace to catch up with the rest of the world and if anything, it transcends the world. The city also houses numerous museums that store a lot of the shared memory of the dark past, and is yet proud of standing tall again. Besides the fast-paced city life, you can also find picturesque gardens, relaxing cafes and fascinating towns to spend your quiet afternoons. Berlin has it all to please everyone that lives or visits here. Coming from a past like this, Berlin has a lot of stories, passing down from generation to generation, to tell. What happened here, how it is now, and where they are at are all that characterize Berlin.

✈ ◀ 柏林 ▶

柏林是德國的首都，同時也是第二次世界大戰時最重要的城市之一。自從柏林的兩端再聯合之後，柏林就迅速發展，而也轉變為一個步調快，令人興奮的城市。它也號稱為全世界最刺激的城市之一。最為摩登的餐廳和走在世界最前線的夜店都穿梭在柏林歷史紀念碑之間。柏林確實有立刻加快它的發展腳步來追上剩下的世界。如果仔細來說的話，它應該是已經超越了世界。這個城市同時也有許多儲存許多黑暗過去的博物館，但它卻又驕傲的站了起來。除了步調快的城市生活之外，你也可以找到如畫般的花園，令人放鬆的咖啡廳，和有趣的小鎮來度過你安靜的午後。柏林可以提供住在這裡或是來觀光的人們各式各樣的需求。來自這麼樣的一個過去，柏林有許多代代相傳的故事。這裡發生過什麼事，它現在如何，之後又何去何從都造就了柏林的特色。

👒 Dialogue 情境對話 ▶

Jenny and Lena are waiting in line to get to Radiohead's concert.

珍妮和黎娜正在排隊進去電台司令的演唱會。

Jenny: I really hope they are going to sing Creep tonight. That song is a classic!

珍妮：我真的希望他們今天會唱 Creep。那首歌真是經典！

Lena: I know. I have been practicing their songs all weeks for tonight! I just hope we can get to a good spot.

黎娜：對啊！我這禮拜都一直為今天晚上練他們的歌！我只希望我們可以佔到一個好位子。

Jenny: Yeah, I didn't realize it's going to be so many people!

珍妮：對啊，我真的不知道今天會那麼多人！

Lena: Did you bring your camera?

黎娜：你有帶你的相機嗎？

Jenny: I did, I hope this is allowed actually.

珍妮：有，我真的希望是允許的。

Lena: What do you mean?

黎娜：什麼意思？

Jenny: They won't let you take pictures in some of the concerts.

珍妮：有些演唱會他們不會讓你拍照。

Lena: Really? That doesn't make any sense to me. Well, I won't be able to throw my camera away that's for

黎娜：真的嗎？那一點道理都沒有。反正確定的是我絕不能把我的相機丟掉。

sure.

Jenny: I don't think they would ask you to do that.

珍妮：我不覺得他們會叫你那樣做。

Lena: I hope not! Wow, look at all the vendors. This is getting so festive.

黎娜：我希望不要！哇，你看那些攤販。現在變的好喜慶噢！

Jenny: It's going to be a fun night!!

珍妮：今天晚上一定會很好玩！

Lena: I'm ready to sing my heart out!

黎娜：我已經準備好要大唱特唱了！

Jenny: Nice, I'm going to need a beer for that!

珍妮：好耶！我需要先來杯啤酒！

Lena: A hot dog for me, please!

黎娜：我要一個熱狗！

Jenny: Okay, I will meet you in there?

珍妮：好，那我們裡面見囉？

Lena: Alright, call me when you are coming in! I'll get a good spot for us!

黎娜：好，等你要進來的時候再打給我！我會幫我們佔個好位子！

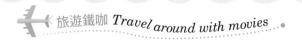

Special Sites Introduction 13: 特別景點報導 ▶

Berlin - Unknown   MP3 25

In the movie Unknown, Martin Harris (Liam Neeson) and Elizabeth Harris (January Jones) went to Berlin for a biotechnology summit. However, Martin realized that he had forgotten his briefcase at the airport, going back to the airport with a cab driven by Gina (Diane Kruger) and a car crash. Being unconscious for 4 days and determined to find out his identity, Martin started an adventure that changed everything with Gina. The suspension builds on more and more as the film progresses. Several scenes were shot in Berlin. If you are a fan of Berlin, try to watch this film and see how many spots you can recognize.

In the movie when Martin and Liz arrived in Berlin, they went to their hotel, the world-renowned Hotel Adlon Kempinski. It is situated at the heart of Berlin where you can go to the iconic Brandeburg Gate and Pariser Platz within walking distance. Hotel Adlon Kempinski is a five star hotel with its own Michelin restaurant, luxurious indoor swimming pool and gigantic fitness and SPA center. A night here might cost you an arm and a leg. However, it will definitely make your stay in Berlin even more memorable.

溫哥華
佛羅倫斯
柏林
洛桑
阿姆斯特丹
阿拉巴馬州
聖安東尼奧
波哥大
太平洋屋脊步道
紐西蘭

柏林 - 狙擊陌生人

在電影狙擊陌生人中，馬丁哈里斯（連恩尼遜）和伊莉莎白哈里斯（珍妮艾莉瓊斯）一同去柏林參加一個生物科技的會議。然而，馬丁突然發現自己把手提箱忘在機場，搭了吉娜（戴安克魯格）開的計程車回機場的路上突然發生車禍。昏迷了四天之後，決心要找出他自己的身份，馬丁和吉娜展開了一個改變一切的旅程。當你更深入這部片，整部片就更轉懸疑。片中許多的場景都是在柏林拍攝。如果你是柏林迷的話，試著看看這部片，並看看你認出幾個景點。

在電影中當馬丁和伊莉莎白抵達柏林，他們就去他們的飯店，世界聞名的阿德隆凱賓斯基飯店。它座落為柏林的心臟地帶，去代表性的勃蘭登堡門和巴黎廣場都只有走路距離而已。阿德隆凱賓斯基飯店是一個五星級的飯店，它有自己的米其林餐廳，豪華的室內游泳池和巨大的健身房和 SPA 中心。在這裡住一晚或許會花了你不少錢，但這也絕對會讓你在柏林的經驗更加的難忘！

East Side Gallery 　MP3 26

The East Side Gallery is a 1.3-kilometer long wall that show-cases 105 paintings from 1990 on the east side of the Berlin Wall. The historical moment and the victory of freedom and peace cannot be better represented in any other way. The artists all around the world rushed to the east side of Berlin after the wall was knocked down. Led by their inspiration from the spirit of liberation, artists left not only colorful murals but also a timeless testimony of joy and reconciliation. The East Side Gallery is by far the largest open-air gallery in the world, and every year visitors from all corners of the world come and witness this heritage of Germany's. Several paintings are all under restoration due to the decay from time. However, the government has taken this restoration project under heritage protection to ensure that more people will be able to see and understand the history of Germany. Various themes of the painting with different painting styles yet all reflect their hope for a better future and joy for all people in the world.

柏林東邊畫廊

　　柏林東邊畫廊是一個在長為一點三公里長的長牆展示一百零五幅在 1990 年柏林牆東邊完成的畫作。這個歷史的時刻和自由和平的勝利不能以其他更好的方式呈現了。許多藝術家在柏林牆被推倒之後立刻趕到柏林牆的東方。被他們的受自由精神啟發的靈感所領導，藝術家們留下的不只是色彩豐富的壁畫，而也是一個歡樂與和解永恆的證據。柏林東邊畫廊是目前為止世界上最大的戶外畫廊，而每年這裡也吸引了許多世界各地的觀光客來見證德國的歷史遺產。現在有許多畫都正在維修，因為時間的關係而腐朽。然而，政府已經將這維修的計劃列為遺跡保護來確保未來更多人可以來看以及瞭解德國的歷史。畫廊中有許多不同的主題以及不同的風格，但他們卻都反映了美好未來的希望和祈求世人喜樂的願望。

Vocabulary and Idioms ▶

❶ **reunification** n 使再聯結　❷ **cutting edge** n 尖端

❸ **transcend** v 超越　　　　❹ **picturesque** adj 如畫的

❺ **classic** n 經典　　　　　❻ **festive** adj 喜慶的

❼ **iconic** adj 標誌性的　　　❽ **mural** n 壁畫

❾ **heritage** n 遺產

1. The reunification of Germany in 1990 is an important part of the history.

   德國在 1990 年再度聯合是歷史是很重要的一部分。

2. With the cutting edge technology, I believe we will have cures for AIDS in no time.

   有著走在尖端的科技，我想我們應該很快就會找到愛滋病的解藥了。

3. A great musician can transcend any genre and create the unique music everyone enjoys.

   一個好的音樂人是可以超越音樂種類並創造出大家所喜愛的音樂。

4. Reading by the picturesque lake at the park really relaxes me.

   在如畫般的湖旁邊看書真的會令我很放鬆。

5. John Lennon's "Imagine" is such a classic that almost everyone can sing it.

   約翰藍儂的 "想像" 真是一首大家都會唱的經典。

6. Christmas is around the corner, and you can tell just by the festive atmosphere all around.

聖誕節快到了，你可以到處都感受到喜慶的氣氛。

7. The iconic Taipei 101 remains one of the most popular tourist attractions in Taiwan.

標誌性的台北一零一還是台灣最受歡迎的景點之一。

8. The murals in the cave really depict the life back then vividly.

洞穴裡的壁畫很生動地描述了以前的生活。

9. Machu Picchu is a very important Mayan heritage for the Peruvians.

馬丘比丘對秘魯人來說是很重要的瑪雅遺址。

旅遊小貼士 ▶

　　曾經聽過當地的柏林朋友說過，當他們在柏林開車，閃了方向燈之後，代表的不是我要左轉或右轉囉，小心噢！而是我要右轉，讓我！其實他們在路上已經大家十分有默契，但是當他們在路上遇間差點和他們擦撞的人，他們就會知道那些人不是柏林人。所以如果有在當地開車的話要謹記這個小提示噢，否則可能會遭到當地柏林人白眼噢！

溫哥華

佛羅倫斯

柏林

洛桑

阿姆斯特丹

阿拉巴馬州

聖安東尼奧

波哥大

太平洋屋脊步道

紐西蘭

141

Unit 14

Lausanne 洛桑
November Man 特務交鋒

城市介紹 ▶

　　Lausanne is located 66 kilometers northeast from Geneva and in the French-speaking part of Switzerland. Lausanne has always been a favorite spot fro many people. It flourished, especially at the Age of Enlightenment, when it was associated with Voltaire, the leading writer in the 18th century. Even till today, Lausanne is an ideal living place for most French-Speaking Swisses because of its low-key elegance and aesthetic atmosphere. In a country of spectacular scenery, Lausanne really lives it up to the standard. With the steep hills overlooking the Lake Geneva (Lac Léman), the glittering water is where many people spend a splendid summer time. The city is divided into two towns and is connected by a small metro. Walking in the city, you will find the aesthetic charm and a cultural tradition. However, over time, Lausanne has given way to the water-skiers, sailors, wind surfers, and roller skaters. It is also the headquarters of the international Olympic Committee. So come down here and enjoy the city the way you want it.

◀ 洛桑 ▶

　　洛桑是位於距離日內瓦東北邊六十六公里的地方，並且位於瑞士的法語區內。洛桑總是許多人很喜歡的一個地方。它尤其在啟蒙時代時方光發熱，因為它和十八世紀的主要作家之一伏爾泰的連結。甚至到今天，洛桑也是大多數瑞士法語區的人最想住的地方，因為它低調的優雅和藝術的氣氛。身在一個風景優美的國家，洛桑真的達到標準。有著陡峭的山丘俯瞰日內瓦湖，那閃閃發亮的湖水是許多人度過許多美好夏日時光的地方。整個城市劃分為兩個小鎮。並由地鐵連接。走在這個城市，你會感受到藝術的魅力，和文化的傳統。然而，隨著時間，洛桑也讓滑水，帆船，風帆和直排輪的人在這裡玩耍。這裡同時也是國際奧林匹克委員會總部。所以來這裡並找到適合你的方式來享受這個城市吧！

溫哥華　佛羅倫斯　柏林　洛桑　阿姆斯特丹　阿拉巴馬州　聖安東尼奧　波哥大　太平洋屋脊步道　紐西蘭

Dialogue 情境對話 ▶

Mike and Grace are touring around the vineyard by Lake Geneva.

麥克和葛瑞斯正在日內瓦湖附近的一個葡萄園逛逛。

Mike: I have never realized how big a part the winemaking business is here.

麥克：我從來不知道這邊製酒的市場是這麼大的。

Grace: Really? This is probably one of the main businesses here. There are 10 kilometers or more of vineyards spreading out along Lake Geneva.

葛瑞斯：真的嗎？這大概是這邊最主要的生意了。這裡到處都有葡萄園酒莊沿著日內瓦湖畔十多公里。

Mike: Oh wow, and the view is just so lovely here. With the lake view down the hill, and organized grape trees lining up neatly. The scene here is impeccable.

麥克：哇，而且這裡的景觀真是可愛。山丘下有湖景，而且葡萄樹直線整齊地排好。這裡的景色是無懈可擊的。

Grace: I know, we gotta taste the wine here, too. Come on now. Let's get inside and try some wine.

葛瑞斯：我知道，我們也一定試試這裡的酒。來吧！我們進去試試看這裡的酒。

Mike: I can't wait.

麥克：我等不及了。

(Grace and Mike are both trying the Rosé)

葛瑞斯和麥客都在試他們的玫瑰紅酒。

Mike: All that hikes up here was totally worth it.

麥克：剛剛那些爬坡都值得了。

Grace: I know, that was what I was thinking about as well.

葛瑞斯：我知道，我也在想一樣的事。

Mike: Actually, I think every hike should end with this.

麥克：其實我想每個爬坡都應該這樣結束。

Grace: Haha! Yes, that does add on to the motivation for hiking.

葛瑞斯：哈哈！對，那的確會為爬山增加動力。

Mike: Why don't we get a few bottles home. They will be good gifts.

麥克：我們來買幾瓶酒回家吧！它們會是很好的禮物。

Grace: Yeah right, I think that's just your excuses for getting more wine for yourself.

葛瑞斯：最好是，我想那只是你想多買幾瓶酒的藉口。

Mike: You know me too well.

麥克：你太瞭解我了！

溫哥華

佛羅倫斯

柏林

洛桑

阿姆斯特丹

阿拉巴馬州

聖安東尼奧

波哥大

太平洋屋脊步道

紐西蘭

Special Sites Introduction 14: 特別景點報導 ▶

Lausanne - November Man  MP3 27

The movie the "November Man" is a story of an ex-CIA agent Peter Deveraux (Pierce Brosnan) who has to protect one of the secret witnesses, Alice (Olga Kurylenko). Alice has an unknown secret that can possibly uncover the biggest scandal of Russia and CIA. In order to investigate, Peter has to be under cover and under great risks from his ex-partner. It is a battle of killers and partners. In the movie, some of the most cutting-edge gadgets are shown and the thrills are unstoppable.

At the beginning of the movie, Peter is retired from the CIA and opened a lakefront coffee shop at Lausanne. It is in front of Lake Geneva. Lake Geneva or Lac Léman, is at the north side of the Alps, and East of Geneva. It's like a giant water mirror that connects the French speaking Vaud and France. It is lined up by several cities, including Lausanne and some smaller towns. By the lake, there are some fairy-tale houses lining up with the Alpes at the back.

溫
哥
華

佛
羅
倫
斯

柏

林

洛

桑

阿
姆
斯
特
丹

阿
拉
巴
馬
州

聖
安
東
尼
奧

波

哥

大

太平洋屋脊步道

紐
西
蘭

洛桑 - 特務交鋒

　　電影特務交鋒是在述説一個前 CIA 探員，彼得德弗羅（皮爾斯佈洛思南飾）必須保護其中一個秘密證人，愛麗絲（歐嘉‧柯瑞蘭寇飾）。愛麗絲有一個不為人知的秘密，那個秘密有可能會揭發俄國和美國 CIA 最大的醜聞。為了要深入調查，彼得必須隱藏身份並因前夥伴的關係深陷極大的危險。這是一個殺手之間和夥伴之間的戰役。在電影中也有許多最新的裝備；而刺激也是隨之而來。

　　在電影的一開始，彼得已經從 CIA 退休並且在日內瓦湖前開了一間咖啡廳。日內瓦湖，是位於阿爾卑斯山的北部，而在日內瓦的東部。這就像是是一個很巨大的，連接法語區瓦特州焊法國的水鏡。它的兩旁有許多的城市圍繞，包括洛桑和一些其他的小城鎮。在湖邊也有許多像童話故事般的房子以阿爾卑斯山為背景。

Notre-Dame de Lausanne MP3 28

When you come to Lausanne, don't forget to visit the iconic Notre-Dame de Lausanne. It is located at the old town side of Lausanne. The construction started in the mid 12th century and it took them nearly 80 years to finish. The grand cathedral is not only the icon of Lausanne, but also became a major tourist attraction here. Different than any other cathedrals, this one is extremely complete with a lot of gothic towers and simply done with perfection. It was also restored in the 19th century by the famous French architect Viollet-le-Duc. Even if it was built centuries ago, this place remains well-reserved and impressive. The rose windows from the 13th century retain their bright colors and the solemnness within the cathedral is just hard to ignore. Upon seeing this majestic cathedral from the outside, it just makes you feel extremely humble and calm. Continue your journey in the cathedral is a total eye-opening experience. The grandness of the space and the high-raised roof makes the cathedral seem even more unreachable. Be sure to stop by here and find your peace of mind.

洛桑聖母大教堂

　　當你來到洛桑，別忘了拜訪代表性的洛桑聖母大教堂。這裡是位於洛桑舊城區。這個建築開始於十二世紀中，並且花費了他們近八十年才完工。這個大教堂不僅是洛桑的象徵，而同時也成為一個很大的觀光景點。不同於其他的大教堂，這個教堂十分的完整，有許多的歌德式尖塔，並且是完美完工。在十九世紀時它是由著名的法屬建築師維奧萊-勒-杜克所修復。即使這個大教堂是在好幾世紀以前所建造，這裡還是保存得十分完善以及還是十分的令人印象深刻。十三世紀的玫瑰窗戶存有鮮艷的顏色，以及教堂中的神聖都令人無法忽略。打從你從外圍看見這個雄偉的大教堂就會令你覺得十分地卑遜和平靜。繼續你的旅程進入大教堂也是一個十分大開眼界的經驗。那廣大的空間和挑高的屋頂都使得這個教堂更加的難以接近。記得來這裡，並找到你的平靜。

Vocabulary and Idioms ▶

❶ flourish Ⅴ 興旺，繁榮

❷ aesthetic
adj 藝術的，美學的

❸ vineyard ⓝ 葡萄園

❹ impeccable
adj 無懈可擊的

❺ excuse ⓝ 藉口

❻ gadget ⓝ 小器具

❼ restore Ⅴ 修復

❽ solemn ⓝ 神聖的，莊嚴的

1. His business really started to flourish last year.

   他的事業真的從去年開始興榮。

2. The illustration made the picture book an aesthetic success.

   這插畫真的使得這個故事書成為一個美學上的成功。

3. We especially love the wines from this vineyard.

   我們特別喜歡從這個葡萄園出來的酒。

4. She has an impeccable taste in fashion.

   他對於時尚有這無懈可擊的品味。

5. She made an excuse to skip work and went to the concert.

   她編了一個藉口翹班並且去看演場會。

6. His recent new gadget is the Google glasses!

   他最新的科技小玩意兒是谷歌眼鏡！

7. I wonder if they could restore this painting. It's way too old.

   我不曉得他們還可不可以修復這幅畫。這真的太古老了。

8. A church is often considered a solemn place. Therefore, you need to keep your voice down when you enter it.

教堂通常被公認為是一個神聖的場所。所以，在進入教堂後音量要壓低。

🎓 旅遊小貼士 ▶

　　如果有打算要在洛桑當上一陣子的話，建議可以到火車站購買洛桑卡（Lausanne Card）。這個洛桑卡可以在一些參觀的景點享受到優惠，並且也可以無限制地搭乘大眾交通工具。所以若是長期來算的話是很划算的噢！若是想要暢遊洛桑的話，建議可以買一張洛桑卡噢！

Unit 15

Amsterdam 阿姆斯特丹
Ocean 12 瞞天過海 2

城市介紹 ▶

Amsterdam is the capital of the kingdom of the Netherlands. Located at the north of Holland, Amsterdam has the nickname "Venice of the North". There are about 160 canals weaving around the city and roughly about 1000 bridges, which resemble the romantic Venice in many ways. Similarly, there are also boat rides that offer you an unforgettable night view of Amsterdam canals. Amsterdam is also one of the most bike-friendly cities in the world. According to the 2003 survey, there were about 1,200,000 bikes and the number is still increasing. The brightly colored tulips, the vast varieties of the cheeses, the romantic canals, and the symbolic windmills can all be spotted during a breezy bike ride at Amsterdam. If you are a fan of museums, there are about 40 museums in the city and more than a million art pieces are stored within them. There is just that magical romantic element in the Amsterdam air that makes the city so elegant and so charming. You would get the feeling that anything could happen here, and strangely, you are kind of looking forward to it!

阿姆斯特丹

　　阿姆斯特丹是荷蘭的首都。位於荷蘭的北部，阿姆斯特丹享有"北方威尼斯"的小名。大約有一百六十條運河交織在整個城市中，以及大約一千座橋，這就如同浪漫的威尼斯一般。更相似的是，也有遊船可以帶給你難忘的阿姆斯特丹夜景。阿姆斯特丹也同時是全世界騎腳踏車最方便的城市之一。根據 2003 年的統計，阿姆斯特丹大約有一百二十萬台腳踏車。而數字都還在爬升。顏色鮮艷的鬱金香，廣大種類的起士，浪漫的運河還有象徵性的風車都可以在微風徐徐的騎單車之旅看見。如果你喜歡博物館的話，市內大約有 40 間博物館，還有超過一百萬個藝術藏品。在阿姆斯特丹的空氣中總是有著那神奇又浪漫的元素使得整個城市如此的優雅和迷人。在這裡你總是有著什麼事都有可能會發生的感覺，而奇怪的是，你還十分期待它發生呢！

溫哥華

佛羅倫斯

柏林

洛桑

阿姆斯特丹

阿拉巴馬州

聖安東尼奧

波哥大

太平洋屋脊步道

紐西蘭

> **Dialogue 情境對話 ▶**
>
> Claire and Kimberly are about to walk in the Red Light District in Amsterdam.
> 克萊兒和金伯利正要走進阿姆斯特丹的紅燈區。

Claire: Wow, are we ready for this?　克萊兒：哇，我們準備好了嗎？

Kimberly: Would they think it's weird that girls walk in this district?　金伯利：不知道他們會不會覺得很奇怪女生走進這裡？

Claire: I'm sure they are used to a lot of tourists walking into this district anyways.　克萊兒：我覺得他們一定已經習慣很多觀光客在這區走來走去。

Kimberly: It is just like its name! This place is covered by red lights! It's so crazy!　金伯利：這真的就跟它的名字一樣！這個地方真的是被紅光籠罩着！真是瘋狂！

Claire: All the girls behind the windows are all so provocatively dressed!　克萊兒：所有在窗戶後的女生都穿得好暴露噢！

Kimberly: Of course, looks like the　金伯利：當然啦，看來這裡

competitions here can be quite fierce as well. | 的競爭應該也很激烈噢。

Claire: I think Amsterdam in a way is pretty avant-garde in many ways. | 克萊兒：我覺得其實阿姆斯特丹在某方面來說也是蠻前衛的。

Kimberly: Yes, indeed, this has been a pretty eye-opening experience since we got here this morning. | 金伯利：對啊，真的，從我們今天早上到這，今天一整天都是很令人大開眼界的體驗！

Claire: No kidding, you would wonder if the crime rates decrease here? | 克萊兒：真的沒在開玩笑，你會想說不知道這裡的犯罪率有沒有比較低？

Kimberly: That would be pretty interesting to look into I guess! | 金伯利：我想那會是個蠻有趣的調查！

Claire: Hey, look at that guy that just walked into the window! | 克萊兒：欸你看那個男生剛走進窗戶內耶！

Kimberly: Oh wow, the lady closed the window with the curtain!! | 金伯利：噢哇！那個女生用窗簾把窗戶關起來了！

溫哥華
佛羅倫斯
柏林
洛桑
阿姆斯特丹
阿拉巴馬州
聖安東尼奧
波哥大
太平洋屋脊步道
紐西蘭

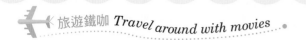

Claire: I wonder if you can get a picture with the ladies here.

克萊兒：不曉得可不可以跟這裡的女生拍張照。

Kimberly: Don't even think about it!

金伯利：想都別想！

Claire: Come on!

克萊兒：拜託！

Special Sites Introduction 15: 特別景點報導 ▶

Amsterdam 阿姆斯特丹 - Ocean 12　　MP3 29

Ocean 12, the sequel to Ocean 11, was equally exciting and witty that was instantly another blockbuster when it came out. The incredible cast of the movie traveled to many different cities in the quest for another masterpiece. In the movie, Ocean (George Clooney), Rusty (Brad Pitt), and Linus (Matt Damon) went to Amsterdam and had a meeting with a local gangster Matsui (Robbie Coltrane). The scene that when Ocean, Rusty and Matsui pulled the "lost in translation" on Linus by saying a bunch of gibberish and seemingly nonsense where they completely lost Linus and forced him to recite a phrase of poem. Only later on Linus was informed that he had been tricked by the three in Amsterdam.

This humorous scene was shot at one of Amsterdam's most famous coffee shop Dampkring. It is said to be one of the friendliest coffee shops in Amsterdam where both first-time visitors and regulars will be welcomed. Many celebrities will stop by this coffee shop, while visiting Amsterdam as well!

阿姆斯特丹 - 瞞天過海 2

　　電影瞞天過海 2，瞞天過海 1 的續集，也是一樣的刺激和機智，當它一上映時就立即變成票房的大熱門！這驚人的卡司去到很多城市拍攝就為了創造另外一個佳作。在電影中，歐遜（喬治克隆尼飾），羅斯（布萊德彼特飾），和萊納斯（麥特戴蒙飾）來到阿姆斯特丹和當地的一個黑幫老大（羅彼‧考特拉尼飾）開會，這就是當歐遜，羅斯和黑幫老大說了一堆沒有意義的話來使出 "無法解釋" 這個花招來耍萊納斯。而萊納斯當下還被逼的朗誦了一小節詩，最後才得知他被這三個人耍了！

　　這個幽默的橋段是在阿姆斯特丹很有名的咖啡店之一 Dampkring 拍攝。那裡聽說是阿姆斯特丹最友善的咖啡店之一。他們歡迎第一次來的客人還有常客。許多名人來到阿姆斯特丹也會來這裡噢！

溫哥華
佛羅倫斯
柏林
洛桑
阿姆斯特丹
阿拉巴馬州
聖安東尼奧
波哥大
太平洋屋脊步道
紐西蘭

One of the confusing parts about Amsterdam is the name of the coffee places. First-time visitors would often confuse themselves while facing 3 different titles: coffee shops, coffee houses, and cafés while only looking for a place to sit down and have a sip of coffee after a long day sightseeing in Amsterdam.

With a legal license, coffee shop owners are allowed to sell cannabis. Most of the coffee shops also sell food and drinks. However, it is illegal for them to sell alcohol. If found selling alcoholic drinks, the store might risk closure. If you are still not sure, looking out for a green and white license outside of the store before you step in. A coffee house, on the other hand, sells coffee and light meals just as our regular coffee place, whereas a café is more or less like a bar. Therefore, next time when you are looking for a good cup of coffee, beware of the names of the places you step in! You may not find what you were looking for in the first place!

咖啡店

　　阿姆斯特丹其中一個令人混淆的是他們很多關於咖啡店的稱呼。第一次來這邊的觀光客只是在阿姆斯特丹觀光了一天，單純想要找地方坐下並喝一口咖啡，遇到三個不一樣的名稱通常都會混淆：coffee shops、coffee houses 和 cafés。

　　有著合法的證照，coffee shops 的店家可以販售大麻。大多數的 coffee shops 也都還是會販賣食物和飲料。然而，對他們而言，販售酒是非法的。如果被發現賣酒的話他們可是會冒著關門大吉的風險。如果你還是不太確定的話，在走進店門前仔細看店門外有沒有一張白綠色的證照。一個 coffee house，另外一方面則指的是像我們一般說的咖啡店，他們有賣咖啡和輕食。而 café 則是多多少少像是酒吧的地方。所以，下次你想找一杯好喝的咖啡時，小心看好店家的名稱，否則你可以會找到你本來沒有料想到的東西噢！

Vocabulary and Idioms ▶

❶ **weave** v 編織

❷ **tulip** n 鬱金香

❸ **symbolic** adj 象徵的

❹ **provocatively** adv 暴露的

❺ **fierce** adj 激烈的

❻ **avant-garde** adj 前衛的

❼ **eye opening** adj 大開眼界的

❽ **witty** adj 機智的

1. She's been weaving her dream of traveling the world ever since she was a kid.

   她從小就開始編織著環遊世界的夢想。

2. She decorated her living room with some tulips.

   她用一些鬱金香來裝飾她的客廳。

3. Red roses are symbolic of love.

   紅玫瑰象徵愛。

4. The dancers at the club have to dress provocatively to attract attention.

   在夜店裡的舞者必須穿著暴露來吸引大家的注意力。

5. They haven't talked to each other since they had a fierce fight last week.

   他們自從上禮拜激烈地吵架後就沒跟對方講過話。

6. Picasso's paintings are very avant-garde at his time.

   畢卡索的畫在他的時代是十分前衛的。

7. It was an eye opening experience to go to the World Expo.

參加世界博覽會真是一個大開眼界的經驗。

8. She always has some witty answers for the reporters.

她對記者總是有機智的回答。

旅遊小貼士 ▶

　　來到荷蘭的阿姆斯特丹，最好的穿梭於城市各處的辦法就是跟當地人一樣騎腳踏車！在荷蘭，他們單車道及腳踏車停車的地方都規劃得很好，而租車店也十分的好找。可是要十分小心的事，荷蘭的偷車賊十分的猖獗！除了不要停在較少人的地方之外，停車之後上的鎖也千萬不要馬虎！如果可以的話，租車時也可以順便買保險！

溫哥華

佛羅倫斯

柏林

洛桑

阿姆斯特丹

阿拉巴馬州

聖安東尼奧

波哥大

太平洋屋脊步道

紐西蘭

Unit 16

Alabama 阿拉巴馬州
Sweet Home Alabama
美麗蹺家人

城市介紹 ▶

Alabama is the southern state of the United States. It derived its name from a Native American. Alabama is always famous for its scenic sights, and also its outdoor activities.

Stepping into Alabama, the blue sky and the white sandy beaches started a long race stretching along the Gulf Shores and Orange beach, while you see the seagulls flying freely in the sky. Not too many people know about this secret spot of the world yet. However, the soft sands, clear seawater, music festivals, great southern cuisine and friendly folks here are definitely worth driving or flying all the way over. If outdoor activities, such as the summer sandcastle-building time are not your cup of tea, there are a lot of historical sites and museums within Alabama. It is after all, the heart of the Civil War. Remember Martin Luther King Jr.'s "I have a dream" speech? Step in the Dexter Avenue King Memorial Baptist Church to know more about the messages he was preaching. Alabama is also where Helen Keller's from. There's nothing better than being there yourself to understand where a great person's from, and that's also where you will get the most authentic stories about them.

◄ 阿拉巴馬州 ►

　　阿拉巴馬州是位於美國南方的一個州。它的名字最一開始是來自一個美洲印第安人。阿拉巴馬總是以它秀麗風景和戶外活動為人所知。踏入阿拉巴馬，當藍天和白沙海灘沿著墨西哥灣區和 Orange Beach 展開了一場賽跑，海鷗正在天空自在地飛翔。還沒有太多人知道世界的這個秘密景點。然而，那細軟的白沙，清澈的海水，音樂盛典，美好的南方美食，和友善的人們是值得你開車或是搭飛機過來一趟的。如果你不是很喜歡戶外活動的人，除了夏天堆沙灘城堡的時光，阿拉巴馬還是有許多歷史景點和博物館。它畢竟是美國內戰的心臟地帶。還記得馬丁路德的 "我有一個夢" 演說嗎？去一趟德克斯特大街浸信會教堂去聊解更多他當時想要傳遞的訊息。阿拉巴馬同時也是海倫凱勒的家鄉。沒有比親自去一趟偉人的家鄉更好的辦法去瞭解他們，以及得到關於他們最真實的故事。

溫哥華
佛羅倫斯
柏林
洛桑
阿姆斯特丹
阿拉巴馬州
聖安東尼奧
波哥大
太平洋脊步道
紐西蘭

Dialogue 情境對話 ▶

Jimmy and Lindsey are on a road trip in Alabama.
吉米和琳熙正在阿拉巴馬里進行公路之旅。

Lindsey: I think we're near the gulf shore areas!

琳熙：我想我們好像快接近墨西哥海灣區囉！

Jimmy: Look at the white sandy beach and the turquoise water! I just want to jump in for a swim!

吉米：看看那些白沙海灘和湛藍的海水！我現在就想跳下去游個泳！

Lindsey: Our hotel is at Orange Beach! We're very close now!

琳熙：我們的飯店在 Orange Beach! 我們現在非常接近了！

Jimmy: We're almost there! Should we go to the hotel first or do you want to stop by somewhere to grab a bite?

吉米：我們快到了！我們要先到飯店還是要去哪裡吃個東西嗎？

Lindsey: It's really up to you! I'm not too hungry yet! I'm just ready to lie down on the soft sand and relax!

琳熙：真的是看你！我現在還沒很餓！我只是很想躺在白沙上放鬆了！

Jimmy: We'll go straight to the hotel

吉米：那我們先直接去飯

first then, and figure it out from there.

店，然後再看之後要幹嘛。

Lindsey: When does the Hangout Festival start again? Can we make it tonight?

琳熙：那個 Hangout 沙灘演唱會是什麼時候開始？我們今天晚上來得及去嗎？

Jimmy: I think so, we got a 3-day pass anyways! Gotta love the music festivals here. I think Red Hot Chilli Peppers are gonna be there tonight!

吉米：我想可以吧。反正我們有三天的門票！一定要很愛這邊的沙灘演唱會的！我記得今天晚上好像有嗆辣紅椒樂團！

Lindsey: We can't miss it then! Let's go check in, get something to eat and get ready to go!

琳熙：那我們就不能錯過了！我們先去飯店 check in，找點東西吃然後就準備出發了吧！

Jimmy: Sounds like a great plan!

吉米：計劃聽起來不錯！

Lindsey: Meanwhile, should we play the theme song of our road trip again?

琳熙：在這同時，我們要不要再來放我們這趟公路之旅的主題曲？

Jimmy: Sweet Home Alabama? That's our jam! Hit it!

吉米：是 Sweet Home Alabama 嗎？那是我們的

溫哥華
佛羅倫斯
柏林
洛桑
阿姆斯特丹
阿拉巴馬州
聖安東尼奧
波哥大
太平洋屋脊步道
紐西蘭

歌！播！

Lindsey: Okie dokie!　　　　　　　琳熙：好低！

 Special Sites Introduction 16: 特別景點報導 ▶

Alabama - Sweet Home Alabama　 MP3 31

In the 2002 Romantic Comedy "Sweet Home Alabama", Melanie (Reese Witherspoon) was a girl from Alabama. However, she was ashamed about her poor southern roots, so she changed her last name, and started a fashion career in New York. She became very successful in both her career and love life. She was engaged to the Mayor's son in New York. Nevertheless, she had to come back to Alabama only to divorce her husband Jake (Josh Lukas).

When Melanie came back to Alabama, one of the roads that showed the historic homes at Melanie's return to Pigeon Creek was shot in Eufaula, Alabama. The stretch of the road, also known as "Sweet Home Alabama Road", has drawn a lot of tourists because of the movie. On top of that, it is one of the most photographed streets around there because of the southern mansions and giant oak trees all lined up nicely along the lanes. The governments are trying to widen the lanes for more tourists to come in the town. However, this has become a debatable issue since some of the residents fear that more people might damage the historical district.

阿拉巴馬州 - 美麗蹺家人

　　在 2002 年的浪漫喜劇片美麗蹺家人中，梅樂妮（瑞絲薇斯朋）是一個從小在阿拉巴馬長大的女孩。然而，她因為對於她在貧窮南部的出生感到很羞愧，於是她改了姓，並開始了她在紐約的時尚生涯。她在事業和愛情都十分的得意，並且和市長的兒子訂婚。不過，她必須要回到阿拉巴馬來和她的老公傑克（喬許盧可斯）離婚。

　　當梅樂妮回到阿拉巴馬的時候，在她要回去小鴿溪時其中的一條路呈現出古老的房子。那裡就是在阿拉巴馬的 Eufaula 所拍攝。這一段路，或稱為 "美麗蹺家人路" 因為電影吸引了許多的觀光客。除此之外，它也是附近最常被拍攝的一條路因為它周邊的南方宅邸和橡樹整齊地排在兩旁。政府正在積極把這條路建寬以便更多人可以進來到這個鎮上。不過，這也成為了十分值得辯論的議題因為有些居民深怕更多人來到這個鎮上會毀損了這個歷史區域。

溫哥華

佛羅倫斯

柏林

洛桑

阿姆斯特丹

阿拉巴馬州

聖安東尼奧

波哥大

太平洋屋脊步道

紐西蘭

 旅遊愛玩咖 ▶

Coming to Alabama, you might run into a side dish called "hush puppies". You are not about to eat any sort of puppies, so there's the relief. So what are hush puppies then? And how did they derive the name? Some said that originally this snack was invented by fishermen and soldiers when they would make this golden snacks for the dogs and say "hush, puppy!" when the dogs are barking and begging for food.

What exactly is it then? It is actually made out of a batter that includes cornmeal, flour, baking soda, salt, onion, butter-milk, and eggs. Once you mix all the ingredients and make the batter, you use a teaspoon to drop the batter in the oil. Fry each of them till golden brown and there, you will have your hush puppies! It is easy, fast, and still allows you to be a dog lover. Try out this hushpuppy and see if it works for both you and your dogs!

南方美食-玉米粉丸子

　　來到阿拉巴馬，你可能會遇到一道菜名為 "hush puppies" （安靜的小狗）。你不會需要吃任何的小狗所以不必擔心。所以那 hush puppies 到底是什麼呢？那他們又是從哪裡得到這個名字的呢？有些人說最一開始是這個點心是由漁人或是士兵們研發，當狗兒們正在吠叫和在乞討食物時，他們就會製作這個黃金色的點心給狗兒們，並說"安靜，小狗！"

　　那這道菜到底是什麼呢？它其實是有玉米粉，麵粉，小蘇打粉，鹽，洋蔥，脫脂乳，和蛋。當你將所有的材料都混和好之後，也將麵糊做好了之後，用一個茶匙來將麵糊丟到油中油炸。將每一球麵糊都炸到金黃色之後就可以！所以，這就是你的 hush puppy 囉！這又簡單，快速，也還允許你繼續身為一個愛狗人士。試試看這個 hush puppy 來看看你和你的狗狗們喜不喜歡這道菜！

溫哥華

佛羅倫斯

柏林

洛桑

阿姆斯特丹

阿拉巴馬州

聖安東尼奧

波哥大

太平洋屋脊步道

紐西蘭

▶ Vocabulary and Idioms ▶

❶ seagull n 海鷗

❷ not someone's cup of tea Idiom 不是某人喜歡的

❸ authentic adj 真實的，道地的

❹ preach v 鼓吹，説教

❺ road trip n 公路之旅

❻ turquoise adj 藍綠色的

❼ debatable adj 可爭辯的

❽ relief n 寬心

1. The seagulls are fighting for the same fish over that side!

   海鷗們在那邊搶奪同一隻魚耶！

2. Hiking is not my cup of tea. It always makes me so tired.

   健行真的不是我喜歡的，我每次都會很累。

3. Stinky tofu is a really authentic Taiwanese dish.

   臭豆腐是一個真正道地的台灣美食。

4. She devoted her life to preaching peace.

   她奉獻了她的一生鼓吹和平。

5. They started their road trip in California last Friday.

   他們上個禮拜五開始展開了在加州的公路之旅。

6. I miss the turquoise warm sea in Florida.

   我想念在佛羅里達州那藍綠色溫暖的海水。

7. To have the death penalty or not remains debatable.

   死刑的必要性還是很有爭議性的。

8. To her relief, all her children were fine.

令她寬心的事，她的小孩們都沒事。

旅遊小貼士 ▶

　　到了美國的南部，他們都會有南部的口音，所以一開始可能會有一點點不習慣，但其實只要聽久了之後也會發現了這個口音的可愛之處。一個明顯的不同是他不會用 you 來説你，他們會用 You all。許多人一開始可能會有一點點聽不懂這邊的口音，以為自己的英文退化，但其實這只要習慣了就好了噢！

溫
哥
華

佛
羅
倫
斯

柏

林

洛

桑

阿
姆
斯
特
丹

阿
拉
巴
馬
州

聖
安
東
尼
奧

波

哥

大

太
平
洋
屋
脊
步
道

紐
西
蘭

Unit 17

San Antonio 聖安東尼奧
Miss Congeniality 麻辣女王

城市介紹 ▶

    San Antonio, or known as the Alamo City, is the second biggest city in Texas. Stepping into San Antonio, you can feel the romantic atmosphere all around you. The Mexican influences can be seen everywhere in the city. Alamo; nevertheless, is the most influential of all. Alamo was built in 1724 as a religious site. However, the Spanish distributed this church to the people as a private property in 1793, so when the Mexicans claimed independency from the Spanish, they claimed Texas as part of Mexico as well. Alamo played a very important role in the Texan history. In 1836, the Texans were troubled by the Mexican law and attempted to fight for their independence. Nonetheless, it was a battle between two hundred Texans and seven thousand Mexican soldiers. The two hundred soldiers fought hard at Alamo and led to the victory for the Texan army in three weeks. Therefore, Alamo is a must see in San Antonio.

Coming into San Antonio, you cannot miss the chance to stroll around the charming River walk. There are several boat rides as well as Mexican restaurants and a few American restaurants for tourists to choose. Spending a night here will definitely give you a romantic experience in Texas.

聖安東尼奧

聖安東尼奧，或是阿拉莫之城，是德州第二大的城市。踏進聖安東尼奧，你立即可以感受到周遭浪漫的氣氛。城市中到處可見墨西哥的影響。阿拉莫，然而，是最有影響力的。阿拉莫是在 1724 年被建立為宗教據點。然而，在 1793 年，西班牙政府將這個教堂分派為私人領土，所以當墨西哥人從西班牙人那裡爭奪到獨立權，他們也將德州劃為墨西哥的領土。阿拉莫在德州歷史上扮演了十分重要的角色。在 1836 年，德州人因為被墨西哥的法律所苦而試圖要爭奪回他們的獨立權。但是，那是一個兩百個德州人對上七千個墨西哥人的戰役。那兩百個士兵在阿拉莫堅強作戰，對三個星期後德州的勝利有很大的影響。所以，阿拉莫是在聖安到尼奧必去的景點噢！

來到聖安東尼奧，也別錯過來到迷人河濱走走。這裡有游船也有墨西哥和少數美式餐廳可供觀光客選擇。來這邊一晚一定會給你在德州浪漫的一晚噢！

溫哥華

佛羅倫斯

柏林

洛桑

阿姆斯特丹

阿拉巴馬州

聖安東尼奧

波哥大

太平洋屋脊步道

紐西蘭

Dialogue 情境對話 ▶

Alex and Jasmine are getting on a boat ride at the River walk at San Antonio.
艾力克思和潔斯敏正在聖安東尼奧河濱的游船上。

Jasmine: This is such a romantic experience. Thanks Alex!

潔斯敏：這真是一個浪漫的體驗。謝謝你艾力克斯！

Alex: You're welcome. I think you definitely made a good call on coming here after thanksgiving. Look at the lights around us.

艾立克斯：不客氣。我想你做了很好的決定說要感恩節過後再來。你看我們周遭的燈！

Jasmine: This is very touristy, but I love it. I'm not going to forget any of this.

潔斯敏：我知道這很觀光客，但是我超愛的。我一定不會忘記這一切的。

Alex: I'm glad you enjoy it! It is our 2nd anniversary after all.

艾立克斯：我很開心你很喜歡！這畢竟是我們的二週年紀念。

Jasmine: People are waving at us from the shore!

潔斯敏：有人在岸上跟我們揮手耶！

174

Alex: Wave back! I'm videotaping all this!

艾立克斯：揮回去啊！我在錄影！

Jasmine: I'm not sure whether it is the wine or the beautiful lights. I'm euphoric.

潔斯敏：我不曉得是因為酒還是這美麗的燈。我好興奮。

Alex: I feel so happy as well. I'm glad we came out here.

艾立克斯：我也覺得好開心。我好高興我們來這。

Jasmine: Should we get some dinner here as well? I'm in love with this side of the city.

潔斯敏：我們要不要也在這裡吃晚餐？我好喜歡這個城市的這一角。

Alex: Don't you worry, my darling, I've made a reservation at one Mexican restaurant already.

艾立克斯：你不必擔心，我親愛的。我已經在這裡的一間墨西哥餐廳定好位了。

Jasmine: Thank you so much. I married the most thoughtful man on earth.

潔斯敏：真的謝謝你。我嫁給了全地球最設想周到的男人。

Alex: The boat ride is about 40 minutes long, so we should be hungry by then. We will have to celebrate afterwards!

艾立克斯：這個游船大概四十分鐘，所以我們結束後應該也餓了。我們等等一定要

溫哥華 佛羅倫斯 柏林 洛桑 阿姆斯特丹 阿拉巴馬州 聖安東尼奧 波哥大 太平洋屋脊步道 紐西蘭

慶祝一下！

Jasmine: Yes, and let's come down here every year!

潔斯敏：好！我們每年都來這裡吧！

Special Sites Introduction 17: 特別景點報導 ▶

San Antonio - Miss Congeniality MP3 33

Miss Congeniality is a comedy released in 2000. A tomboy FBI agent Gracie Hart (Sandra Bullock) was transformed into a beauty pageant contestant to hunt down the possible suspect. It is indeed one of those ugly duckling's swan becoming movies. But Hart's boyish clumsiness and kindness won the hearts of many households, including the other contestants'. That's what makes her Miss Congeniality. It's the perfect film to bring you and your family a few chuckles.

In the movie when Hart and the other contestants are doing the swimming suit competition, it was shot at the very Arneson River Theater. It is an outdoor performance theater on the north side of the river. The audience usually sits on the grass-covered steps on the opposite side to enjoy the performance. There are 13 rows of seats, which can seat up to 800 members for a show. If you wish to see a show here, be sure to look up the performances in advance!

聖安東尼奧 - 麻辣女王

麻辣女王是一部在 2000 年上映的喜劇片。一個男孩子氣的聯邦調查員葛蕾絲哈特（珊卓布拉克飾）轉變為選美比賽的參選者去捕捉一個可能的嫌犯。這的確是那些醜小鴨變天鵝的電影之一，但是哈特男孩子氣的笨拙和好心腸為她贏得許多人的心，包括其他參選人的。這也就是為什麼她在比賽中得到最佳人緣獎。它是一部可以帶給你和你的家人一些歡笑的片。

在電影中當哈特和其他參選人在競選泳裝比賽時，他們就是在艾尼遜河劇場所拍攝。觀眾們通常坐在對面觀賞表演。大約有十三排的座位，可以坐大概八百個觀眾。如果你想要來觀賞一個表演的話，記得要事先查詢有什麼表演噢！

溫哥華

佛羅倫斯

柏林

洛桑

阿姆斯特丹

阿拉巴馬州

聖安東尼奧

波哥大

太平洋屋脊步道

紐西蘭

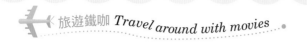
 旅遊愛玩咖 ▶

 Schlitterbahn Water Park · MP3 34

Schlitterban is about 40 minutes drive from San Antonio. However, it is a must visit if you are around the town. Over seventy acres of space with thrilling facilities and exciting rides within the park ensure you and your family have a great time in Texas. It is one of the most fun-filled water parks in the world. Without exaggeration, each year, tons of people rush in to the park to look for some summer excitement. Despite the fact that people have to wait in long lines, everyone seems to have a great time. One little tip to avoid the long wait is to visit the park from April to June 30th or from August 15th to September 18th, which is their off-season time. Schlitterbahn is a family-owned business that is based in New Braunfels, Texas. They first opened in 1979 and have developed four parks in Texas and one in Kansas City. Therefore, if you wish to try their different locations, look them up and see which one is the next!

施利特班水上樂園

　　施利特班水上樂園大約離聖安東尼奧四十分鐘的車程。然而，如果你在這個附近的話，這是一個一定要來的地方。在超過七十英畝的空間設置刺激的設施和乘坐設施可以確保你和家人都可以在德州玩得很開心。這是全世界最好玩的水上樂園之一。不誇張，每年有許多人都會來到這裡尋求夏日的刺激。儘管大家需要大排長龍，每個人似乎都還是玩得十分開心。一個小小的避開人潮的辦法是盡量選擇在四月到六月三十之間，或是趁八月十五到九月十八之間來玩。因為這正是這裡淡季的時候。施利特班水上樂園是一個以紐布朗費爾斯為中心的家族企業。他們在 1979 年開幕，而至今也已經在德州和坎薩斯城加開了四個樂園。所以如果你想要試試不同的樂園的話，查查看下一個要去哪裡吧！

溫哥華

佛羅倫斯

柏林

洛桑

阿姆斯特丹

阿拉巴馬州

聖安東尼奧

波哥大

太平洋屋脊步道

紐西蘭

Vocabulary and Idioms ▶

❶ influential
    adj 有影響力的

❷ attempt v 試圖

❸ touristy adj 觀光客的

❹ euphoric adj 非常高興的

❺ thoughtful
    adj 設想周全的

❻ transform v 轉變

❼ clumsiness n 笨拙

❽ thrilling adj 刺激的

1. He used to be a very influential figure here, but not anymore.

   他以前在這裡是很有影響力的人物，可是再也不是了。

2. They attempt to finish the task by July.

   他們試圖要在七月完成所有的工作。

3. Taking pictures with a selfie stick can be very touristy, but it captures great pictures.

   用自拍桿照相可能很觀光客，可是它都可以捕捉到很好的照片。

4. I felt euphoric, thrilled and grateful when I graduated.

   我當時畢業的時候覺得很開心，興奮以及感激。

5. She has always been very thoughtful and sweet ever since she was a kid.

   她從小就是一個很設想周全和貼心的人。

6. He transformed the old office into a very modern space to work.

   他將老舊的辦公室轉變為摩登的工作空間。

7. Her clumsiness often keeps her from getting jobs.

她的笨拙總是使她找不到工作。

8. It's a fast-paced, and thrilling movie.

這是一個步調快，又刺激的電影。

旅遊小貼士 ▶

　　因為聖安東尼奧的地理位置距離墨西哥邊境十分地接近，許多遊客來到這邊都喜歡到邊界也一睹墨西哥的風情。在墨西哥邊界的地帶也設立了許多墨西哥的紀念品店。然而，許多暴力事件或是暴動卻時常在邊界發生。所以在前往到邊界的景點之前，請務必查詢當下的情況在前往，千萬不要貿然前往噢，避免危險發生！

溫哥華

佛羅倫斯

柏林

洛桑

阿姆斯特丹

阿拉巴馬州

聖安東尼奧

波哥大

太平洋屋脊步道

紐西蘭

Unit 18

Bogota 波哥大 - Cities on Speed 急速都市

城市介紹 ▶

    As the capital of Colombia, Bogota does a great job representing Colombia to the world. Visitors traveling to Bogota will find the transportation in this city rather convenient. The bus system and bike routes are all very well-planned and well-organized. There are the yellow taxis driving around the city as well if you do not feel like busing it down to your destinations. Foodies are in very good hands in this city. Bogota has traditional meals peppered around the city for you to try. They also have high-class restaurants that provide you with both Colombian food and international cuisine. Follow the aroma to the world famous Colombian coffee and try their traditional sweets and chocolates if you're not stuffed yet. Bars are everywhere with a variety of music, such as salsa, Reggeaton, house, or a mixture of all. You can always have a good time there. There are also a lot of world-class museums in this historical city. Plan your stay in Bogota a little bit longer. Chances are that you might not have finished exploring the city before you need to leave!

波哥大

身為哥倫比亞的首都，波哥大十分出色地代表哥倫比亞呈現到世界。來到哥倫比亞的觀光客們會發現波哥大的交通系統很方便。他們的公車系統和腳踏車道都規劃和整理的十分完善。如果你不想要坐公車到你的目的地，城市中也到處都看得到黃色的計程車。饕客們來到波哥大會好好受到照顧。波哥大城市到處都有傳統哥倫比亞美食。他們也有高級的哥倫比亞和國際美食的餐廳。如果你還沒吃飽的話，跟著香味來到世界聞名的哥倫比亞的咖啡，再試試他們傳統的點心和巧克力。酒吧也是隨處可見，放著各式各樣的音樂，例如騷沙，雷鬼，豪斯，或者混合，你總是會在這裡度過美好的時光。這裡也有許多世界級的博物館，所以把你在波哥大的時間計劃的長一些，因為你很有可能在你還沒探索完整個城市前就得離開了。

Dialogue 情境對話

Timmy is learning how to dance salsa from his local friend Natalia.

提米正在跟他當地的朋友娜塔麗雅學怎麼跳騷沙舞。

Natalia: Are you ready to salsa?　　娜塔麗雅：你準備好要騷沙了嗎？

Timmy: I hope so!　　提米：我希望如此！

Natalia: Okay, so let's listen to the tempos first.　　娜塔麗雅：好，那我們先來聽節奏。

Timmy: Okay, 1, 2, 3, 4…　　提米：好，1，2，3，4…

Natalia: No, in Salsa, we do 1, 2, 3 hold a little bit, and then 5, 6, 7, hold a little longer. Now it's your turn.　　娜塔麗雅：不，在騷沙，我們是，1，2，3 停留一下下，然後再 5，6，7 停留一下下。現在換你試試看。

Timmy: 1,2, 3, hold. 5, 6, 7 hold. 1, 2,3, hold. 5, 6, 7 hold.　　提米：1，2，3 停。5，6，7 停。1，2，3，停，5，6，7 停。

Natalia: Yes, you're very talented Timmy. Do you play any instruments? Or do you dance?　　娜塔麗雅：很好，你很有才華耶提米。你會任何樂器嗎？或是你有在跳舞嗎？

Timmy: I was in the dancing club back in High School, but I haven't　　提米：我以前高中是熱舞社的，但是我已經很久沒有跳

danced for a very long time. Thanks for the compliment though Natalia!

舞了。不過謝謝你的贊美娜塔麗雅！

Natalia: You're welcome, so here are the basic steps in Salsa. 1, 2, 3. 5, 6, 7. (Natalia demonstrates the steps) Come join me.

娜塔麗雅：不客氣，所以這是基本的騷沙舞步。1，2，3，5，6，7（納塔利雅在示範舞步）

Timmy: Okay. Am I doing it right?

提米：好，我這樣做對嗎？

Natalia: Yes, muy bien! Very good! Keep doing it. I'm gonna play the salsa music now.

娜塔麗雅：對，很好（西文）！非常好！繼續。我現在要放騷沙音樂來跳舞了。

Natalia plays the music for them to dance.

（娜塔麗雅播放音樂讓他們跳舞）

Timmy: Wow the tempo is very fast.

提米：哇這個節奏很快耶！

Natalia: Just follow the music and remember the tempo. Most importantly, you have to enjoy it! Let's have some fun!

娜塔麗雅：只要跟著音樂然後記得基本的節奏。最重要的是，你一定要享受騷沙！我們來跳得開心一點吧！

Timmy: Okay! I think I like Salsa a

提米：好！我想我很喜歡騷

溫哥華
佛羅倫斯
柏林
洛桑
阿姆斯特丹
阿拉巴馬州
聖安東尼奧
波哥大
太平洋屋脊步道
紐西蘭

lot! 沙！

Special Sites Introduction 18: 特別景點報導

Bogota - Cities on Speed MP3 35

The documentary Cities on Speed is sponsored by the Danish Film Institute, a collection of 4 films that are directed by 4 different directors with the same theme of the fast-paced, character-based stories in the cities. One of the films, Bogota Change, is documented in Bogota. The film is about two distinguished mayors in Bogota that brought changes to the corruption and violence in Bogota. One of the mayors, Antanas Mockus, was the president of the National University of Colombia. He resigned from the University after the day he mooned the protesting students. He soon became a popular character in Bogota and was later on chosen to be the mayor of Bogota. Because of his integrity and honesty, he did bring about some positive changes in Bogota. In the movie, the director presented an unbiased view of the recorded situation, leaving the audience to make a fair judgment of their own.

The National University of Colombia is one of the best universities in Colombia. There are several campuses distributed around the country. Near the one in Bogota, there are 17 historical buildings that represent the architecture for the last 60 years

波哥大 - 急速都市

　　這個電影是由丹麥電影協會所贊助的四個電影所組成的紀錄片。四個電影也是由四個不同的導演，但是四部片的共同點都是是步調快速，角色為主的紀錄片。其中的一部片，波哥大的改變，是在波哥大城市所拍攝記錄。這部片是以兩個著名的波哥大市長為波哥大腐敗和暴力所帶來的改變為主。其中一個市長，安塔那厮莫庫斯（**Antanas Mockus**）是公立哥倫比亞大學的前校長，他在抗議學生前脫褲子秀屁股的隔天辭掉校長一職。他立刻在波哥大變為一個十分受歡迎的人物並被選為市長。因為他的正直和誠實，他為波哥大帶來了許多正面的改變。在電影中，導演呈現了一個公正的角度來拍攝，留給觀眾判斷是非的抉擇。公立哥倫比亞大學是哥倫比亞最好的大學之一。國內有許多不同的校區，其中在波哥大的校區附近有十七個代表了哥倫比亞六十年前的建築的歷史建築。

 Food (Ajiaco) 馬鈴薯燉雞湯　　MP3 36

Coming to Bogota, you cannot leave without trying their hearty soup, Ajiaco! Ajiaco is made with mostly Chicken, three different types of potatoes, and a local herb called guascas. It is often served with rice and a slice of avocado. First-time visitors might misunderstand that the avocado is the after meal fruit. However, any local will show you the proper way to eat this dish is to have a spoonful of Ajiaco soup followed by a bite of avocado. The marriage of the two is unexpectedly great. The richness of the avocado melted finely within the chicken soup, adding on a fresh, but creamy taste in your mouth. Nothing can beat having an Ajiaco soup in a chilly night at Bogota. This fine Colombian cuisine says it all in Ajiaco. A bowl of this will offer you energy and all the nutrition you need. I think this is the secret for Colombian people so that they can work so hard and play even harder. This soup is very popular in this city as well as in Cuba. Don't miss the chance to try this traditional Colombian dish!

溫哥華

佛羅倫斯

柏林

洛桑

阿姆斯特丹

阿拉巴馬州

聖安東尼奧

波哥大

太平洋屋脊步道

紐西蘭

　　來到波哥大，你絕對不能在沒試過他們豐盛的馬鈴薯燉雞湯（Aji-aco）前就離開！這道菜主要是以雞肉，三種不同的馬鈴薯，和一個當地叫做 guascas 的香料所組成。通常都會和米飯，和一片酪梨一起吃。第一次來玩的人可能會誤以為酪梨是飯後水果。但是，每一個當地人都會是飯給你看正確的吃法是先喝一匙馬鈴薯燉雞湯，接著再吃一口酪梨。這兩者的結合是出乎意料之外的好！酪梨的濃郁會在馬鈴薯燉雞湯中融化結合得很好。在你的口中增添了一分新鮮卻又濃郁的口感。沒有什麼可以打敗在一個寒冷的波哥大夜晚喝一碗馬鈴薯燉雞湯。一碗馬鈴薯燉雞湯中說盡了哥倫比亞精湛的烹飪。一碗馬鈴薯燉雞湯就會提供了你所需要的精力和營養。我想這就是哥倫比亞人可以辛勤工作並更盡情享樂的秘密了！這道菜在這個城市還有古巴都十分受到歡迎。不要錯過試試這道傳統哥倫比亞菜餚的機會噢！

Vocabulary and Idioms ▶

❶ **represent** v 代表	❷ **destination** v 目的地
❸ **aroma** n 香味	❹ **instrument** n 樂器
❺ **demonstrate** v 示範	❻ **documentary** n 紀錄片
❼ **hearty** adj 豐盛的	❽ **avocado** n 酪梨

1. The white in the Taiwanese flag represents freedom.

   台灣國旗中的白色代表自由。

2. It will still take us two hours to reach our destination.

   還要兩小時我們才會抵達目的地。

3. No one can resist the aroma of a good roast chicken.

   沒有人可以抵抗的了好的烤雞的香味。

4. He can play several instruments.

   他會很多不同的樂器。

5. Kelly demonstrates how to make fried eggs in her class today.

   凱利今天在班上示範了怎麼做炒蛋。

6. Documentaries are very informative, but it can be a little bit dry sometimes.

   紀錄片有許多資訊，但是有的時候會有一點枯燥。

7. She came home to a hearty meal her mom prepared for her.

   她回家看到她媽媽為她準備了一桌豐盛的菜。

8. Avocado is a fruit full of nutrition.

   酪梨是一個充滿營養的水果。

旅遊小貼士 ▶

　　來到波哥大，要注意的是亞州人的臉孔在這邊是十分少見的，所以一個不會令人意外的事是可能走在路上隨時會被當地人盯著看。甚至是整台公車可能都會盯著你看的程度。一般走在路上可以享有大明星的待遇，成為眾人的目光焦點，但是當波哥大正在進行抗議的遊行，盡量避免參加以免發生危險噢！

溫哥華

佛羅倫斯

柏林

洛桑

阿姆斯特丹

阿拉巴馬州

聖安東尼奧

波哥大

太平洋屋脊步道

紐西蘭

Unit 19

Pacific Crest Trail
太平洋屋脊步道
Wild - Bridge of the Gods
那時候我只剩下勇敢 - 眾神之橋

城市介紹 ▶

The Pacific Crest Trail is a 2,663 miles or 4,265 kilometers scenic trail in length ranging from the boarder of Mexico and crosses 9 mountains: Laguna, San Jacinto, San Bernardino, San Gabriel, Liebre, Tehachapi, Sierra Nevada, Klamath, and Cascades; and extends to the boarder of Canada. It is a hiking and backpacking trial that penetrates national parks, wilderness, desserts, and rainforests. Going on the hike usually takes months of preparation and training, and when you are actually on the hike, it takes about 4 to 6 months to complete the hike depending on your pace. Each year, Pacific Crest Trail attracts thousands of hikers. Some hikers would only come here hiking for a few days, while others resolved to cover every mile of the trail. Taking every bit of the beauty in the trail and turn it into a precious story to remember and share for a lifetime. Whether you need a break from life, or you just want to add this trail onto your adventures, Pacific Crest Trail will not let you down. The long trail offers a challenging, yet rewarding experience for you to explore.

◀太平洋屋脊步道▶

太平洋屋脊步道是從墨西哥橫跨九座山脈：拉古納山，聖加希圖山，聖伯納狄諾山，聖蓋博山，列夫雷山，德哈查比山，內華達山脈，克拉馬斯山，喀斯喀特山；到加拿大邊界，長為兩千六百六十三英里或是四千兩百六十五公里長的秀麗步道。它是一個貫穿國家公園，荒野，沙漠，和雨林的健行或是背包旅行的步道。要走上這個步道通常需要好幾個月的準備和訓練，而當你真正在這個步道上時，取決於每個人走路的速度，通常需要花費四到六個月的時間才能完成整個步道。每年太平洋屋脊步道都吸引了上千人來拜訪，有些健行者只會來健行幾天，其他的則決心走完步道上的每一英里。他們會帶走步道上的美麗並把它轉變為一個一生珍貴的故事去回憶或是分享。不論你需要在人生暫停休息一下，或是只是想添加這個步道到你的冒險，太平洋屋脊步道都不會讓你失望。這個冗長的步道提供了一個具有挑戰性並且值得的經驗來讓你來探索。

溫哥華

佛羅倫斯

柏林

洛桑

阿姆斯特丹

阿拉巴馬州

聖安東尼奧

波哥大

太平洋屋脊步道

紐西蘭

Dialogue 情境對話 ▶

Brandon and Erin ran into each other in the Pacific Crest Trail together.
布蘭登和艾琳在太平洋屋脊步道遇到彼此。

Brandon: How are you doing so far?

布蘭登：你目前為止怎麼樣？

Erin: I'm doing good. I just wish I packed lighter for this trip.

艾琳：我很好。我只希望我當初來的時候打包輕一點。

Brandon: How long are you going to hike?

布蘭登：你要健行多久呢？

Erin: I'm just trying not to quit every day. My goal is to stay in here for a month.

艾琳：我現在每天只希望我不要放棄。我的目標是在這裡待一個月。

Brandon: That's neat! I'm trying to finish the trail.

布蘭登：好棒！我要把整個步道走完！

Erin: Wow, the whole thing? How long have you been here?

艾琳：哇，整個步道？你在這裡多久了？

Brandon: I have been here for 2 months already. I'm enjoying every bit of it.

布蘭登：我已經在這裡兩個月了。我很享受每一個部分。

Erin: Have you seen any wild life yet?

艾琳：你有看到任何野生動物了嗎？

Brandon: Plenty. I saw bears last week. They are such gorgeous animals.

布蘭登：很多。我上禮拜看到熊。牠們真是令人驚艷的動物。

Erin: Wow, weren't you scared?

艾琳：哇，你不怕嗎？

Brandon: Not too much. I made some noises the whole way, so I guess they knew I was coming. They were not too close to me, but enough for me to appreciate their beauty.

布蘭登：不太怕。我整路都有在發出一點噪音，所以我想牠們知道我來了。牠們沒有很靠近我，但是還是在我可以欣賞牠們的美的距離。

Erin: Wow, that sounds pretty amazing! What kind of noises were you making? I saw quite a few deer the other day as well.

艾琳：哇，聽起來好棒噢！你是在製造什麼噪音呢？我前幾天也有看到一些鹿。

Brandon: I was mostly talking to my-

布蘭登：我大部分都是在跟

溫哥華

佛羅倫斯

柏林

洛桑

阿姆斯特丹

阿拉巴馬州

聖安東尼奧

波哥大

太平洋屋脊步道

紐西蘭

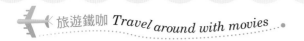
self. You have no idea how happy I am to run into you!

我自己說話。你不知道遇到你我有多開心！

Erin: I have seen your name for a long time, and have been trying to catch up with you. Sorry it took me so long.

艾琳：其實我已經看到你的名字很久了，而且一直要追趕上你。對不起花了我這麼久才追上你。

Brandon: Haha, better late than never!

布蘭登：哈哈，遲到總比沒來好！

Special Sites Introduction 19: 特別景點報導 ▶

Pacific Crest Trail - Wild - Bridge of the Gods MP3 37

In the movie "Wild" Cheryl Strayed's (Reese Witherspoon) final destination for herself was at the Bridge of the Gods. After a journey on the Pacific Crest Trail, and also her mental journey to get over her mother's death, the movie ends with Cheryl on the Bridge of the Gods. For the author, when she first finished the trail, she did not know that she would once again come back to the same place four years later and say yes to the love of her life. And fifteen years later, she came back with her family of four to eat ice cream and share her story on the trail.

The Bridge of Gods is a steel bridge that connects northern

Oregon and southern Washington State. It crosses the Columbia River and is about four miles long. It is also the lowest part of the whole trail. If you just wish to check this cool site out, you do not have to hike in the trial to be here. You can simply drive here. It is around seventy kilometers away from northeast Portland, Oregon.

太平洋屋脊步道 - 那時候我只剩下勇敢 - 眾神之橋

在電影"那時候我只剩下勇敢"中，雪兒史翠德（瑞斯薇斯朋）自己設定的最後的目的地是眾神之橋。經過了太平洋屋脊步道旅程，還有她自己內心克服了喪母之痛的旅程之後，電影終結在雪兒走到了眾神之橋。而對作者而言，當她一開始結束了他的徒步旅行，她並不知道他四年之後會回到這裡，並對她一生的最愛說我願意。而十五年後，她和她一家四口回到這裡吃冰淇淋以及分享他在步道上的故事。

眾神之橋是一座連接北奧勒剛和南華盛頓州，由鋼鐵造成的架橋。它橫跨了哥倫比亞河，大約四英里長。它也同時是整個不到上最低的地方。如果你想要來這個很棒的景點看看，你不需要徒步旅行到這裡。你可以開車到這個地方。它大約是離波特蘭，奧勒岡七十公里的地方。

溫哥華

佛羅倫斯

柏林

洛桑

阿姆斯特丹

阿拉巴馬州

聖安東尼奧

波哥大

太平洋屋脊步道

紐西蘭

 MP3 38

One of the rather popular hikes near the Pacific Crest Trail is the Jefferson Park trail. It is an 11.95-mile-long trail round trip. Expect a lot of hikers on this trial, especially during summer times and fall. Spectacular lake views, full-bloomed wild flowers, and the magnificent mountain views all make this trial so scenic and special for many people. The hike ranges from moderate to strenuous with the elevation up to 1800 feet. Since this is a very popular hike, the restrictions in this hike are a bit stricter. Look up where you can camp in advance and campfire is banned throughout the whole trail. For those who enjoy hiking and are not ready for hardcore backpacking trips, Jefferson Park trail is the one for you. Setting foot on the beautiful meadow and camp under the shooting stars by the lakes, you are guaranteed a fantastic time when you make the decision to come here. The hike feeds directly into the Pacific Crest Trail, so if you feel like you can go on a little longer for your adventure, continue the hike to the Pacific Crest Trail, which would probably offer more than what you are looking for.

傑佛森公園

　　在太平洋屋脊步道旁有一個蠻受歡迎的步道，傑佛森步道。它是一個來回長為十一點九五英里長的步道。預期會遇到很多健行者在這個步道上，尤其是在夏天和秋天。這裡壯麗的湖景，綻開的野花，和浩大的山景都讓這個步道對很多人來說更加的秀麗和特別。它是中等到艱難程度的步道，提升的高度會到達一千八百英尺。因為這個步道十分的受歡迎，這裡的規定也比較嚴格。來這個步道之前記得查詢在哪裡可以露營，而營火在這個步道到處都是禁止的。對於喜歡健行而對於艱難地背包行程還沒準備好的人，傑佛森公園步道很適合你。走進這漂亮的草園，在湖邊和流星下露營，當你做了要來這裡的決定時，你就已經保證一定會有一個難忘的時光。這個步道也直接可以接上太平洋屋脊步道，所以如果你想要繼續你的冒險，繼續走上太平洋屋脊步道，它會提供的可能比你需要的還多。

溫哥華

佛羅倫斯

柏林

洛桑

阿姆斯特丹

阿拉巴馬州

聖安東尼奧

波哥大

太平洋屋脊步道

紐西蘭

Vocabulary and Idioms ▶

❶ penetrate Ⓥ 穿過；穿入　　**❷ wilderness** Ⓝ 荒野

❸ resolved adj 下定決心的　　**❹ rewarding** adj 值得的，有報酬的

❺ pack Ⓥ 打包　　**❻ appreciate** Ⓥ 感激；欣賞

❼ restriction Ⓝ 限制，規定　　**❽ meadow** Ⓝ 草地

1. The rain penetrated his shirt.

   雨水滲透入他的襯衫。

2. You will need a lot of survivor skills to live in the wilderness.

   在荒野中存活你需要很多的求生技能。

3. He's resolved to finish his work tonight.

   他下定決心要在今天晚上完成他的工作。

4. Running in winter mornings can be very hard, but very rewarding.

   在冬天的早晨跑步可能會很難，但卻也十分的值得。

5. He has to finish packing tonight since he has an early morning flight.

   他今天晚上一定要打包完因為他是坐明天一早的飛機。

6. I really appreciate all your help at the meeting.

   我真的很感謝你在會議中所有的幫助。

7. There are more and more traffic restrictions.

   現在有越來越多的交通規定。

8. I miss the open meadows in the mountains.

我好想念在山上開放的草地。

旅遊小貼士 ▶

　　當你真的來到太平洋屋脊步道時，可以去買太陽能充電板來為你的手機充電。帶手機的好處是如果你在步道中迷了路，就算沒有網路也還是可以藉由先前下載的地圖來指引你前進。建議的是在途中最好都是使用航空模式，而紙本的地圖和指南針也都還是要帶，當然也要帶防水的手機噢！否則好不容易走了很遠若是迷路或是手機故障的話可是會很令人懊惱的！

Unit 20

New Zealand 紐西蘭
The Lord of the Rings 魔戒

城市介紹 ▶

New Zealand is a wonderful place that consists of two main islands and numerous other small islands. With the population of 4.5 million, New Zealand is about 7 times bigger than Taiwan. What's there to fill up all that extra space? Forests, lakes and limitless beauty. New Zealand houses many of the best hiking trials in the world. They are even called the "Great Walks" So if you are big in hiking, this just might be the pilgrim for you to come check it out. With the lush forests and magical nature to explore, hiking might be one of the popular things to do here. However, there are more than 30 national parks in the country and they spread out evenly in both islands. The spectacular nature and friendly locals all make this place one of the best living environment for people. I once heard people said, "Do not make New Zealand the first place you go. Otherwise, the rest of the world would seem ugly." Perhaps it was said with a bit exaggeration. However, this tends to grow on me a little. Where else can be this dreamy in the world?

紐西蘭 ▶

　　紐西蘭是一個主要以兩個島嶼以及其它一些較小的島嶼所組成的很棒的地方。它有著四百伍拾萬人口，而紐西蘭竟是比台灣大上七倍的國家。那是什麼填補了多餘的空間呢？森林，湖泊，和無止境的美景。紐西蘭也同時是全世界有很多最棒的踐行步道的國家。他們還甚至叫那些步道 "偉大步道"。所以如果你很喜歡健行，這裡應該是你朝聖的地方。有著翠綠的森林和神奇的大自然去探索，健行只是這裡很受歡迎的活動之一。然而，這個在這個國家裡有超過三十個國家公園，而他們也是平均的分佈在兩個島上。有著極致的自然景色，和友善的當地居民都使得這個地方成為最適合人居住的環境之一。我曾經聽過別人說：「不要第一次出國就去紐西蘭，因為這樣會使得你接下來去的地方都很醜。」雖然這是有一點誇張。但是，我也漸漸地開始同意這個說法。還有什麼地方比這裡更夢幻呢？

溫哥華　佛羅倫斯　柏林　洛桑　阿姆斯特丹　阿拉巴馬州　聖安東尼奧　波哥大　太平洋屋脊步道　紐西蘭

Dialogue 情境對話 ▶

Cait and Chris are on a Waitomo Caves boat tour. They are whispering to each other.

凱特和克里斯正在懷托摩螢火蟲洞的導覽船上。他們正在跟彼此小聲說話。

Cait: I have never seen anything like this!

凱特：我從來沒看過這樣的地方！

Chris: Why do we have to whisper again?

克里斯：為什麼我們講話要這麼小聲？

Cait: The glow worms are very sensitive to sounds and lights! This is just so breathtaking!

凱特：因為這些螢火蟲是對燈光和聲音都十分敏感的！這真是美的太壯觀了！

Chris: I mean, I have seen fireflies before, but these glow worms here have taken things to a whole new level!

克里斯：我的意思是說，我之前也有看過螢火蟲，可是這個種類的已經又是另外一個境界的！

Cait: I feel like I'm in the middle of the Milky Way or something.

凱特：我覺得我好像在銀河系中間還什麼的。

Chris: I heard that these glow worms are only found in New Zealand and Australia.

克里斯：我聽説這種螢火蟲只有在紐西蘭和澳洲可以找到。

Cait: Wow, we're very lucky then. The tour guide said that this cave was first discovered by Maori people. I can only imagine how stoked they must have been!

凱特：哇，那我們很幸運耶。導遊説這個洞穴一開始是被毛利人發現的。我能想像他們一開始發現的時候一定很興奮！

Chris: This would totally be my own secret spot if I found it.

克里斯：如果是我發現的話，這裡一定是我自己的秘密基地。

Cait: Well, good thing you didn't find it then. Otherwise, I won't be able to see this today.

凱特：嗯，那還好沒被你發現。不然我現在就看不到了。

Chris: Then you should thank me then.

克里斯：那你應該要謝謝我。

Cait: I'd rather thank the Maori people. Haha

凱特：我寧願謝謝毛利人。哈哈

溫哥華
佛羅倫斯
柏林
洛桑
阿姆斯特丹
阿拉巴馬州
聖安東尼奧
波哥大
太平洋脊步道
紐西蘭

New Zealand 紐西蘭

The Lord of the Rings 魔戒 - 哈比村　MP3 39

Written by the English author J.R.R. Tolkien between 1937 and 1949, The Lord of the Rings is perhaps one of the best selling novels around the world. It has been translated into many different languages and many films were made of this story. The story first started in a hobbit land where you can also find the place in its other movie The Hobbit.

The charming Hobbiton is actually located at a private farm, Alexander Farm in Matamata in the North Island of New Zealand. You will not be able to drive in the private property by yourself unless you join a tour. Its lushness, and quaint houses are set just for the film. You can see that this is where the scene when Bilbo had his birthday party. This private farmland will perhaps be one of the most picturesque places you have ever witnessed. There are several local tours that would guide you through the whole setting. You will be able to see the Hobbit holes, the Green Dragon Inn, the Mill and several other iconic scenes from the movies. It is a must if you are a Hobbit fan! Come and check out this enchanting village!

魔戒 - 哈比村

　　由英國作家 J.R.R. 托爾金在 1937 年和 1949 年之間所著作，魔界大概是世上最暢銷的小說之一。它已經被翻譯為好幾個語言，也有好多部電影為了這個故事而拍攝。故事一開始是由哈比人的屬地開始，而這個地方你在後來的哈比人電影中也可以看見。

　　這個迷人的哈比村是在位在一個紐西蘭北島的馬塔馬塔一個私人的農場，亞力山大農場中。你沒辦法直接開車進去因為這裡是一個私人領地，除非你跟團才進得來。它的翠綠和古色古香的房子都是為電影所設立的。你也可以看見這裡就是比爾博過生日趴的地方。這個私人的農地將是你看過風景最好的地方之一。這裡有很多當地的導遊可以帶領你穿越整個場景。你可以看到哈比洞，綠龍客棧，磨坊和很多其他電影中代表性的地方。這裡是哈比迷必去！你快來這裡看看這魔幻的小村子。

溫哥華

佛羅倫斯

柏林

洛桑

阿姆斯特丹

阿拉巴馬州

聖安東尼奧

波哥大

太平洋屋脊步道

紐西蘭

旅遊愛玩咖

Maori Culture MP3 40

When you see two men say "kiaora! kiaora!" and rub their noses. It is the Maoris that are greeting each other. Maori culture can be spotted through out the whole country. Their crafts are especially skillful and you will be able to see them all around. The Maori welcoming dance has become the official way to welcome a very important guest. The national anthem of New Zealand, God Defend New Zealand, is also sung in Maori:

"E I ho ā A tu wa On gā I wi mā tou rā Ā ta wha ka ron go na Me a ro ha no — a Ki a hu a ko te pai Ki a tau tō wa ta whai Ma na a ki ti a mai A o te a ro — a"

Here's the English version:

"God of Nations at Thy feet In the bonds of love we meet Hear our voices we entreat God defend our free land Guard Pacific's triple star From the shafts of strife and war Make her praises heard afar God defend New Zea — land"

毛利文化

　　當你聽到兩個男人說 "kiaora！kiaora！" 並且摸摸他們的鼻子。這就是毛利人打招呼的方式。毛利文化在整個國家都隨處可見。他們的手工藝尤其技術精湛，而你也可以到處都見識的到。毛利人的迎賓舞也成為了官方迎接貴客時的方式。紐西蘭的國歌，天佑紐西蘭，也是有以毛利文演唱：

　　"E I ho ā A tu wa On gā I wi mā tou rā Ā ta wha ka ron go na Me a ro ha no — a Ki a hu a ko te pai Ki a tau tō wa ta whai Ma na a ki ti a mai A o te a ro — a"

在主宰這個國家的上帝腳下，因為愛我們在此相聚。

請主聽到我們的聲音，與我們的虔誠。

祝願上帝保佑我們的自由之境。

守護太平洋上的三 明星，

遠離爭鬥與戰爭的紛亂，

讓她的美名遠傳天際，

上帝保佑紐西蘭。

溫哥華
佛羅倫斯
柏林
洛桑
阿姆斯特丹
阿拉巴馬州
聖安東尼奧
波哥大
太平洋屋脊步道
紐西蘭

Vocabulary and Idioms ▶

❶ **numerous** adj 很多的	❷ **tend to** Phrase 傾向
❸ **dreamy** adj 夢幻的	❹ **whisper** v 低聲説
❺ **rub** v 摩擦	❻ **crafts** n 手工藝
❼ **anthem** n 國歌	❽ **praise** n 讚揚

1. The countless hills and numerous sheep make a good scenery in New Zealand.

   無數的山丘和許多羊使得紐西蘭有很好的風景。

2. He tends to make decisions too impulsively.

   他有太衝動做決定的傾向。

3. The melody of the song is so dreamy that it becomes very popular.

   這首歌的旋律很夢幻所以變得十分熱門。

4. The students that were whispering in class were asked to the teacher's office after class.

   剛剛上課在低聲説話的學生下課後被叫去老師的辦公室裡。

5. They can not stop rubbing their hands because of the cold weather.

   他們無法停止摩擦他們的手因為天氣實在是太冷了。

6. She is very good at crafts.

   她的手工藝非常厲害。

7. He never seems to remember the lyrics of his national anthem.

他好像永遠都記不得國歌的歌詞。

8. He doesn't deserve so much praise since he didn't really try his best.

他不值得那麼多的讚賞，因為他並沒有全力以赴。

旅遊小貼士 ▶

　　來到紐西蘭，這邊的紫外線十分地強，所以進行戶外活動時，十分容易曬傷，建議出門前記得要擦防曬乳！避免曬傷。還有就是因為這邊的氣候相對之下比較乾燥，所以出門也都要帶水，否則這裡的人口並沒有那麼多，可能會面臨想喝水卻買不到的窘境喔！

溫
哥
華

佛
羅
倫
斯

柏

林

洛

桑

阿
姆
斯
特
丹

阿
拉
巴
馬
州

聖
安
東
尼
奧

波

哥

大

太
平
洋
屋
脊
步
道

紐
西
蘭

Unit 21
Argentina 阿根廷
On the Road 浪蕩時代

城市介紹 ▶

If you have sleeping on your agenda, Buenos Aires may be a city to skip. Buenos Aires is known as the sleepless city thanks to attractions of the tourist sites that last from day throughout the night. You will also notice that tourists and locals are deeply attracted by these enduring attractions.

The city's daytime activities have an artistic and cultural expression that would impress even a queen. Some of these noteworthy destinations would include the colorful La Boca neighborhood, San Telmo Antique Market, and Costanera Sur. You will also find the world's first religious theme park, an amazing

Zoo, and a botanic Garden showcasing some of South America's treasures. Boca Stadium hosts the Boca Juniors, one of the most famous South American soccer teams. If you do not make it to Boca Stadium to watch a match, you must try to squeeze in one at another stadium before you leave to experience the intense and rejuvenating culture that surrounds South American soccer.

After the tours and visitations close down for the day, which is strikingly late. The nighttime comes alive with concerts, theaters, coffee shops, pubs, and even casinos. Once you think your day is finally coming to a close, one of your friends will be dragging you into a disco or "discoteca" which will keep you dancing away until the wee hours of the morning.

◀ 阿根廷 ▶

　　如果你的行程上有睡覺，那你可能要跳過這個城市。布宜諾斯艾利斯以『不睡覺』的城市而聞名，是由於城市景點的吸引力是從早到晚。你可能也會發現觀光客和當地人都深受觀光客和當地人吸引。

　　這個城市白天的活動有著藝術和文化的面貌，連皇后都會印象深刻。有一些著名的景點例如色彩鮮艷的 La Boca 社區，San Telmo 古董市集和南濱生態保護區。你也可以找到全世界第一個宗教主題樂園，一個超棒的動物園，和一個展現南美洲珍貴的植物的植物園。Boca 體育館是南美洲知名足球隊 Boca Juniors 的主場。如果你在離開之前無法去 Boca 體育館的話，一定要試試看擠進其他的體育館去體驗那環繞南美洲足球的緊張又使人充滿活力的文化。在很晚的時候，白天的遊覽和參觀都關門了。夜晚正隨著演唱會，電影院，咖啡廳，酒吧，和甚至賭場而醒來。當你正覺得你的一天終於要結束的時候，你的其中一個朋友會來拉你到一個小舞廳（discoteca）來跳舞到早上很早的時候。

 Dialogue 情境對話 ▶

Beth is picking up Sue to go out for shopping in the afternoon.
貝絲下午正要接蘇一起去逛街。

Beth: Knock knock! What's taking you so long?

貝絲：叩叩叩！你怎麼那麼久？

Sue: Hold on, I just woke up.

蘇：等等，我剛醒來。

Beth: You just woke up!! It's 3 in the afternoon! How on earth can you be sleeping this late!?

貝絲：你剛醒來！！現在是下午三點了耶！你到底怎麼可以睡這麼晚！？

Sue: You won't believe it! Jorge took me to disco Alle Bevoli last night and we were partying there until 8 am this morning!

蘇：你不會相信的！荷黑昨天晚上帶我到 Alle Bevoli 舞廳，我們在那裡狂歡到今天早上八點！

Beth: Are you serious! How were you able to stay up that late?

貝絲：真的假的！你怎麼可以熬夜到那麼晚？

Sue: I didn't even notice! There were so many lights and exciting electronic music!

蘇：我也沒注意到！那裡有好多燈光和刺激的電子音樂！

Beth: So cool! Were you dancing?

貝絲：好酷！你有跳舞嗎？

Sue: We danced so much! Everybody was! So many people all really got into the music!

蘇：我們一直跳！大家都在跳舞！很多人都很投入音樂！

Beth: Well, I hope you take me next time!

貝絲：我希望下次你會帶我去！

Sue: Oh! I will! But you'd better put your dancing shoes on and get ready for an amazing time!

蘇：噢我會的！但你最好把你的舞鞋穿上，並準備渡過一個美好的時光！

Special Sites Introduction 21: 特別景點報導 ▸

Argentina - On the Road 💿 MP3 41

"On the Road" is a movie released in 2012 that was based off of a book that was published back in 1957. Loosely based on the author's (SalParadise) own life as he traveled with his friend Dean and Dean's ex-wife Marylou (kristen Stewart). Dean is a wild and rambunctious type of character which ends up leading these two on inspirational trips on and off over a period of 4 years.

This movie holds a lot of deep themes and lessons that are based around a period filled with jazz, drugs, and alcohol. As the movie goes on, one of the scenes is taped in the beautiful Bariloche of Argentina in the Patagonian lake district. It's located at the base of the Andes, which provides for stunning views and scenery. Bariloche has a somewhat Swiss feel and is consisted of many small lakes with rolling green hills. For the more adventurous traveler, options, such as trekking, water sports, and climbing will keep you busy for your entire stay.

阿根廷 - 浪蕩時代

　　浪蕩時代是一個在 2012 年上映並根據一本在 1957 年出版的書改編。劇中主要以作家（山姆萊利飾）和他的朋友狄恩（蓋瑞特荷德倫飾）和狄恩的前妻瑪莉露（克莉絲汀史都華飾）旅行時的生活為主。迪恩是一個狂野，不受管束的角色，並最後帶領其他兩個角色踏上為期四年鼓舞人心的旅程。

　　這部電影根據爵士，毒品，和酒精充斥的時代提出深入的主題和教訓。跟著電影，其中的一個場景是在阿根廷巴塔根尼雅的湖區，美麗的巴里洛切所拍攝。它是位於安第斯山脈的根部，那裡有著驚人的景觀和風景。巴里洛切有著如同瑞士般的感覺並且由許多小湖和起伏的綠山巒。對於比較喜歡冒險的旅客，這裡有健行，水上活動，和爬山可以讓你一整天都空閒不下來喔！

阿根廷
庫斯科
紐奧良
新德里
拉斯維加斯
伊斯坦堡
西雅圖
班夫鎮
可愛島
冰島

Argentina is known among the world as producing some of the best tasting beef. One of the greatest culinary treats of visiting is being able to taste the rich flavor first hand. Even better, because Argentina exports all of the different cuts of beef to other countries, it saves the most tender and juicy part, the tenderloin, for its own restaurants. You will find this treat in almost every restaurant, from small bars to fine dinning restaurants.

What is it that makes this beef taste so delicious? It starts with the cow being able to roam freely in pastures. The warmer climate and large amount of rainfall make for a pasture full of a sweet grass for the cows to feed on. In turn, the end product is very sweet and flavorful meat. Argentinians also do a very good job of showcasing their prized beef by cooking it only with salt and most often on an Argentine wood grill known as the Asado.

Not to worry though, there are many other options, such as empanadas, blood sausages, and robust vegetable dishes if you are not a beef eater. Along with your meal, don't miss out on a wonderful glass of the countries well-known Malbec wine!

阿根廷的牛肉

　　阿根廷在全世界是公認有著某些最美味的牛肉。來到阿根廷的其中一個最棒的料理獎賞就是可以吃到第一手的濃郁香味。甚至更好的是，阿根廷會出口各個不同部位的牛肉到別的國家去，而留下了最嫩，和多汁的嫩腰肉給自己的餐廳。你可以在各大餐廳吃到這個好東西，從小酒吧到高級餐廳都有。

　　是什麼使得這裡的牛肉這麼好吃呢？這要從這裡的牛都可以自由地在牧場裡漫步。溫暖的氣候和大量的雨量都使得牛有充分的香甜牧草可以吃。而換來的也是非常香甜，風味十足的肉。阿根廷人也十分充分地展示這備受讚賞肉質。他們通常只加鹽，並且大多時候在一個阿根廷的木製烤肉架 Asado 上烤。

　　如果你不吃牛肉的話，也不必擔心，他們還有其他的選項，例如阿根廷餡餃，血餡香腸，和許多蔬菜。也別錯過了這個國家聞名的馬爾貝克紅酒來搭配你的餐點喔！

Vocabulary and Idioms ▶

❶ **antique** n 古董

❷ **rejuvenating** adj 使人變年輕的，恢復精神的

❸ **on earth** Phrase 到底

❹ **rambunctious** adj 粗暴的，不受管制的

❺ **consist** v 包含

❻ **culinary** adj 烹飪的

❼ **tender** adj 嫩的

❽ **robust** adj 強壯的，健全的

1. He has a habit of collecting antiques.

   他有搜集古董的習慣。

2. The hot spring water is extremely rejuvenating and good for your skin.

   溫泉水是會使人變年輕而且還對你的皮膚很好。

3. What on earth are you doing?

   你到底在做什麼？

4. His rambunctious behaviors always get him into troubles.

   他不受管制的行為常常為他帶來麻煩。

5. The winning team consists two boys and two girls.

   贏的隊伍包括兩個男生和兩個女生。

6. He is truly a culinary legend.

   他真是烹飪界的傳奇。

7. The lamb is very tender and flavorful.

   這羊肉實在是十分的嫩和風味十足。

8. The robust athlete is able to finish the marathon in record time.

這強壯的運動家以最快紀錄的時間完成馬拉松。

旅遊小貼士 ▶

　　由於阿根廷位於南美洲，所以一個明顯和我們不同的是我們的季節是顛倒的喔！也就是我們夏天的時候就是他們的冬天，反之亦然。還有就是阿根廷境內隨著不同的位置有著不同的氣候。北部和西北部為乾燥熱帶氣候，東部為潮溼氣候，中部為草原氣候，以及南部有冰原型的氣候。所以要根據自己的行程好好地微調需要帶的衣服喔！

Unit 22

Cusco 庫斯科
The Motorcycle Diaries
革命前的摩托車日記

城市介紹▶

Perched among the high clouds in the Andes, Cusco is definitely more breathtaking than anyone has imagined. Given the nickname, navel of the world, Cusco was the economical, political, educational center of the old empire. Even till this day, Cusco still for sure has what it takes to be the potential of the world center. The beautiful city preserved the colonial architecture, indigenous Quechua culture as well as the Inca stone-built walls. The town itself feels like a pop-up history book, wherever you go, you will find layers history. Today, Cusco has developed itself into a somewhat modern retreat for adventurers from the world to come and worship. The beautiful setting, colorful festivals, and convenience makes Cusco one of the most exciting places to visit in Peru. There are inexpensive hotels and hostels, bars and restaurants for visitors to choose. After being the center of the world for centuries, Cusco remained its place, only switching to the center of the tourist attraction. Each year, Cusco has drawn hundreds of thousands of tourists. However, due to the fact that Cusco is located on the high altitude, it usually takes the visitors a while to get used to. Nevertheless, according to many, it is worth being sick for.

庫斯科

　　座落於安第斯山脈的雲之中，庫斯科絕對比任何人想像的都還要美麗。有著世界的肚臍之稱，庫斯科曾經是古帝國的經濟，政治，和教育的中心。甚至到今天，庫斯科都還是有著成為世界中心的潛力。這個美麗的城市保留著殖民時期的建築，原住民克丘亞文化和印加文化的石牆。整個城市感覺像是立體的歷史課本。你去的每一個地方，都可以找到層層的歷史。今天，庫斯科已經發展為冒險家們來參拜的現代去處。漂亮的場景，色彩繽紛的慶典，和便利性都使得庫斯科成為秘魯最刺激的地點之一。這裡有便宜的飯店或青年旅社，酒吧，和餐廳供觀光客選擇。在當今世界中心好幾世紀之後，庫斯科還是保有它的地位，只是現在轉換為觀光重鎮。每年庫斯科都會吸引了成千上萬的觀光客。然而因為庫斯科位於高海拔，許多人都需要一些時間來習慣。但是根據許多人說，庫斯科是值得你為它患得高山症的。

阿根廷

庫斯科

紐奧良

新德里

拉斯維加斯

伊斯坦堡

西雅圖

班夫鎮

可愛島

冰島

Dialogue 情境對話 ▶

Dennis and April are going to try the traditional food in Peru.
丹尼斯和艾波正要試秘魯的傳統食物。

Dennis: What should we order? Ceviche?

丹尼斯：我們要點什麼呢？Ceviche?

April: What exactly is a Ceviche again?

艾波：Ceviche 到底是什麼？

Dennis: It's basically raw seafood with citrus juice.

丹尼斯：其實就是生海鮮和酸橘汁。

April: Sounds like food poison!

艾波：聽起來像是食物中毒！

Dennis: No, it does not, the acid from the citrus juice will cook the raw meat. It's good. Let's give it a try.

丹尼斯：才不會，酸橘汁中的酸會把生肉煮熟。很好吃！我們試試看！

April: Look at this one "Cuy". Did I read it correctly? Traditional roasted guinea pig?

艾波：你看這個 "Cuy"。我剛剛有讀錯嘛？傳統的烤天竺鼠？

Dennis: Oh yeah, it is actually one of the main dishes here.

丹尼斯：噢對，那其實是這裡的主菜之一。

April: What? Aren't guinea pigs pets? And they are some sorts of rodents, right?

艾波：什麼？天竺鼠不是寵物嗎？而且他們是不是鼠類的一種嗎？

Dennis: Well…if you want to put it that way…

丹尼斯：嗯…如果你要那麼說的話…

April: No, I don't want to eat rats. Next.

艾波：不要，我不要吃老鼠。下一個。

Dennis: Hey we have to try it. You can't find this dish anywhere else! We're getting it!

丹尼斯：欸我們要試試看。你在別的地方找不到的！我們要點這個！

April: What? I refuse to eat it.

艾波：什麼？我拒絕吃這道。

Dennis: That's okay. Just for the sake of it. We'll order and see what we think!

丹尼斯：沒關係。就試試看。我們點了再看我們到時候覺得怎麼樣！

April: You can't trick me into eating

艾波：你這次騙不了我吃這

阿根廷

庫斯科

紐奧良

新德里

拉斯維加斯

伊斯坦堡

西雅圖

班夫鎮

可愛島

冰島

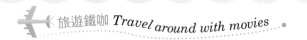
it. I'm not falling for this one. | 個。我這次不會上當。

Dennis: It will be a memorable experience. | 丹尼斯：這會是一個難忘的經驗。

April: Can I have a big bowl of rice and a big bottle of beer then, please!! | 艾波：那我可以點一大碗白飯和一大瓶啤酒嗎，拜託！！

Dennis: You got it!! | 丹尼斯：沒問題！！

Special Sites Introduction 22: 特別景點報導 ▶

 Cusco - The Motorcycle Diaries   MP3 43

The Motorcycle Diaries is a 2004 film based on the written memoir of Erneto Guevara(Gael Garcia Bernal), who become the commander, Che Guevara in the revolution. In the movie, Erneto and his friend Alberto Garnado (Rodrigo de la Serna) started a motorcycle expedition in South America where they witness a lot of inequalities and poverty. Inspired by their trip, Erneto started a revolution to change the economic inequalities after their trip.

When Erneto and Alberto arrived in Cusco, the scene when they were shown around the city by a little boy who explained the way to differentiate stones built by the Incas and incapables

(Spaniards) was shot at the famous twelve angle Inca Stone.

The twelve angle stone showcased how skillful the Incas were to build stonewalls back then. It was originally the wall of the old palace Hatunrumiyoc, but it is the wall of the museum of the religious art today. If you are not going there with a tour guide, look for the twelve angle stone carefully. However, chances are that, you might be able to run into a tour group there. Don't forget to tip the tour guide if you like their explanation!

庫斯科 - 革命前的摩托車日記

革命前的摩托車日記是一個 2004 年根據回憶錄埃內斯托格瓦拉（蓋爾賈西亞貝那飾）。埃內斯托格瓦拉也就是後來革命的頭頭的切格瓦拉。在電影中，埃內斯托和他的朋友阿爾貝托·格拉納多（羅德里格 德拉 塞納飾）開始了一個在南美洲的摩托車探險，他們在途中也目睹了許多的不平等以及貧窮。因為這個旅程的啟發，埃內斯托在旅途後開始了一個決心改變經濟不平等的革命。

當埃內斯托和阿爾貝托抵達了庫斯科，有一個小男孩帶領他們四處逛庫斯科，他同時也向他們解釋了如何分辨由印加人建造的石牆和由無能的人（小男孩指的是西班牙人）所建造。這個場景就是在十二角牆所拍攝。

十二角牆呈現了印加人以前製造石牆的技術。其實這道牆一開始是 Hatunrumiyoc 宮殿的牆，但是現在是宗教藝術博物館外的牆。如果

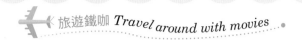
你不是和導遊去那裡的話，要小心地找出這塊十二角牆。然而，你很有可能會遇到另外一個觀光團。如果喜歡當團導遊的解釋的話，別忘了給他小費噢！

 Machu Picchu 🎧 MP3 44

Machu Picchu is located 2,430 meters above the sea and around 80 kilometers from the northwest of Cusco. It is a tangible evidence of the Incas. Most of the archaeologist believed that Machu Picchu is built for the emperor Pachacuti.

Going to Machu Picchu has been many people's dream. Trekking through the Andes Mountain to see this lost city covered in dense forest where the Incas worshiped the stone temples some 500 years ago. The fact that the Incas constructed such impressive and intricate stone temples with sheer manpower has always been both miraculous and mysterious. They did not have any knowledge of iron, steel, or even wheels. However, this impressive work seemed only to benefit a few. Only less than a thousand people were living in this city. Nevertheless, the city was abandoned a century after it was built. Today, if you wish to explore this old Inca trail to Machu Picchu, it is not so hidden anymore. Expect to see groups of people coming up the trail with you. Therefore, plan to sign up for a hiking trail in advance. You will need a tour guide in this trail as well as a permit. That said, plan ahead and book your tour as soon as possible.

馬丘比丘

馬丘比丘是一個位於海拔兩千四百三十公尺，距離庫斯科西北部大約八十公里。它是一個印加文化存在的具體證據。大部分的考古學家都認為馬丘比丘是為了君王帕查庫特克所建造。

去馬丘比丘一直是許多人的夢想。在安第斯山脈上健行去看這被茂密的雨林覆蓋，古印加人在石廟裡敬神的失落之城。印加人以純人力建造這個令人敬佩以及複雜精細的石廟真是令人覺得神奇又神秘。他們並沒有任何關於鐵，鋼，或輪子的概念。然而，這令人印象深刻的作品似乎只有少部分人受益，只有少於一千人居住在這裡，而這個地方也在建造後的一百年左右被拋棄。今天，如果你想要來探索這個馬丘比丘印加古道來到馬丘比丘，這裡不再那麼的隱秘了。預期看到許多人跟你在印加古道上。所以，計劃提早報名健行。在這個步道你會需要導遊和許可證。也就是說呢，提前計畫和儘早訂你的行程。

Vocabulary and Idioms ▶

❶ **perch** Ⅴ 座落，棲息 　 ❷ **breathtaking** adj 驚人的

❸ **memoir** n 回憶錄 　 ❹ **witness** Ⅴ 目擊

❺ **tangible**
　 adj 具體的，有形的 　 ❻ **dense** adj 茂密的

❼ **worship** Ⅴ 崇拜，敬仰 　 ❽ **permit** n 許可證

1. The birds perch high on a tree branch.

   小鳥們高高地棲息在樹枝上。

2. I will never forget the breathtaking view at Machu Picchu.

   我永遠不會忘記馬丘比丘那驚人的景色。

3. He decides to write a memoir when he retires.

   他決定當他退休之後他要寫一個回憶錄 。

4. He witnessed the car accident this morning when he was jogging.

   他今天早上慢跑的時候目擊了一個車禍。

5. A table is a tangible object.

   桌子是一個具體的物體。

6. The bamboo forest is so dense that it is so dark hiking inside.

   這個竹林十分的茂密所以在其中健行時都十分的昏暗。

7. A lot of people worship Buddha in Taiwan.

   有許多在台灣的人敬仰佛陀。

8. Do we need a permit to camp here?

我們在這裡露營需要許可證嗎？

🎓 旅遊小貼士 ▶

　　來到秘魯，尤其是去馬丘比丘的印加古道上難免會遇到克丘亞人（Quechua），他們時常會在古道旁邊販售各種在印加古道健行的人們需要的東西。他們雖然工作辛勤，但是絕對是待人公道。在當地克丘亞人有一個概念是 ainy，這是一個輪迴福報的概念，當你今天幫了你的鄰居，他們有一天也會為你做一樣的事。所以雖然努力地想要賣掉帶去的東西，但他們也不會詐騙你的錢。

阿根廷

庫斯科

紐奧良

新德里

拉斯維加斯

伊斯坦堡

西雅圖

班夫鎮

可愛島

冰島

Unit 23

New Orleans 紐奧良 - Chef 五星主廚快餐車

城市介紹 ▶

　　Located in the southern state, Louisiana, you will find a unique city, New Orleans. There's no city like such in the U.S.A. Perhaps it is the colonial influences that make New Orleans stand out. Its effortless beauty can be spotted in even the smallest corner. It is, nevertheless, the atmosphere in this city that makes it so enchanting. New Orleans is the birthplace for Jazz, so it's not hard to imagine walking down the street with all sort of music, such as Jazz and Blues, coming out from the doors. We just wish we were born in the time when Louis Armstrong is still here running around to make all his gigs in town. Romance is certainly in the air. Why would it not be? With great music, delicious delicacies, and Mardi Gras, it is really hard to have a terrible time here. After spending some time in New Orleans, maybe you will understand why some people never leave here. You got fun, good food, and good music to dance to, why leaving? But when you do, it will be like a great conversation you cannot forget.

紐奧良 ▶

　　位於美國南部的路易斯安那州你可以找到一個很獨特的城市，紐奧良。在美國沒有一個城市像紐奧良。或許是那些殖民文化的影響使得紐奧良這麼突出。它輕鬆自如的美即使在最小的角落都可以被看見。然而，是它的氣氛使得這個城市這麼的迷人。紐奧良是爵士音樂的出生地，所以不難想像走在街上，聽著許多音樂，例如爵士和藍調從門口流出。我們只希望能夠在路易斯阿姆斯壯還在城中奔波於他的工作時出生。空氣中確實有浪漫情調。怎麼會沒有呢？有著好音樂，美食，和馬蒂格拉嘉年華會，實在很難在這邊度過很糟的時光。在紐奧良一陣子後，或許你會瞭解為什麼有些人不離開這裡。在這裡度過歡樂的時光，有好的音樂可以跳舞，為什麼要離開呢？但是如果你要走，這裡就會像是一個你曾有過的很棒的對話，使你難以忘懷。

阿根廷
庫斯科
紐.奧.良
新德里
拉斯維加斯
伊斯坦堡
西雅圖
班夫鎮
可愛島
冰島

Dialogue 情境對話 ▶

Charles and Patty are going to Mardi Gras.
查爾斯和佩蒂要去馬蒂格拉嘉年華會。

Patty: How do I look? Look at the beads and the mask I made last night!

佩蒂：我看起來怎麼樣？看看我昨天做的這些串珠和面具！

Charles: You look amazing! Nice outfit Patty! I just bought the mask this morning at the store!

查爾斯：你看起來棒透了！很棒的服裝佩蒂！我今天早上只在店裡買了面具！

Patty: That will do! I should know this… but what does Mardi Gras mean anyways?

佩蒂：那也可以阿！我應該知道這個的…但是馬蒂格拉到底是什麼意思？

Charles: It is actually a festival from France. Mardi Gras means Fat Tuesday in English.

查爾斯：這其實是來自法國的節慶。馬蒂格拉在英文是肥膩星期二的意思。

Patty: Fat Tuesday? How come?

佩蒂：肥膩星期二？為什麼？

Charles: They usually have a big

查爾斯：他們通常在他們禁

celebration before their fast, so before the Ash Wednesday, they have the fat Tuesday. They will eat lots on this day.

食前都會有一個很大的慶祝，所以在聖灰星期三前，他們會有肥膩星期二。他們通常會在這天吃很多。

Patty: Are we going to eat lots later? Is that what's gonna happen?

佩蒂：我們等下也會吃很多嗎？這是等下會發生的事嗎？

Charles: You can. But eating lots on Mardi Gras was the original idea. To have a feast before they started a fast. However, it became a big festival through time. Now people have parades, and all sorts of celebration.

查爾斯：可以啊。可是在這天吃很多是最一開始的意思。在開始禁食前有一個大餐。可是現在他已經演變為一個很大的慶典。現在人們有遊行，還有各式各樣的慶祝。

Patty: Wow, that sounds fun! Thanks Charles.

佩蒂：哇，聽起來真好玩！謝啦查爾斯。

Charles: You're welcome!

查爾斯：不客氣！

Patty: So I guess we should head to the French Quarter for the parade now, right?

佩蒂：所以我們應該要去法國區看遊行隊吧？

Charles: Yes, unless you want to eat lots now! Haha

查爾斯：對啊，除非你想要先大吃！哈哈

Patty: Hey that's not a bad idea, either! Let it be the real fat Tuesday!

佩蒂：嘿！那也是一個很好的主意啊！就讓今天成為真正的肥膩星期二吧！

Special Sites Introduction 23: 特別景點報導 ▶

New Orleans - Chef 五星主廚快餐車　 MP3 45

"Chef" is a 2004 comedy drama that captured everyone's attention with not only the joyful plot but also the exuberance and passion of the Chef. In the film, Carl (Jon Favreau) was the head chef at a restaurant in California. However, he had a conflict with the restaurant owner about their never-changing "classic menu" and ended up getting a very bad review from a food critic and even quit his job as a head chef. He then started a food truck business that showed his passion for Cuban food. He went on a cross-country trip with the food truck and his partner and son. The three started a bonding trip and a new chapter of their lives.

In the movie, when they stopped at New Orleans, Carl took his son, Percy, to Café du Monde for their beignets. Beignets are basically a French doughnut that is fluffy and sprinkled with sugar powder. It is not too greasy nor too sweet. Café Du Monde was opened in 1862 at the French Market. If you wish to taste the beignet as Carl and Percy did, stop by this place. Chef knows food better!

紐奧良 - 五星主廚快餐車

　　五星主廚快餐車是一部 2004 年的喜劇劇情片。它不僅以輕鬆喜悅的劇情並且以廚師的活力和熱情來抓住大家的注意力。在片中，卡爾（強費爾魯飾）是一家在加州的餐廳的主廚。然而，他和老闆對於他們從未改變的 "經典菜單" 起了衝突，並且因此得到一個美食評論家的負評和辭掉了主廚一職。他開始了他快餐車的生意也展現了他對古巴食物的熱情。他和他的搭擋和兒子，波西，踏上了一個跨越美國的快餐車旅行。三個人開始這個聯絡感情的旅程並且開始了各自人生的下一章。

　　在電影中，當他們在紐奧良停留，卡爾帶波西到度夢咖啡館去吃法式甜甜圈（beignet）。beignet 其實就是法式的甜甜圈。吃起來口感鬆軟，並且灑滿糖粉。它並不會太油膩或是過甜。度夢咖啡館是在 1862 年在法國市場開店。如果你也想要嚐嚐卡爾和波西在片中吃的法式甜甜圈，來這邊試試看。廚師比較懂美食！

阿根廷
庫斯科
紐奧良
新德里
拉斯維加斯
伊斯坦堡
西雅圖
班夫鎮
可愛島
冰島

Preservation hall　　MP3 46

Sitting in the heart of the French Quarter, the Preservation Hall stands firmly despite the fact that it was established in 1961. If you are looking for the real New Orleans Jazz, this is the right place to go to. It vowed to preserve and protect the traditional New Orleans music. It's open 7 nights a week to offer traditional New Orleans Jazz for locals and the tourist. Unlike other music venues, Preservation Hall offers an intimate experience for the Jazz fans all over the world. They also have a house band, the Preservation Hall Jazz Band, touring around the world to showcase the New Orleans's music heritage. As Louis Armstrong once said: "Preservation Hall. Now that's where you'll find all the greats." If you are looking for some authentic and great music, this place is highly recommended! By us, and Louis Armstrong.

典藏廳

　　座落於法國區的心臟地帶，儘管典藏廳設立於 1961 年，它還是堅定地站在這裡。如果你想要找真正的紐奧良爵士音樂，這裡就是對的地方。它決心要保存並且保護傳統的紐奧良音樂。一個禮拜七天晚上都有開門來提供當地居民或是全世界的觀光客傳統紐奧良爵士。不像其他的音樂廳，典藏廳提供了全世界爵士迷一個十分親密的體驗。他們同時也有一個當家樂團，典藏廳爵士樂團，在全世界巡迴並呈現紐奧良的音樂遺產。如同路易斯阿姆斯壯所說：「在紐奧良典藏廳，你可以聽到所有的好音樂。」如果你在找道地的好音樂，這個地方是大大地被我們，還有路易斯阿姆斯壯推薦的。

Vocabulary and Idioms ▶

❶ effortless adj 輕鬆的	❷ beads n 串珠
❸ feast n 盛宴	❹ exuberance n 活力蓬勃
❺ critic n 評論家	❻ bonding adj 人際關係結合的
❼ fluffy adj 蓬鬆的	❽ intimate adj 親密的

1. I really like her effortless style.

   我真的很喜歡她輕鬆自在的風格。

2. Marie is wearing a very colorful string of beads.

   茉莉正穿著一串色彩繽紛的串珠項鍊。

3. The chef is busy preparing the feast for the wedding.

   主廚正忙著準備婚禮的盛宴。

4. You can see from the painting that the painter paints with exuberance and passion.

   你可以從畫中看出畫家的活力和熱情。

5. As a fashion critic, she has to be very blunt and straightforward sometimes.

   身為一個時尚評論家，她有時必須要非常的直率和直接的。

6. They are having a bonding moment together talking at the backyard.

   他們正在後院聊天聯絡感情。

7. The pancakes my mom make are always very fluffy and delicious.

我媽媽做的鬆餅總是十分的鬆軟和美味。

8. The two becomes very intimate after the graduation trip.

他們兩個在畢業旅行之後變得十分的親密。

旅遊小貼士 ▶

　　需要注意的是典藏廳並非一般酒吧，那裡既沒有吧臺，也不提供餐飲。所以要去典藏廳一探爵士樂的迷人之處之前，可以先吃過東西，或這是也可以帶有容器裝的飲料進去典藏廳內。另外，典藏廳是沒有廁所的喔，記得要先去廁所一趟再來排隊進場喔！

Unit 24

New Delhi 新德里
Eat, Pray, Love
享受吧！一個人的旅行

城市介紹 ▶

New Delhi is a city that is always happening. Imagine a population of 14 million people living in some 1500 square kilometers together. Yes, that means, cows, women, men, kids, cars, tuk tuks, taxis, and more are all on the road. Everywhere you go, you will not be alone. Did I mention cows? Yes, cows are considered holy animals in this country, so wherever they wish to go, you cannot move them. If they decide to take a nap in the middle of the traffic, so be it. It is a really interesting place with one of the most ancient history in the world. If you decide to explore the history here, lots of historical sites await you. Despite its historical attractions, Indian people here are all very friendly. Be it that whether they want to sell things or not, they are mostly hospitable. However, People intending to look for relaxation, might find it hard to find peace here, unless you are practicing yoga or meditation in one of the ashrams here, Otherwise, with different arrays of the goods on the streets, you hear shop owners hustling to sell, and tourists trying to bargain. New Delhi will never be a boring city.

德里

　　新德里是一個蓬勃的城市。想像一千四百萬人一同居住在大約一千五百平方公里。沒錯，意思就是説，牛，女人，男人，小孩，車子，嘟嘟車，計程車還有更多都在路上。不論你到哪裡，你都不會是一個人。我剛剛是説牛嗎？對，牛在這個國家是十分神聖的動物，所以不管她們想要去哪裡，你都不可以移動她們。如果她們打算在路中間睡午覺，那她們就可以。這是一個十分有趣並有著世界上最古老的歷史的城市。如果你想要探索這裡的歷史的話，有許多的歷史景點在此等著你。除了歷史景點，印度人大部分都十分的友善，不論他是不是想要賣你東西，大部分都十分的好客。然而，如果你是想要來放鬆的話，你可能會發現在這裡很難找到平靜。除非你是去印度的修行場，不然的話，有這不同的商品陳列在街上，你會聽見店家汲汲營營地想賣東西，而觀光客試圖殺價。新德里永遠都不會是一個無聊的城市。

Dialogue 情境對話 ▶

Jody and Tom are trying out the Indian curry in a local restaurant.

裘蒂和湯姆在印度當地的餐廳試試他們的咖哩。

Jody: I can't believe we are going to try the real Indian curry now!

裘蒂：我真不敢相信我們要吃到道地的印度咖哩了！

Tom: You've always been a big fan of curry. I'm a little bit concerned about mine. I hope it's not too spicy.

湯姆：你一直都很喜歡咖哩。我有點擔心我點的。我希望它不要太辣。

Jody: I'm sure you will be fine! Here we go!

裘蒂：我相信你可以的！我們來試試看吧！

Tom: Mine is very rich, and you can taste so many spices inside. Oh, wait, lots of chili peppers for sure.

湯姆：我的十分的濃郁，而且你可以吃到很多香料。噢，等等，好多辣椒噢！

Jody: Are you okay? Do you want some water?

裘蒂：你還好嗎？你要水嗎？

Tom: No, look at this. They always put sugar and chili powder on the ta-

湯姆：不，你看這個。他們總是會放糖和辣椒粉在桌上

ble so that you can adjust the flavor yourself.

所以你可以調整口味。

Jody: I get the chili powder, but what's with the sugar?

裴蒂：我懂辣椒粉，可是糖要幹嘛？

Tom: (adds lots of sugar to his curry) Sugar helps neutralize the burning sensation from the chili peppers.

湯姆：（將許多糖加入他咖哩裡）糖可以幫助中和辣椒帶來的灼燒感。

Jody: Really? Does it work?

裴蒂：真的嗎？有用嗎？

Tom: Oh yeah, it's a lot better.

湯姆：噢有，好多了。

Jody: Oh man, I'll be needing a nap after finishing this meal.

裴蒂：我的天啊。我等下吃完這些需要睡個午覺。

Tom: It is a pretty heavy meal. Do you want to order some yogurt drink? I heard they help you digest!

湯姆：這是蠻重的一餐。你想要點個優格飲料喝嗎？我聽說那會幫助消化。

Jody: That'll be great!

裴蒂：聽起來很不錯！

Special Sites Introduction 24: 特別景點報導 ▶

New Delhi - Eat, Pray, Love   MP3 47

Eat, Pray, Love is a 2010 romantic comedy that is based on Elizabeth Gilbert's memoir of the same name. Liz (Julia Roberts) is a woman who failed her marriage and life and is on a quest to look for the passion and desire for life once again. She spent one year on the road, in three different countries, and several unknown adventures. However, by traveling to Italy, India and finishing with Bali, Liz not only finds herself back, but also finds her significant other half and learns how to love herself and someone else once again.

Within this inspiring, yet joyful movie, Liz (Julia Roberts) traveled to India and practiced meditation within one ashram. The ashram in this film is actually the Ashram HarI Mandir. An ashram is a place where it allows you to look into your inner self and inspect your spiritual aspects. It is not a place where you come to, for when you need a break from life. On the contrary, it is a place where it helps you to activate your mental activities and practice to be more mindful at whatever you do. Come experience what Liz had experienced and you might find it useful for you in some way!

新德里 - 享受吧！一個人的旅行

　　享受吧一個人的旅行是 2010 年的一部根據伊莉莎白·吉兒伯特的同名回憶錄的浪漫喜劇片。莉茲（朱莉亞蘿柏茲飾）是一個婚姻和人生失敗的女性，並且在再次尋求對於人生的熱情和渴望。她花了一年在路上，三個不同的國家，和許多未知的冒險。然而，藉由去義大利，印度，並結束在峇里島，莉茲不僅找回自己並也找到她的另外一半。她學會如何再次愛自己和愛別人。

　　在這個激勵卻又歡樂的片中，莉茲（朱莉亞蘿柏茲飾）到印度旅遊並且在印度的修行場學習如何靜坐靈修。而在片中的修行場正是 HarI Mandir 修行場。一個印度修行場是個允許你看進內心深處並且檢視你靈魂的地方。它並不是你在人生需要休息來的地方，而相反的，它是一個能夠幫助你開啟內心活動的地方，而且練習更深切注意做每件事情的地方。來體驗看看莉茲的體驗，你可能會發現這個練習某方面對你也是有幫助的！

旅遊愛玩咖 ▶

Lotus temple   MP3 48

Lotus Temple is the Bahai House of Worship that finished its construction in 1986. Its Lotus-flower shape earned many architectural awards and is featured in many magazines. Designed by an Iranian-Canadian Architect, people can come and enjoy peace and tranquility in this holy space. The goal of the temple is to bring faiths together despite the different religions, races, languages, and genders. Upon entering the place, you will see stairs leading you to the actual Lotus Temple. From there, you need to take off your shoes and just walk in the temple with your barefeet. There will be people passing out brochures about this temple and how they do not mind if everyone has a different religion as long as everyone prays in silence within the temple. The idea of this temple may seem ideal but it is practiced every open day of the temple. If we can project this idea to the world, then imagine how many unnecessary conflicts can be avoided. The space allows you to hold different beliefs, but everyone still shares the common space peacefully with respect. And that's the way it should be, right?

蓮花廟

　　蓮花廟是在 1986 年完成的巴哈伊靈曦堂（崇拜上帝的啟明之處）。它蓮花的外型為它奪得了許多建築的獎項和成為許多雜誌的主題。由一位加拿大籍的伊朗建築師所設計，人們可以來這個神聖的空間享受和平和寧靜。這個廟的目標是無論不同的信仰，種族，語言和性別地把所有的信念聯合起來。一進這個地方，你會看到有樓梯帶引你進入蓮花廟。從那裡，你必須要脫鞋，並赤腳走入蓮花廟。那裡也有人會發給你關於這個廟的小冊子，並且告知他們並不介意大家有不一樣的信仰，只要大家在祈禱的時候都可以以靜默的方式。如果我們可以把這個點子投射到全世界，那試想有多少非必要的衝突可以被避免呢？這個空間允許你有不同的信念，但是大家都還是可以尊敬平和的分享共用的空間。而這本來就該是這樣，不是嗎？

阿根廷
庫斯科
紐奧良
新德里
拉斯維加斯
伊斯坦堡
西雅圖
班夫鎮
可愛島
冰島

Vocabulary and Idioms ▶

❶ **hospitable** adj 好客的　　❷ **concern** v 擔心

❸ **spice** n 香料　　❹ **neutralize** v 中和

❺ **sensation** n 感覺，轟動　　❻ **quest** n 探索

❼ **inspect** v 檢視　　❽ **feature** v 以⋯為特色

1. He is always very hospitable with everyone that comes to his house.

   他總是對每個來他家的人非常好客。

2. My mom is always concerned about my little brother.

   我媽媽總是很擔心我的弟弟。

3. I cannot resist any Italian spices.

   我無法抵抗任何義大利香料。

4. Milk can neutralize the spiciness from food.

   牛奶可以中和食物中的辣。

5. Brad Pitt created a bit of a sensation at the airport this morning.

   布萊德比特今天早上在機場造成了小轟動。

6. She is on a quest for food now. Don't get in her way.

   她現在在找食物。不要擋到她的路。

7. The landlord came and inspected our room before we moved out this noon.

   今天中午在我們搬離開之前房東有來檢視房間。

8. The movie is featured by Julia Roberts.

這部電影是朱利亞羅勃茲主演。

旅遊小貼士 ▶

　　來到新德里，買東西要一定殺價。而不同於去其他的國家，這裡殺價你可以從原價的十分之一開始殺價。有的時候你甚至要起價的更低。千萬不要過意不去因為有的時候店家為了賺取更多的錢，通常都會開出一個超級高價，而不知道的旅客也常常白白花了許多冤枉錢。所以來到新德里買東西，除了比價三家之外，一定要殺價噢！還有就是在印度，這裡的人會搖搖頭表示 OK，所以當你問他們問題當他們搖搖頭卻又跟你說 OK 的話，千萬不要太困惑噢。

阿根廷

庫斯科

紐奧良

新德里

拉斯維加斯

伊斯坦堡

西雅圖

班夫鎮

可愛島

冰島

Unit 25

Las Vegas 拉斯維加斯
What happens in Vegas
頭彩冤家

🏛 城市介紹 ▶

Las Vegas, the Entertainment Capital of the World, offers all sorts of entertainments from slots, casinos, to exhibitions and shows. Whether you are here for a wild celebration or a relaxing experience, Las Vegas has it all covered. It is a place where the visual effects go mad, and all the others push the rest of your senses to their limits. The lights, the music, and the big flashy signboards are all testing your fun and novelty tolerance. It is indeed very much like walking into the gaming center when you were a kid, only this time, you're walking into an adult one. Another way to describe it is that Las Vegas is like a combination of 10 different festivals. Its is fun-guaranteed and has lots to try and see. However, this is not to say that Las Vegas is not kids-friendly. On the contrary, there are plenty of magic shows, or acrobatic shows in Vegas that are suitable for a family outing. Planning a different kind of adventure? Come to Las Vegas!

✈ 拉斯維加斯 ▶

　　拉斯維加斯，世界娛樂首都，提供了各式各樣的娛樂。從吃角子老虎，賭場，到展覽和表演。無論你是為了一個狂野的慶祝，或是一個放鬆的經驗來到拉斯維加斯，它都有這些。這是一個視覺效果瘋狂，還有其它也都在刺激你剩下的感官到極限的地方。燈光，音樂，和大又閃爍的看板都在測試你享受樂趣和新奇事物的限度。這其實感覺很像你還小的時候走進娛樂場所的感覺，但只是這次，你以大人的身份走進來。另一個來描述的方式是拉斯維加斯就像是十種節慶加在一起。絕對保證很多樂趣，以及很多可以看和嘗試的。然而，這並不是說拉斯維加斯是不適合小孩子來的。相反的，這裡有許多的魔術秀和特技表演都很適家族旅行來觀賞。正在計劃一個不一樣的冒險嗎？來拉斯維加斯吧！

 Dialogue 情境對話 ▶

Elaine and Betty are by one slot machine and decide to give it a try.
伊蓮和貝蒂正在角子吃老虎旁，並決定要試試看。

Betty: How does this work? I've never played slot machines before. Some hints, please?

貝蒂：這個要怎麼玩？我從來沒玩過角子老虎。可以給我一些提示嗎，拜託？

Elaine: it's pretty self-explanatory. Just put in the money and spin the reels. I guess we will know if we win!

伊蓮：其實這個還蠻直接的。就把錢放進去，旋轉輪盤。我想如果我們贏了的話，我們會知道。

Betty: Alright, that sounds easy. How much money should we put it? I'm sorry. I really have no idea.

貝蒂：好吧，聽起來蠻簡單的。我們要放多少錢？對不起，我真的完全不知道怎麼玩。

Elaine: Here's a quarter. I guess we can start small!

伊蓮：這裡是一個二十五分硬幣。我想我們開始先玩一點點就好。

Betty: Do you want me to spin the reel?

貝蒂：你想要我轉輪盤嗎？

Elaine: Sure, go ahead! Good luck!

伊蓮：好啊，你來！祝你好運！

(Betty spins the reels and the ma-

（貝蒂轉了輪盤而機器開始

chine rings!)

鈴聲大響！）

Betty: Oh my god, what just happened? Is that normal? How do we get this to stop ringing? This is getting embarrassing!

貝蒂：我的天啊，發生了什麼事？這是正常的嘛？我們要怎麼停止這個鈴聲？我開始覺得很難為情了！

Elaine: We won!! That's so awesome! Let's see how much we win!

伊蓮：我們贏了！太棒了！我們來看看我們贏了多少！

Betty: Really? Oh my god, this is incredible. How much did we win?

貝蒂：真的嗎？我的天啊，這太神奇了。我們贏了多少？

Elaine: It says we have 125 dollars now, do we want to cash it or continue?

伊蓮：它說我們現在有一百二十五美元，我們要兌現還是繼續？

Betty: Let's cash it! That was just the beginner's luck! Let's make good use of this money!

貝蒂：我們兌現好了！剛剛只是第一次玩的好運！我們來好好利用這些錢！

Elaine: It's your call. It is your money anyways! You spun the reels.

伊蓮：給你決定。這畢竟是你的錢！你轉的輪盤！

Betty: Don't be silly. We're gonna spend this on a very good dinner! It's your quarter!

貝蒂：別傻了。我們要把錢花在很好的晚餐上！是你的二十五分硬幣！

Elaine: Sounds terrific! Thanks Betty!

伊蓮：聽起來不錯！謝啦貝蒂！

Special Sites Introduction 25: 特別景點報導 ▶

Las Vegas - What happens in Vegas MP3 49

There's a famous saying in Vegas, "what happens in Vegas, stays in Vegas." What happens if you did something in Vegas, and you just could not get out of it that easily? This is what happened in the movie What Happens in Vegas. When the reserved and serious Joy (Cameron Diaz) got dumped by her boyfriend, and Jack (Ashton Kutcher) got fired by his own father, both feeling distressed, went to Vegas with their friends. Randomly, the two groups met up in Vegas and started a mad evening. Jack used Joy's quarter to win the jackpot from the slots. To make the matter even more complicated, the two got married over the alcohol influence over the night. Flying back to New York, the two were forced to honor the marriage and try to work things out instead of getting a divorce.

In the movie, when Joy showed up in a limo with her friends

in front of their hotel, the scene was shot in front of the famous fountains at the Bellagio Hotel. The fountains are featured with performances set to the light and music. There will be shows every 30 minutes in the afternoon, and every 15 minutes in the evening. Be sure not to miss this free and memorable fountains show when you are here!

拉斯維加斯 - 頭彩冤家

在拉斯維加斯有一個很有名的俗諺 "在賭城發生的，就讓它留在賭城吧。" 但是如果你在賭城做了讓你無法輕易脫身的事怎麼辦呢？這就是在電影頭彩冤家中的情節。當保守又較嚴肅的喬伊（卡麥蓉狄亞茲飾）被她的男友甩了，而傑克（艾希頓庫奇飾）則是被自己的老爸開除，兩個人都感到十分的苦惱，所以都和朋友去了拉斯維加斯。隨機的兩組人馬在拉斯維加斯遇上，並且展開了在拉斯維加斯一個十分瘋狂的夜晚。傑克用喬伊的二十五分硬幣贏得吃角子老虎的大獎。使事情更複雜，他們兩個前一晚在酒精的影響下還結了婚。飛回紐約後，他們被迫履行婚約並且試著解決他們的難題，而不是離婚。在電影中，當喬伊和朋友搭乘大型豪華轎車抵達飯店，這個場景是在百樂宮前的噴水池所拍攝。這裡的噴水池是以設定好的燈光和音樂為特色。在下午時，每隔三十分鐘會表演一次，而在晚上則是每隔十五分鐘一次。在拉斯維加斯的你，不要錯過這個免費又令人印象深刻的噴水池表演喔！

阿根廷

庫斯科

紐奧良

新德里

拉斯維加斯

伊斯坦堡

西雅圖

班夫鎮

可愛島

冰島

Cirque du Soleil is certainly not strange to most people. Based in Québec, Cirque du Soleil began to evoke the imagination of people from 1984. Today, Cirque du Soleil has over 4,000 employees and around 1,300 artists worldwide.

When you come to Las Vegas, one thing you must not miss is to see "O" before you leave. Among all the performances, "O"is chosen to be the best performance among all. Going beyond the limit of stages, "O" is an aquatic performance weaved with art, surrealism and with theatrical effect. "O" is often called a timeless production. With 85 of the international performers, artists, and professional divers, they make this production and show perfect even if it is alive. Each scene can be captured as a painting or a picture. Fans that want to come in to see this breathtaking and lavish show must reserve your tickets way ahead of time, for that it is a must-see for most of the visitors here. Therefore, be ready to embark on a magical journey with Cirque du Soleil. This just might be one of the most unforgettable experiences in your life.

阿
根
廷

庫
斯
科

紐
奧
良

新
德
里

拉
斯
維
加
斯

伊
斯
坦
堡

西
雅
圖

班
夫
鎮

可
愛
島

冰
島

太陽劇團 "O"

太陽劇團對大多數的人一定不會很陌生。以魁北克為總部,太陽劇團從 1984 年開始喚起大家的想像力。今天,太陽馬戲團在全球已經有超過四千個員工,一千三百個藝術家。

當你來到拉斯維加斯,在你走之前,你一定不能錯過 "O"。在他們所有的表演中, "O" 被選為是最精彩的一個。超越了舞台的極限, "O" 是一個水上的表演,並交織了藝術,超現實主義和舞台效果。 "O" 也常被稱為永恆之作。有八十五位國際表演者,藝術家,專業潛水家,他們完美地呈現整個製作和表演,即使是現場表演。每一個場景都可以被捕捉為一幅畫或是一張照片。想要來一探這個驚人又豐富表演的粉絲們,一定要超提前訂票,因為這幾乎是大多數來這裡的觀光客必看的表演。所以,準備好一同和太陽劇團一起開啟這個神奇的旅程吧!這可能會是你一生最難忘的經驗之一。

◉◉ Vocabulary and Idioms ▶

❶ exhibition n 展覽

❷ incredible adj 難以置信的，驚人的

❸ beginner's luck Phrase 新手的好運氣

❹ reserved adj 含蓄的

❺ randomly adv 隨機地

❻ aquatic adj 水上的，水中的

❼ timeless adj 永恆的

❽ embark v 開始

1. The newest alien exhibition at the science museum is amazing!

   在科學博物館最新的外星人展覽真的超棒的！

2. Both the design and the execution of that dress are incredible.

   那件洋裝的設計和做工都十分的驚人。

3. He won the first game with the beginner's luck. He will have to practice more for the next ones.

   他以新手的好運氣贏了第一場比賽。他為了之後的比賽必須多加練習。

4. She is very reserved and never shares too much about her personal life.

   她是一個非常含蓄並且從不分享她私人生活的人。

5. We saw each other randomly at the movie theater.

   我們隨機地在電影院看到彼此。

6. We went to a local aquatic park to see dolphins.

我們去了一個當地的水上公園去看海豚。

7. She is a timeless beauty in his eyes. 30 years of marriage, she is still the apple of his eye.

她在他眼中是永遠的美人。結婚三十年,她依舊是他的摯愛。

8. He is ready to embark on another chapter of his life.

他已經準備好開始他人生的下一章節。

旅遊小貼士 ▶

　　當你正沈浸在賭桌上,口渴了怎麼辦?手氣正旺的時候,一個貼心的小提醒是角子老虎前,賭桌前,調酒都免費,但是一定要給小費喔!不然的話服務生可能會不會再朝你的方向走來。所以雖然説是免費,還不如説是飲料很便宜噢!也不要忘了記得要給小費的國際禮儀噢!

阿
根
廷

庫
斯
科

紐
奧
良

新
德
里

拉
斯
維
加
斯

伊
斯
坦
堡

西
雅
圖

班
夫
鎮

可
愛
島

冰
島

Unit 26

Istanbul 伊斯坦堡
Skyfall 空降危機

城市介紹 ▶

The location of this city has attracted and connected many people from the East and West for a long time. This magical meeting place collides with a variety of cultures and through time, they have decorated the city with what was considered the best architectures and establishments of the time. Persians, Romans, Ottomans, all you can think of, have all been attracted to this mysterious city and decided they would stay. It is not hard to imagine the various cultures here. Most people would visit the Sultanahmet district and visit most of the important buildings there on foot. It's amazing how concentrated the area is and it is, to be honest, quite easy to make a historic trip day all at once.

Venturing out to the other sides of the district you can find hip restaurants and edgy bars. Have a coffee at one of their coffee houses and talk about the city's glorious past and get your fortune told. What a wonderful way to know the city and yourself!

伊斯坦堡

　　這個城市的地點已經吸引，並連結從東方和西方來的人很久了。這個神奇的碰面地點撞擊出許多不同的文化，而隨著時間他們也以當時最好的建築以及建設來裝飾這個城市。波斯人，羅馬人，奧圖曼人，你想得到的，都被吸引到這個神秘的城市並決定他們不離開了。這的確不令人難想像這裡多種的文化。大多數人會到蘇丹艾哈邁區拜訪，並且以走路的方式拜訪許多重要的建築。這區如此的集中真的很驚人，而且老實説，蠻容易一次安排一個歷史之旅。走出這區你可以找到流行的餐廳和時髦的酒吧。在咖啡廳喝杯咖啡並且談談這城市光榮的過去，並且算算你的命運。真是一個了解這個城市和你的好辦法！

阿根廷
庫斯科
紐奧良
新德里
拉斯維加斯
伊斯坦堡
西雅圖
班夫鎮
可愛島
冰島

Dialogue 情境對話 ▶

Rebecca and her local friend Cansin are at a local coffee house.

瑞貝卡和她當地的朋友坎欣正在當地的一個咖啡廳裡。

Rebecca: Wow this is so nice. There are coffee houses everywhere here.

瑞貝卡：哇這裡好棒喔。到處都有咖啡廳。

Cansin: Yes, we love to drink coffee. It's just a nice place to hang out with friends or enjoy a book to yourself you know.

坎欣：對啊，我們很愛喝咖啡。這就是一個和朋友見面很棒的地方或是自己來這邊讀一本書。

Rebecca: That's so cool. The coffee seems so thick here. I can see the sediments at the bottom of the cup.

瑞貝卡：好酷喔。這裡的咖啡感覺好濃喔。我可以看到杯底的沈澱物。

Cansin: Yeah, we grind the coffee into very fine powers that's why. You can really taste the real coffee flavor that way. It's quite strong though. I have to warn you. I can tell your fortune by reading the coffee grind. Do

坎欣：對啊，那是因為我們把咖啡磨的很細。那樣你才可以品嚐到咖啡真正的風味。那還蠻濃的喔，我必須先警告你。我還可以從咖啡渣來算你的命喔。你想要試

you want to try?

試看嗎？

Rebecca: A coffee grind fortune telling? Yes, please!

瑞貝卡：咖啡渣算命？好，拜託！

Cansin: Okay, so first drink the coffee and leave the grind behind. (Rebecca sips the coffee)

坎欣：好那首先你先喝咖啡，然後把咖啡渣留下。（瑞貝卡啜飲咖啡）

Rebecca: Okay. Done! Wow, it is quite strong.

瑞貝卡：好，喝完了！哇，真的很濃。

Casin: Then make a wish before you cover the coffee cup with the dish.

坎欣：然後在你把杯蓋放在咖啡杯上前許個願望。

Rebecca: Okay.

瑞貝卡：好了。

Casin: Alright. Gently flip the cup upside down. And now we wait till the grind to settle and dry.

坎欣：好，現在輕輕地把杯子整個翻過來。然後我們現在要等到咖啡渣沈澱和乾掉。

(10 minutes later)

（十分鐘過後）

Casin: Okay, let's see what we

坎欣：好，讓我們來看看我

阿根廷
庫斯科
紐奧良
新德里
拉斯維加斯
伊斯坦堡
西雅圖
班夫鎮
可愛島
冰島

have here. I see a circle, which means everything is going well, and your wish is most likely to come true.

們有什麼。我看到一個圈圈，意思是説每一件事情都很順利，而且你的願望很有可能會實現。

Rebecca: Hooray! What else does it say?

瑞貝卡：萬歲！它還説了什麼？

Casin: Oh no…

坎欣：噢不…

Rebecca: What?

瑞貝卡：怎麼了？

Casin: It also says that you will lose some money. Cansin forgot to bring her wallet, so you might have to pay for her first…

坎欣：它説你會破財。坎欣沒帶錢包所以你要先幫她付錢…

Rebecca: Really?? That's no problem. But will you tell me more first before I pay?

瑞貝卡：真的嗎？那沒問題。可是你可以在我付錢之前先多告訴我一點嗎？

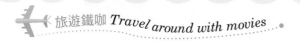
Special Sites Introduction 26: 特別景點報導 ▶

In the 2002 007 movie, "Skyfall", it continued from what James Bond (Daniel Craig) did with his last assignment tremendously jeopardizes the real identities of the undercover agents around the world. Desperately, M was forced to turn to Bond for help to relocate the agency.

At the beginning of the movie, Bond was chasing a man on the rooftop of a very busy market in Istanbul. That is the very Grand Bazaar that most tourists would not miss. It was built between 1445 to 1461, and it is one of the biggest and oldest markets in the world. It covers around 58 streets, and some 4,000 stores. You can find just about anything here, from accessories, spices, carpets, scarves, leather products, or old weaponries. It is like a mini community within the Grand Bazaar, too, because you will be able to find mosques, banks, restaurants and post offices. It is extremely fun treasure hunting and playing mind games with the shop owners. It is the perfect place shopping for souvenirs as well.

伊斯坦堡 - 空降危機

在 2002 年 007 的電影，空降危機中，它延續了因為詹姆士龐德（丹尼爾克雷格飾）上次的任務而危害到世界各地臥底探員的真正身份。情急下，探員 M 被迫來向龐德請求幫助重置總部。

在電影的一開始，龐德在一個繁忙的屋頂上追逐一個男子。那個市集就是大多數觀光客都不會錯過的大市集（Grand Bazaar）。它是在 1445 年到 1461 年之間建立，並且也是世界上最大和最古老的市集之一。它涵蓋了大約五十八條街，和約莫四千個店家。你可以在這邊找到幾乎任何東西，從首飾，香料，地毯，圍巾，皮製品或是古老的武器。在大市集裡也就像是一個小型的社區一樣因為你也可以找到清真寺，銀行，餐廳和郵局。在這裡尋寶和和店家玩心理遊戲都十分地好玩。這也是購買紀念品的好去處喔！

阿根廷

庫斯科

紐奧良

新德里

拉斯維加斯

伊斯坦堡

西雅圖

班夫鎮

可愛島

冰島

 MP3 52

The Hagia Sophia, or Ayasofya in Turkish is definitely one of the wonders of the world. It was built more than a thousand and five hundred years ago. Constantine the Great first built it as a church. The huge dome on the exterior is their legacy. And then when the Ottoman took over the empire, they changed the church into a mosque. However, as the Republic of Turkey was established, the Hagia Sophia lost its purpose as a mosque, so it is served as a museum nowadays. Even if the line outside of this marvelous building might be quite long, it will be worthwhile as you step in and see this jaw-dropping building that stunned you with its grand space and delicate details. You can hear the hum once you are inside. It is as if you are walking in a seashell. This gigantic Byzantine building really showcases the architecture skills over time. What an interesting space that shared the space, history, religions, and it stands still even till today. Remember to drop by and say hello to this ancient beauty. Perhaps it will share some stories with you!

阿
根
廷

庫
斯
科

紐
奧
良

新
德
里

拉
斯
維
加
斯

伊
斯
坦
堡

西
雅
圖

班
夫
鎮

可
愛
島

冰
島

聖蘇菲亞大教堂

　　聖蘇菲亞大教堂，或是土耳其文中的 Ayasofya 絕對是世界的奇景之一。它是遠在超過一千五百年前建造的。康斯坦丁大帝最先把這裡建立為一個教堂。在外面那巨大的圓屋頂就是他們的遺產。之後當奧圖曼人搶攻帝國，把這個教堂改為清真寺。然而，隨著土耳其共和國的建立，蘇菲亞大教堂也漸漸地失去它身為清真寺的意義，所以現在改為博物館。即使在這雄偉的建築外面大排長龍，但是當你進入這個以巨大的空間和精細的細節來令你吃驚的博物館內，一切都是值得的。當你可以進入博物館內你能聽見嗡嗡聲就像是你走在貝殼裡一般。這個巨大的拜占庭建築著實隨著時間展示了建築技巧。這真是一個分享了空間，歷史，信仰的有趣的空間，而它到今日都還是穩穩地站著。記得來這裡看看並和這個古典美人打招呼。或許它會跟你分享更多的故事喔！

Vocabulary and Idioms ▶

❶ collide v 撞擊 ❷ sediment n 沈澱物

❸ grind v 磨 ❹ jeopardize v 危及

❺ desperately adv 絕望地，拼命地 ❻ exterior n 外部

❼ legacy n 遺產 ❽ jaw-dropping adj 吃驚的

1. His car collided with a scooter.

   他的車和一個摩托車相撞。

2. Look at the sediments in the bottle. I think this is bad already.

   你看這瓶子裡的沈澱物。我想這已經壞了。

3. He grinds his teeth when he's sleeping.

   他睡覺的時候會磨牙。

4. If you keep skipping classes, you might jeopardize your chance to become an intern later on.

   如果你繼續翹課，你可能會危及你之後成為實習生的機會。

5. She looks for her kid in the department store desperately.

   她在百貨公司裡拼命地找她的小孩。

6. You cannot judge this place just by its exterior.

   你不能憑外觀就評斷這裡。

7. A good environment is the best legacy we can leave for our children.

   一個好的環境是我們可以留給我們的孩子最好的遺產。

8. This has been a really jaw-dropping experience to really get to know what kind of person she is.

認清她是怎麼樣的一個人真是一個令人吃驚的經驗。

旅遊小貼士 ▶

　　如果有計劃要到著名的藍色清真寺拜訪的話，要切記他們有一些衣著上的規定，男士不能穿短褲，女士不能露出四肢和胸口。入內都要拖鞋。若是不合格的話，會得到一條大絲巾作掩蓋。若是不習慣公用的絲巾的話，建議可以自己帶一條絲巾喔！

阿根廷
庫斯科
紐奧良
新德里
拉斯維加斯
伊斯坦堡
西雅圖
班夫鎮
可愛島
冰島

Unit 27
Seattle 西雅圖 - Sleepless in Seattle 西雅圖夜未眠

城市介紹 ▶

  Urban explorer and adventure seekers might find Seattle a real gem. You can find fantastic city scenes with the convenient transportation. Walking down the streets with a cup of coffee at hand—perhaps from the very first Starbucks, you can wander around the pike Place Market where they sell excellent seafood and just about anything you can find in a farmer's market. After shopping around and trying all the fresh food, stop by the famous Space Needle for a great view of the city and continue your tour with the art and history museums. If these activities are not your

旅遊鐵咖 *Travel around with movies*

cup of tea, turn into the suburbs to look for the world-class camp-sites, and just be in line with nature. The stunning nature will impress you like no others. You can kayak, ski, run, and sail to discover your piece of Seattle beauty. It seems like everyone can appreciate Seattle in his or her own way, whatever you do, have fun in this Emerald City!

◀ 西雅圖 ▶

　　城市探險家和冒險者可能會覺得西雅圖是一個珍寶。你可以以便利的交通系統來到這美好的城市街景。走在街上手中拿這一杯咖啡一可能是從第一家星巴克買來的，在派克市場遊走，你可以在買到美味的海鮮的和你在農夫市集需要的任何東西。在到處逛逛並且嚐試了許多新鮮的食物之後，來有名的太空針塔停留一下並且享受城市美景並去美術和歷史博物館繼續你的觀光。如果這些活動都不是你喜歡的話，轉進市郊去找世界級的露營營地，並和大自然同步。這美麗的大自然會讓你十分的印象深刻。你可以在這裡划小艇，滑雪，慢跑，和風帆來找到屬於你的西雅圖之美。似乎每個來到西雅圖的人都可以以自己的角度來欣賞西雅圖。無論你做什麼，在翡翠城玩得開心點！

Dialogue 情境對話 ▶

Erin and Sylvia are walking in the Pike Place Market by the fish vendors.
艾倫和蔣維雅正走在派克市場的魚攤旁。

阿根廷庫斯科
紐奧良
新德里
拉斯維加斯
伊斯坦堡
西雅圖
班夫鎮
可愛島
冰島

Erin: What's going on there? Are those people bargaining for fish?

艾倫：那裡發生什麼事了？那些人是在殺價買魚嗎？

Sylvia: Yeah, they're pretty loud. I feel like I'm in a stock market or something.

蕭維雅：對啊，他們好大聲。我覺得我現在好像在股票市場之類的。

Erin: Well, what do you say? Should we join them?

艾倫：嗯，你覺得如何？我們要加入他們嗎？

Sylvia: Sure, why not. I'm very intrigued now. We should get a yummy fish for dinner as well.

蕭維雅：好啊，有何不可。我現在也十分有興趣。我們也該買條好吃的魚當晚餐。

Erin: Roger that! Let's go!

艾倫：收到！走吧！

(Erin and Sylvia walk closer to the crowds)

(艾倫和蕭維雅走近人群)

Sylvia: Oh my god, they're throwing fish all around. That's so neat!

蕭維雅：我的天啊，他們把魚丟得到處都是。好酷噢！

Erin: The guy at the front throws the fish to the counter once someone buys something! They must have

艾倫：如果有人買東西的話，在前面的這個人會把魚丟到櫃台！他們一定已經丟

done this for many times. Look how skillful they are.

過好幾次了。你看他們技術有多好！

Sylvia: I know! He didn't even look! That is such a good marketing strategy to get more people.

蔫維雅：我知道！他根本就沒看！這真是一個很好的行銷手法來吸引人群。

Erin: Should we buy one?

艾倫：我們要買一條嗎？

Sylvia: Haha! Okay! I'll order it.

蔫維雅：哈哈！好啊！我來點。

Sylvia: Excuse me, we'd like this snapper over here, please!

蔫維雅：不好意思，我們要在這邊的這隻鯛魚！

(The fisher mongers throw their snapper to the guy at the counter at once.)

（魚販馬上把他們的鯛魚丟給櫃台的人）

Erin: Nice throw and nice catch!!

艾倫：丟得好也接得好！！

Sylvia: This is the best fish shopping experience ever!

蔫維雅：這真是最棒的買魚經驗！

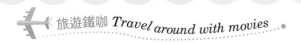

Special Sites Introduction 27: 特別景點報導 ▶

Seattle - Sleepless in Seattle 西雅圖夜未眠 MP3 53

Sleepless in Seattle, a 1993 classic is which still touches many people's hearts even till this day. Sam Baldwin (Tom Hanks) lost his wife to cancer and was randomly sharing the story on air in a radio show. Annie Reed (Meg Ryan) was listening to the radio show as well. Drawn by Sam's love for his wife, Annie wrote a letter to Sam to meet up on Valentine's Day. The moving plots and scenes remain in its fans' hearts for a very long time.

At the scene when Sam is talking to his friend Jay. Jay sheds some light on dating when they were at Athenian Inn. It is a brunch place located in the Pike Place Market at 1517 Pike Place. The restaurant itself is over a century old, and thus it is a very old school, yet very charming in its own fashion. It is said that they serve the coldest beer in the world. It still draws lots of tourists and Sleepless in Seattle fans even till today. Come by and see for yourself!

西雅圖 - 西雅圖夜未眠

西雅圖夜未眠，一部在 1993 年上映的經典但時至今日都還是觸動了很多人的心。山姆包溫（湯姆漢克飾）的妻子因癌症過世，巧合之下在電台上分享了他的故事。安妮瑞德（梅格萊恩飾）正在收聽一樣的電台。被山姆對妻子的愛所吸引，安妮寫了一封信給山姆並約他在情人節當天見面。這動人的情節和片段都還久留在粉絲們的心中。

在山姆正在和他的朋友傑談天時，傑在雅典客棧解釋了他對約會的意見。雅典客棧是位於派克市場的 1517 號。這家餐廳本身已經超過一個世紀，所以這邊十分的老舊但卻十分的有自己的魅力。聽說他們有全世界最冰涼的啤酒。它至今都還吸引了許多的觀光客以及西雅圖夜未眠的影迷。你來這邊自己看看吧！

旅遊愛玩咖 ▶

Starbucks 102 Pike St., Seattle, Washington 98101.

MP3 54

The global coffee chain, Starbucks, not only serve hot and cold beverages, sandwiches, pastries, but also sell their own mugs and related products. Carrying a cup of Starbucks is more than what it looks like. It is also trendy and sometimes makes your life better. It has over 21,000 stores in over 63 countries. Nonetheless, all big corporations must start somewhere. This global coffee giant started its first store in 1971 at a corner of Pike Place Market. Because this is a historical district, this Starbucks gets to retain what it looked like at the beginning. One significant difference is the Starbucks logo. The one today is very different from the original one. We can actually tell it is a mermaid in the original logo. Why not drop by this very first store where they remain humble just as it started at the beginning. That is a living proof that dream does come true and become bigger! Come and have a cup of coffee and dream dreams.

阿
根
廷

庫
斯
科

紐
奧
良

新
德
里

拉
斯
維
加
斯

伊
斯
坦
堡

西
雅
圖

班
夫
鎮

可
愛
島

冰
島

星巴克 - 派克街 102 號，西雅圖，華盛頓州 98101

　　這個世界連鎖咖啡店，星巴克，不只賣冷熱飲品，三明治，糕點，他們也賣他們自己的馬克杯，和其它相關產品。拿著一杯星巴克不只是看起來這樣。這同時也是十分時髦而且有的時候會讓你的生活更好過些。它有超過兩萬一千家店分散在六十個國家。然而，每個大企業都一定從哪裡開始起步。這個全球咖啡大咖開始於 1971 年在派克市場的轉角開了第一家店。因為這裡是歷史區，所以這家星巴克還是保有它一開始的時候的樣貌。一個很大的不同是星巴克的商標。現在的商標和最一開始的十分不同。我們可以看出商標原來是美人魚。為什麼不來這第一家店看看它就像一開始一般的謙卑。這是一個夢想會成真也會變大的活生生的例子！來喝杯咖啡並且發個夢吧！

Vocabulary and Idioms ▶

❶ **urban** adj 城市的

❷ **gem** n 寶石，可貴的人

❸ **intrigued** adj 好奇的

❹ **strategy** n 策略

❺ **shed light on**
  Idiom 照明，解釋

❻ **mug** n 馬克杯

❼ **trendy** adj 時髦的

❽ **retain** v 保留，保持

1. In urban areas, there are usually more cars.

  在市區通常都會比較多車。

2. He's a real gem in an era like now. Make sure you don't lose him.

  他在現在這個時代，真的是難能可貴的人。你千萬不要失去他了。

3. I am intrigued by the sound dolphins make.

  我對海豚發出來的聲音感到十分的好奇。

4. What is the best strategy to get high scores efficiently?

  什麼是有效率地得高分的最好策略？

5. As a doctor, he is able to shed light on the problem.

  身為醫生，他可以幫忙解釋問題的徵兆。

6. He felt much more awake after a mug of coffee.

  他在喝完一馬克杯的咖啡後感到清醒了許多。

7. Where did she get that trendy bag?

  她從哪裡買來那麼時髦的包包？

8. Review what is learned will help retain the knowledge.

復習學過的東習可以幫助你記住知識。

旅遊小貼士 ▶

　　當你在西雅圖想要到當地的唐人街逛逛，並吃些中式的食物解解鄉愁時，記得特別的是在西雅圖，有別於別的地方的唐人街稱呼為 China Town，這裡的唐人街稱為 International District，避免找不到路和誤會，記得找路的時候要查 International District 喔！別迷路啦！

阿
根
廷

庫
斯
科

紐
奧
良

新
德
里

拉
斯
維
加
斯

伊
斯
坦
堡

西
雅
圖

班
夫
鎮

可
愛
島

冰
島

Unit 28

Banff 班夫鎮
River of No Return
大江東去／弓河瀑布

城市介紹 ▶

The town of Banff is in the heart of the Banff National Park. This is a small town of 7000 people, and each year, millions of visitors will come here for skiing, biking, hiking, and soaking in the hot springs! With the great amenities, the town offers visitors comfortable stay during their visit. The main street in the town is the Banff Avenue where the street is filled with souvenir stores, restaurants, and galleries. Besides that, most of the street names in this town are named after animal names. For instance, you might see Buffalo street or Deer street. At first, you might find it bizarre. However, local people explained that since animals are the first residents of this town, they feel obliged to name their streets after them in order to acknowledge the animals. It is indeed true that wildlife can be spotted easily here, and with Mountain Cascade at the background, the town of Banff truly becomes one of the most scenic cities in the world.

◀ 班夫鎮 ▶

　　班夫鎮是班夫國家公園的中心。這是個有七千人的小鎮，而每年，上百萬的旅客會來到這裡滑雪，騎腳踏車，和泡溫泉！有著完善的設施，小鎮提供了旅客來訪時舒適的停留。這裡主要的路是班夫大道。這個大道上充滿了紀念品店，餐廳和畫廊。除此之外，這裡大部分的路名都是由動物名稱來命名。例如，你可能會看到水牛街，或是花鹿街。剛開始你可能會覺得很奇怪，可是在當地人解釋因為動物們才是最先住在這裡的居民，所以他們覺得有義務用他們的名字來命名這裡的街道，以便感謝這裡的動物們。這裡的確常能看到野生動物，而有卡斯喀山為背景，班夫鎮著實是世界上風景最好的城市之一。

Dialogue 情境對話 ▶

Jonathan and Jamie are walking around in the Chateau Lake Louise.
強納森和潔咪正在路易絲湖城堡裡走走。

阿根廷
庫斯科
紐奧良
新德里
拉斯維加斯
伊斯坦堡
西雅圖
班夫鎮
可愛島
冰島

Jonathan: This is such a spectacular spot to stay.

強納森：這真是一個超棒的住宿地點。

Jamie: It is definitely luxurious. I think it's a good call that we decide to splurge a little and stay here.

潔咪：真的十分的奢華。我覺得我們花多一點錢來住這裡真是一個很好的決定。

Jonathan: Yeah definitely. Come here Jamie. I think this is the reason why this hotel is claimed to have the most beautiful window.

強納森：對啊，真的。潔咪你來這裡一下，我想這就是為什麼這個飯店有最美的窗戶之稱。

Jamie: Oh wow, with mountain Victoria at the back and lake Louise in the front. I'm not leaving here! Ever!

潔咪：噢哇，維多利亞山在後面，路易斯湖在前景。我不要離開這裡，永遠都不要！

Jonathan: Well, I'm sure we can find you a dish-washing job here.

強納森：嗯，我想我們應該可以幫你在這裡找個洗盤子的工作。

Jamie: It'll be worth it.

潔咪：那也會很值得。

Jonathan: It sure is a good investment to build a hotel here. We had to

強納森：在這裡蓋這個飯店一定會是一個很好的投資。

make a reservation here like 6 months ago! It is packed every single day.

我們要在六個月前就預訂了！這裡每天都客滿！

Jamie: Perhaps I can earn more tips here than from working back home.

潔咪：搞不好我在這裡靠小費賺錢還比現在工作的地方賺得多。

Jonathan: You might be right. I wouldn't be surprised.

強納森：你搞不好是對的。我並不會驚訝。

Jamie: But thanks again for planning this trip. It's been a real treat!

潔咪：但謝謝你規劃這個旅行。真的是很棒的旅行！

Jonathan: No problem. What do you think? Should we venture out and go hiking around here?

強納森：沒問題。你覺得怎麼樣？我們要不要出去冒險一下去健行一下？

Jamie: Sure! Let me grab a jacket.

潔咪：好！讓我拿個外套！

 Special Sites Introduction 28: 特別景點報導 ▶

Banff - River of No Return   MP3 55

In the classic movie, River of No Return, Kay (Marilyn Monroe), a singer at a local saloon, Matt (Robert Mitchum), an ex-convict that has recently been released from prison, and Matt's son float on a raft, they encounter an attack from hostile Indians. The exciting scene of the three trying to escape the attack from the fierce Indians gets even more exciting when the raft is passing through a very narrow valley. This memorable scene was shot in the Bow River in Banff national park. The theme song of this movie is also called the River of No Return. It is sung by Marilyn Monroe and it still comes up in the visitors' head whenever they come to visit Bow River. Just as the lyrics suggest, sometimes it's peaceful, and sometimes wild and free. Bow River is an extremely scenic river, which starts from the Rockies. The river cuts through the town of Banff and flows 645 kilometers long. It is mighty and the best way to explore this river is by a guided rafting trip from the town.

班夫鎮 - 大江東去/弓河瀑布

在經典的電影，大江東去中，凱（瑪麗蓮夢露飾）是一個在酒吧的歌手，馬特（勞勃米契飾）是一個剛從監獄釋放出來的前囚犯，和馬特的兒子馬克三人在木筏上飄流。他們在途中遇到了有具敵意的印第安人攻擊。當木筏通過一個極為狹隘的峽谷這三人試圖逃脫印第安人攻擊，這刺激的一幕變得更刺激。這令人印象深刻的場景就是在班夫國家公園的弓河所拍攝。而這部片的主題曲也叫做大江東去。是由瑪麗蓮夢露所錄唱，這首歌在遊客來訪弓河時還是時常會盤旋在他們的腦海中。就像是歌詞所說的，這條河有的時候平靜，有的時候狂野而自由。弓河是一個從洛基山脈開始景觀美麗的河水。它貫穿了班夫鎮而長蔓延六百四十五公里長。探索這條河最好的方式是從鎮上找一個有導遊的泛舟行程！

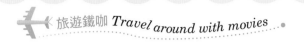

 旅遊愛玩咖 ▶

 Moraine Lake   MP3 56

Coming to Moraine Lake is like walking into a fantasy movie, such as the Lord of the Rings. It is the closet possible place you can find fairies and unicorns roaming around without feeling too surprised. The place that is so well-preserved, pure, and clean. The exquisite and spectacular scenery is also usually the subject of many photos or paintings. You will marvel at the dramatic turquoise glacial water and feel the tranquility at the same time. Make sure you make the trip down here when you are in the Rockies because this might strike you as a more beautiful place than any other attractions within the area. There are some accessible trails around Moraine Lake. You may also rent a canoe and enjoy the view from the center of the lake. Without exaggeration, it is hands down one of the most peaceful places on earth.

夢蓮湖

　　來到夢蓮湖就像走進了奇幻電影一般，例如魔戒。這是你最接近可以找到精靈和獨角獸自由漫遊也不會太驚訝的地方。這裡還是被保存得十分完善，純淨，乾淨。那精緻和壯麗的景象通常是許多攝影和畫畫的主題。你會驚嘆那誇張湛藍的冰河水，而卻又同時感受到內心寧靜。如果你在這附近的話，一定要來一趟夢蓮湖。因為它可能會讓你覺得這裡是在這區更為漂亮的景點。夢蓮湖附近也有許多步道。你也可以租一個獨木舟並在湖中享受它的美景。沒有誇大，這裡真的是地球上最平靜安寧的地方之一。

▶ Vocabulary and Idioms ▶

❶ **amenities** n 便利設施　　❷ **bizarre** adj 奇異的

❸ **oblige** v 使不得不　　❹ **luxurious** adj 奢華的

❺ **splurge** v 揮霍金錢　　❻ **hostile** adj 懷敵意的

❼ **exquisite**
adj 精美的；精緻的

❽ **tranquility** n 平靜，安寧

1. The amenities in this place are over the top.

   這個地方的設施真是最頂級的。

2. Many people find it bizarre that John does not have a Face-book.

   很多人都覺得約翰沒有臉書是一件很奇怪的事。

3. I feel obliged to offer him a job.

   我覺得我不得不給他一個工作。

4. Everybody is jealous of his luxurious life.

   大家都很羨慕他奢華的生活。

5. It feels good to splurge once in a while as a reward for your hard work.

   偶爾揮霍金錢當作是努力工作之後的酬勞感覺很好。

6. He is always hostile to the staff in that company.

   他總是對這個公司的員工充滿敵意。

7. The exquisite presentation makes this dish even more desirable.

這個精美的擺盤使得這道菜讓人更想要享用。

8. I felt nothing but tranquility after an hour of practicing yoga.

我在練習完一個小時候的瑜伽後只感到平靜。

旅遊小貼士 ▶

　　在加拿大，室內是全面禁煙，所以千萬不要在飯店或是室內場所抽煙。罰金由最少 200 加幣起跳，所以絕對要小心這個規定噢！還有就是來到洛基山脈這區之前一定要先調查好天氣狀況，若是河上結冰，許多的水上活動也會隨之取消，避免遺憾，一定要先查好天氣噢！

阿根廷

庫斯科

紐奧良

新德里

拉斯維加斯

伊斯坦堡

西雅圖

班夫鎮

可愛島

冰島

Unit 29

Kauai 可愛島
Avatar 阿凡達

城市介紹 ▶

This is the place where your imagination can roam free. There are no limits to your laughing, dancing, and singing. Kauai still keeps its rawness, and it is the simplicity and free spiritedness that make Kauai so beautiful. With the nickname "The Garden Island", Kauai painted its garden with bright green forests and colorful tropical plants.

If you are a nature enthusiast, congratulations, you have come to the right place. However, if not, you might want to consider changing your flight ASAP because Kauai might be "boring" for you. On the other hand, nature enthusiasts, you are about to start probably one of the best adventures in your life. Get ready to soak in the moment and give Kauai everything you have in return! Hike as far as you can, dive as deep as you can, and see as much and as far as you can. Don't even blink too much for that. Life is transient. Enjoy Kauai while you can. There are all sorts of trails, snorkeling, diving, surfing, and kayaking spots. Even if you just want to enjoy a quiet beach time, Kauai also has lots of world-class beaches for you to choose from. So come to Kauai and find your piece of paradise!

可愛島

這是一個你可以讓想象力漫遊，而對歡笑，跳舞，和唱歌也完全沒有限制的地方。可愛島還是保有它的天然，而也正是它那簡單和自由精神使得可愛島那麼的美麗。有 "花園之島" 這個暱稱，可愛島以鮮艷的綠雨林和色彩豐富地熱帶植物來彩繪它這花園。

如果你是一個大自然愛好者，恭喜你，你來對地方了。不過如果你不是的話，你可能想要儘快考慮更換你的班機因為你可能會覺得可愛到很 "無聊"。另外一方面，對大自然愛好者來說，你即將展開你人生最棒的冒險之一。準備好沈浸在每一個時刻，並且回報可愛島你的一切！健行時越遠越好，潛水時潛得越深越好，能夠看得越多越遠越好。甚至不要眨眼因為人生稍縱即逝。在你還可以的時候盡情享受可愛島。那裡有很多的步道，浮潛，潛水，衝浪，獨木舟的地方，即使你只是想要享受一個安靜的海灘，可愛島也有許多世界級的海灘供你選擇。所以來可愛島吧，來找你自己的一小片天堂！

阿根廷

庫斯科

紐奧良

新德里

拉斯維加斯

伊斯坦堡

西雅圖

班夫鎮

可愛島

冰島

Dialogue 情境對話 ▶

Tammy and Matt decided to kayak along Napali coast.
譚咪和麥特決定要沿著 Napali 沿岸划輕型獨木舟。

Tammy: Wow, this is absolutely mind blowing!

譚咪：哇，這真是太令人興奮了！！

Matt: Yeah, It's such a beautiful day today, too. The water is so glassy.

麥特：對啊，今天也真是美麗的一天。海水像玻璃般的光滑。

Tammy: Yeah, this is such a great idea, Matt! Sorry, I chickened out on the Kalaulau trail!

譚咪：對啊，這真是一個好主意麥特！對不起我因為害怕而沒去 Kalaulau 步道！

Matt: Not a problem at all. This is not too bad, either. We can still make it to the Kalaulau beach this way!

麥特：沒關係。這也不差阿。我們這樣還是可以去到 Kalaulau 海邊！

Tammy: I hope so!

譚咪：我希望如此！

Matt: We can do it. We just have to keep an eye on our position. We don't want to drift too far from the shore.

麥特：我們可以做到的。我們只是要留心注意我們的位置。我們不想要漂到離岸邊太遠的地方。

Tammy: No, that does not sound fun at all. Luckily it's not too windy today!

譚咪：不，那一點也不好玩。幸運的是今天風沒有很大！

Matt: No. We are very lucky! Wait!! Do you see the fin that's swimming towards us?

麥特：嗯沒有很大。我們真的很幸運！等等！！你有看到朝我們游過來的魚鰭嗎？

Tammy: What?! Don't scare me! Is it a shark?

譚咪：什麼？！不要嚇我！是鯊魚嗎？

Matt: I am not sure! Keep your hands in the kayak!

麥特：我不確定！你的手不要超出獨木舟！

Tammy: What?! What can we do besides that?

譚咪：什麼？！除了那個我們還能做什麼？

Matt: Whatever you do, don't jump off this kayak!

麥特：不管你做什麼，千萬別跳下這獨木舟！

Tammy: Why would I do that?

譚咪：為什麼我會想要那樣做？

阿根廷
庫斯科
紐奧良
新德里
拉斯維加斯
伊斯坦堡
西雅圖
班夫鎮
可愛島
冰島

Tammy: Matt?

譚咪：麥特？

Matt: Wait a second…

麥特：等等…

Tammy: Talk to me Matt, I'm freaking out!

譚咪：現在是什麼狀況麥特，我快嚇死了！

Matt: I think…

麥特：我想…

Tammy: What are you thinking? This is driving me nuts!

譚咪：你想什麼？這快把我逼瘋了！

Matt: I think they are a pod of dolphins, Tammy! This is amazing!

麥特：我想這是一群海豚譚咪！這真是太神奇了！

Tammy: What? Really? Where's our GoPro??

譚咪：什麼？真的嗎？我們的 GoPro 呢？

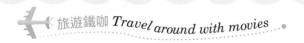
 Special Sites Introduction 29: 特別景點報導 ▶

 Avatar MP3 57

Remember the blockbuster released in 2009, Avatar? The epic science fiction that was set in the 22nd century when humans discovered a way to mine on the Pandora Planet where lushness is everywhere and mysterious creatures habituate on the island. The blue-skinned tribute called Na-Vi is the indigenous people on Pandora. The sensationally beautiful scenes of Pandora are one of the selling points of the movie.

Most of the rainforest scenes were shot in Kauai's Keahu Arboretum. In the movie when Jack Sully (Sam Worthington) was under the training of the Na Vi Princess Neytiri (Zoe Saldana), the background was mostly shot in Keahu Arboretum. Keahu Arboretum is a nature preserve surrounding the Wailua River on the east coast of Kauai. There are trails, picnic areas, and swimming spots within the place. This peaceful site is also home to several different trees and plants. If you wish to visit the Pandora Planet in real life, why not pay a visit to Kauai? Who knows? Perhaps you can find some Na Vi people within the Arboretum!

阿凡達

　　還記得在 2009 年上映的熱門大片：阿凡達嗎？這個壯麗的科幻大片是設定在二十二世紀，當人類發現了可以在潘朵拉星球上採礦。潘朵拉星球是一個十分翠綠的星球，而星球上也居住了許多神秘的生物。其中一個稱為納美的藍皮膚的族群是潘朵拉星球上的原住民。片中在潘朵拉星球上那不同凡響的美景也是該片大受歡迎的原因之一。

　　片中大部分雨林的場景都是在可愛島的 Keahu 植物園中拍攝。在電影中當傑克蘇利（麥山姆沃辛頓飾）正在接受納美人公主妮特麗（柔伊莎達娜飾）特訓時，許多的背景也是在 Keahu 植物園所拍攝的。Keahu 植物園是一個環繞著可愛島東邊的 Wailua 河的自然保護區。在這裡有步道，野餐區，還有可以游泳的地方。這個平靜的地方也是許多不同的樹和植物的家。如果你想要在現實生活中去一趟潘朵拉星球，不妨去一趟可愛島？誰知道呢？説不定你真的會在植物園中遇見納美人呢！

 **Kalaulau Trail** MP3 58

In Kauai, there is one major hidden gem that is known to many people, but only few dare to venture through the whole trail. It is an 11-mile trail along Napali coast that started from Ke'e beach till Kalaulau beach, meaning you will be hiking by the ocean throughout the whole trail. It covers five valleys in total and if you are determined to go all the way to Kalaulau Valley (the last valley), you will need a permit to enter the trail. The trail can be pretty strenuous, but everyone that has done the trail will tell you it will definitely be worthwhile. It is one of the most breathtaking trails in the world. The lushness in Kauai, the shimmering blue of the ocean and the carefree sky will all help you forget the weight of your backpack. The drops of your sweat and the racing heartbeats of yours make you become aware of the present moment; it is right then and there that you are walking through the trail with your able body. Some claimed that when you reach the end of the trail, you would surrender yourself to the Mother Nature for its raw beauty that you're about to witness her if you decide to take the challenge.

Kalaulau 海灘的步道

在可愛島有一個很多人知道卻很少人走完整個步道的終極秘密景點。這是一個十一英里（或是大約十八公里）並沿著 Napali 從 Ke'e 海灘到 Kalaulau 海灘的步道，意思也就是說全程步道都你都可以沿著海洋健行。這個步道包含了總共五個山谷，而如果你決心要走到 Kalaulau 山谷（最後一個山谷），那樣話你會需要拿入山證。這個步道會蠻艱辛的，但是每個去過的人都會告訴你這絕對是值得的！這是全世界最令人屏息的步道之一。可愛島的翠綠，海水閃爍的藍，還有那無憂無慮的藍天都會幫助你忘記你背包的重量。每一滴汗水和你激烈的心跳都令你意識到當下的那個時刻：就是那時，在那個地方，你以你有能力的身體走過那個步道。有些人宣稱當你抵達步道的終點，你將會將自己全然交給孕育萬物的大自然只因為你將目睹她那全然未加工的美麗，如果你決定要接受這個挑戰的話。

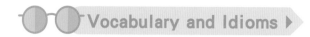
Vocabulary and Idioms ▶

❶ **roam** Ⓥ 漫遊		❷ **rawness** Ⓝ 天然	

❸ **enthusiast** Ⓝ 愛好者   ❹ **transient** adj 稍縱即逝的

❺ **glassy** adj 像玻璃般光滑的   ❻ **epic** adj 壯麗的

❼ **indigenous** adj 土著的   ❽ **strenuous** adj 艱辛的

1. The sheep roam freely in the spacious ranch.

   羊群們都在寬敞的牧場中自由地漫步。

2. I like the picture for its rawness and how it captures the most direct emotion from the subject.

   我喜歡這張照片的天然和直接還有它捕捉到被拍者的最直接情緒。

3. He is a fishing enthusiast. He fishes almost every day.

   他是一個釣魚愛好者。他幾乎每天都釣魚。

4. Beauty is transient on the outside. However, inner beauty is timeless.

   外在的美是稍縱即逝的。但是內在美卻是永恆的。

5. The water is so glassy today. It is such a treat just to look at the ocean and relax on the beach.

   今天的海面就像玻璃船的光滑。在海邊放鬆並且看著海洋真是個享受。

6. After days of hiking, we finally reached the epic Machu Pic-chu.

   在健行了好幾天之後，我們終於到了壯觀的馬丘比丘。

7. The indigenous people in the mountain taught us how to hunt and fish in the jungle.

在山中的原住民教我們如何在叢林中打獵和捕魚。

8. The hike is more strenuous than what he can take.

這個健行比他能承受的還要艱辛。

旅遊小貼士 ▶

　　來到可愛島時，白天四處觀光可能會發現島上充滿了公雞，他們可不是有人飼養的，他們是當地最原始的住民喔！遇到公雞時，也千萬不要害怕，只是如果有紮營的話，早上可能很早就會被號稱為天然鬧鐘的公雞們給叫醒囉！另外就是在可愛島，所有的店家在八點前就會關門，所以切記，若是有需要買一些補給品的話，千萬記得白天遇到店家就要先買齊喔！

阿根廷
庫斯科
紐奧良
新德里
拉斯維加斯
伊斯坦堡
西雅圖
班夫鎮
可愛島
冰島

Unit 30

Iceland 冰島
The Secret Life of Walter
Mitty 白日夢冒險王

城市介紹 ▶

Perhaps the flag of the Republic of Iceland best describes Iceland. The blue in the flag represents ocean, the white for glaciers and the red is the lava from the volcanoes. This is the meeting place of ice and fire, hot, and cold, where nothing seems impossible here. As its romance rolls on, Iceland was first discovered by the pirates. This volcanic island cradles the most hot springs in the world. There are around 100 volcanoes with more than 30 of them are active till this day. It is not hard to imagine the natural scenes here must be one of a kind. However, there's more to it on this island. On the southern side of the island, you can find pastures and grown vegetables from the residents there. Therefore, most of the people reside on the south of the island. Trekking through the lava field, exploring on the glaciers, whale watching sails and bathing in hot springs are all the popular things to do here, but if you are feeling adventurous, try sampling the sheep's head, slátur (Icelandic tripe sausage) and hákarl (fermented shark meat). It will be an adventure like no others.

冰島

　　或許冰島共和國的國旗把冰島描述的最好。國旗裡的藍色代表的是海洋，白色代表的是冰河，而紅色代表的是火山的熔岩。這是一個冰與火，冷與熱的交界點，也是一個看起來什麼事都是有可能發生的地方。就隨著這浪漫的描述，冰島也是最先被海盜所發現。這個火山島是孕育著全世界最多溫泉的地方。一共有大約一百個火山，而其中超過三十個到今天還是活火山。不難想像這裡大自然的風貌一定是獨一無二。然而，這個火山還有更多。在島上的南邊你可以找到牧場以及居民種植的蔬菜。所以，大多數的居民都是住在島上的南邊。在火山熔岩上健行，在冰河上探索，賞鯨的風帆，以及在溫泉裡泡澡都是在這裡十分受歡迎的行程，但如果你想要多冒險，你可以試試看羊頭，slátur（冰島香腸）和 hákarl（醃鯊魚肉）。這會是很不一樣的冒險。

Dialogue 情境對話 ▶

Billy and Sherry are on a tour to see the aurora.
比利和雪莉正在看極光的團裡。

Sherry: It is freezing! I can't feel my feet already.

雪莉：好冷喔！我的腳已經沒感覺了。

Billy: I know, but I can't wait to see aurora. This is definitely one of the things on my bucket list.

比利：我知道，但是我等不及要看極光了。這絕對在我的人生清單上。

Sherry: I checked the weather today. It's not too cloudy tonight. I think we are very likely to see it!

雪莉：我今天有查天氣。今天晚上不會很多雲。我想我們應該很有可能看到極光！

Billy: Wait a minute! Is that it? The green bands in the sky! Look at that Sherry!

比利：等等！是那個嗎？在天空綠色的帶狀！雪莉你看！

Sherry: Wow, this is amazing. Look! It's moving! This is incredible!

雪莉：哇，好棒喔。你看！它在動耶！真是太神奇了！

Billy: I'm in tears. Nature always has a way to amaze me.

比利：我已經要哭了。大自然總是有辦法給我驚喜。

Sherry: This is like a dreamland. I bet we can find fairies here if we take a closer look.

雪莉：這裡好像夢境喔。我打賭如果我們仔細找，一定可以找到精靈。

Billy: It's just so stunning and peaceful out here. Hey, how are you doing cold wise? Do you want my scarf?

比利：這裡就是好美，好平靜。欸你會冷嗎？你要我的圍巾嗎？

Sherry: I'm fine. This is worth the cold. Hey! We should take pictures like everyone else!

雪莉：我很好。這值得這麼冷。嘿！我們應該要和其他人一樣照個相！

Billy: Yes, we should. Should we ask other people to take a picture of us?

比利：對，應該的。我們要叫別人幫我們合照嗎？

Sherry: Yes, I'm going to keep that photo forever and ever.

雪莉：對啊，我一定會一輩子好好保存那張相片！

Billy: Um… Sherry…?

比利：啊…雪莉…？

Sherry: Yeah? What's wrong?

雪莉：嗯？怎麼了？

Billy: The camera's dead…

比利：相機沒電了…

阿根廷

庫斯科

紐奧良

新德里

拉斯維加斯

伊斯坦堡

西雅圖

班夫鎮

可愛島

冰島

Special Sites Introduction 30: 特別景點報導 ▶

The Secret Life of Walter Mitty MP3 59

Walter Mitty (Ben Stiller) is an employee at the Life magazine. Like many of the people, he works day in and day out in an office and spends life as a quiet worker. However, inside of Walter's mind lives an adventurous hero, who at times comes out and does impossible actions in real life. At times like those, Walter usually freezes in real life, while none of his imaginations come true. Nonetheless, on his last assignment, in order to obtain the final perfect shot, he needs to find the photographer Sean O'Connell (Sean Penn) who is traveling in Greenland, Iceland, and Afghanistan.

Walter followed Sean to Iceland, one impressive scene of him long boarding down the hills to the empty town to catch the flight. The road is named 'Seydisfjordur' located in Seydisfjordur. Seydisfjordur is a little town full of wooden houses, artists, and craftmen. It is located on the east side of Iceland. Make sure to stop by this scenic spot to check out what Walter saw here.

白日夢冒險王（塞濟斯菲厄澤市）

　　華特米提（班史提勒飾）是一個在生活雜誌上班的員工。就像是許多人一樣，他每天在辦公室裡上班，過著安靜的辦公室生活。然而，在華特的心裡住著一個熱愛冒險的英雄。他有的時候會跑出來，並且做出在現實生活中不可能的行為。在那些時候，華特通常是在現實生活中靜止不動當所有的白日夢都其實沒有發生。但是，在他最後的一個任務，為了要得到那最後一張完美的照片，他必須要找到攝影師尚恩歐康諾（西恩潘飾）。尚恩正在格林蘭，冰島，和阿富汗旅行。

　　華特跟隨著尚恩到冰島，一個令人印象深刻的一幕是當他一路上用長板滑下山坡到一個空無一人的鎮上去趕飛機。那條路的名字是塞濟斯菲厄澤，位於塞濟斯菲厄澤市。塞濟斯菲厄澤市是一個充滿了木屋，藝術家，和木匠的小鎮。它位於冰島的東邊。記得來這邊看看華特在片中所看到的風景喔。

 Blue Lagoon 　　 MP3 60

Blue Lagoon is probably one of the most popular tourist attractions in Iceland. Many people swear that soaking in the hot spring in the blue lagoon is by far one of the most blissful experiences they have ever had. So what's so special and blissful about this place then? Funny how there are so many natural hot springs in Iceland. Blue Lagoon is actually a man-made outdoor hot spring SPA center. The lagoon is fed by the water output of the nearby geothermal power plant Svartsengi and is renewed every two days. The warm waters are rich in minerals like silica and sulfur, and it is said that bathing in the water here is very rejuvenating and relaxing. To top off the wonderful experience, there is a bar in the middle of the lagoon just in case you are in the mood for a cold drink. Having a cold beer in the outdoor hot spring in Iceland. How do you spell stress again?

阿根廷

庫斯科

紐奧良

新德里

拉斯維加斯

伊斯坦堡

西雅圖

班夫鎮

可愛島

冰島

藍湖

　　藍湖大概是冰島最受歡迎的景點之一。許多人發誓浸泡在藍湖的溫泉裡是目前為止最令他們覺得幸福的經驗之一。所以到底哪裡幸福呢？奇妙的是冰島有那麼多的天然溫泉，而藍湖其實是人工的露天溫泉水療中心。這裡的湖水是有附近地熱發電廠 Svartsengi 所排放出，而他們也會每隔兩天換一次水。這溫暖的水充滿了礦物質例如白矽泥和硫磺，而聽説他們會使人變年輕，以及放鬆。再繼續使得整個經驗更加完美，如果你剛好想要喝冰飲的話，在湖的中間有一個小吧。在冰島的露天溫泉中喝一杯冰啤酒。你剛剛説壓力怎麼寫？

Vocabulary and Idioms ▶

❶ **lava** n 火山熔岩   ❷ **active** adj 活躍的

❸ **fermented** adj 發酵的   ❹ **aurora** n 極光

❺ **freeze** v 靜止不動   ❻ **lagoon** n 潟湖

❼ **blissful** adj 幸福的   ❽ **sulfur** n 硫磺

1. Lava rocks are very popular for decorating the gardens.

   火山石是很常被用來裝飾花園。

2. He's a super active person. I've never seen him tired.

   他是一個十分活躍的人。我從來沒看他累過。

3. Nato are basically fermented beans.

   納豆其實就是發酵的豆子。

4. There are so many legends about aurora.

   有好多關於極光的傳說。

5. The thief freezes when he sees the cops.

   當小偷看到警察時，他立刻靜止不動。

6. There's nothing more relaxing than swimming in a calm lagoon.

   沒有什麼比在平靜的潟湖裡來更令人放鬆了。

7. Thanks for the blissful summer time.

   謝謝你給我一個幸福快樂的夏日時光。

8. I can smell sulfur from the hot springs.

   我可以聞到溫泉中的硫磺。

旅遊小貼士 ▶

　　有打算要在冰島寄明信片的要注意喔，冰島並不像在其他地方十分地方便，冰島的雷克雅維克機場也沒有郵局喔！所以，我建議在買明信片的時候，也要一起買郵票，以免到時候找不到郵票從這邊寄出！那就太可惜囉！

阿
根
廷

庫
斯
科

紐
奧
良

新
德
里

拉
斯
維
加
斯

伊
斯
坦
堡

西
雅
圖

班
夫
鎮

可
愛
島

冰
島

Learn Smart! 046

Follow 30 場票房電影實現你的旅遊英語夢

作　　　者	李佩玲/Bella
發　行　人	周瑞德
企　劃　編　輯	陳韋佑
封　面　設　計	高鍾琪
內　文　排　版	菩薩蠻數位文化有限公司
校　　　對	陳欣慧、饒美君

印　　　製	大亞彩色印刷製版股份有限公司
初　　　版	2015 年 5 月
出　　　版	倍斯特出版事業有限公司
電　　　話	(02) 2351-2007
傳　　　真	(02) 2351-0887
地　　　址	100 台北市中正區福州街 1 號 10 樓之 2
E - m a i l	best.books.service@gmail.com
定　　　價	新台幣 380 元

港澳地區總經銷　泛華發行代理有限公司

地　　　址	香港新界將軍澳工業邨駿昌街 7 號 2 樓
電　　　話	(852) 2798-2323
傳　　　真	(852) 2796-5471

國家圖書館出版品預行編目(CIP)資料

Follow 30 場票房電影實現你的旅遊英
語夢 / Bella 作. -- 初版. -- 臺北
市 : 倍斯特, 2015.05
　　　面　;　　公分. -- (Learn
smart! ; 46)
ISBN 978-986-90883-9-8(平裝)
1. 英語 2. 旅遊 3. 會話
　805.188　　　　　104005507

Simply Learning, Simply Best

Simply Learning, Simply Best